THE TRAIL BOOK
Western Literature Series

"'Arr-rr-ump!' I said" (*chapter* 3)

THE TRAIL BOOK
MARY AUSTIN

With Illustrations by Milo Winter
Afterword by Melody Graulich

UNIVERSITY OF NEVADA PRESS ▲▲ RENO / LAS VEGAS

Western Literature Series

The Trail Book was first published by Houghton Mifflin Company,
The Riverside Press Cambridge, in 1918.

University of Nevada Press, Reno, Nevada 89557 USA
www.unpress.nevada.edu
New material copyright © 2004 by University of Nevada Press
All rights reserved
Manufactured in the United States of America
Design by Carrie House
Library of Congress Cataloging-in-Publication Data
Austin, Mary Hunter, 1868–1934.
The trail book / Mary Austin ; with illustrations by Milo
Winter.—University of Nevada Press paperback ed. / afterword by
Melody Graulich.
p. cm. — (Western literature series)
ISBN 978-0-87417-588-2 (pbk. : alk. paper)
1. American Museum of Natural History—Fiction. 2. Indians of
North America—Fiction. 3. Nature stories, American. 4. West
(U.S.)—Fiction. I. Title. II. Series.
PS3501.U8T73 2004
813'.52—dc22   2003022017
The paper used in this book meets the requirements of American
National Standard for Information Sciences—Permanence of
Paper for Printed Library Materials, ANSI Z.48-1984. Binding
materials were selected for strength and durability.

University of Nevada Press Paperback Edition, 2004
This book has been reproduced as a digital reprint.

[*Frontispiece:*] " 'Arr-rr-ump!' I said" (*chapter* 3)

To Mary, My Niece
In The Hope That She May Find
Through The Trails Of Her Own Country
The Road To Wonderland

CONTENTS

ILLUSTRATIONS

I

HOW OLIVER AND DORCAS JANE
FOUND THE TRAIL

From the time that he had first found himself alone with them, Oliver had felt sure that the animals could come alive again if they wished. That was one blowy afternoon about a week after his father had been made night engineer and nobody had come into the Museum for several hours.

Oliver had been sitting for some time in front of the Buffalo case, wondering what might be at the other end of the trail. The cows that stood midway in it had such a *going* look. He was sure it must lead, past the hummock where the old bull flourished his tail, to one of those places where he had always wished to be. All at once, as the boy sat there thinking about it, the glass case disappeared and the trail shot out like a dark snake over a great stretch of rolling, grass-covered prairie.

He could see the tops of the grasses stirring like the hair on the old Buffalo's coat, and the ripple of water on the beaver pool which was just opposite and yet somehow only to be reached after long travel through the Buffalo Country. The wind moved on the grass, on the surface of the water and the young leaves of the alders, and over all the animals came the start and stir of life.

And then the slow, shuffling steps of the Museum attendant startled it all into stillness again.

The attendant spoke to Oliver as he passed, for even a small boy is worth talking to when you have been all day in a Museum where nothing is new to you and nobody comes.

"You want to look out, son," said the attendant, who really liked the boy and had n't a notion what sort of ideas he was putting into Oliver's head. "If you ain't careful, some of them things will come downstairs some night and go off with ye."

And why should MacShea have said that if he had n't known for certain that the animals *did* come alive at night? That was the way Oliver put it when he was trying to describe this extraordinary experience to his sister.

Dorcas Jane, who was eleven and a half and not at all imaginative, eyed him suspiciously. Oliver had such a way of stating things that were not at all believable, in a way that made them seem the likeliest things in the world. He was even capable of acting for days as if things were so, which you knew from the beginning were only the most delightful of make-believes. Life on this basis was immensely more exciting, but then you never knew whether or not he might be what some of his boy friends called "stringing you," so when Oliver began to hint darkly at his belief that the stuffed animals in the Mammal room of the Museum came alive at night and had larks of their own, Dorcas Jane offered the most noncommittal objection that occurred to her.

"They could n't," she said; "the night watchman would n't let them." There were watchmen, she knew, who went the rounds of every floor.

But, insisted Oliver, why should they have watchmen at all, if not to prevent people from breaking in and disturbing the animals when they were busy with affairs of their own? He meant to stay up there himself some night and see what it was all about; and as he went on to explain how it would be possible to slip up the great stair while the watchmen were at the far end of the long hall, and of the places one could hide if the watchman came along when he was n't wanted, he said "we" and "us." For, of course, he meant to take Dorcas Jane with him. Where would be the fun of such an adventure if you had it alone? And besides, Oliver had discovered that it was not at all difficult to scare himself with the things he had merely imagined. There were times when Dorcas Jane's frank disbelief was a great comfort to him. Still, he was n't the sort of boy to be scared before anything has really happened, so when Dorcas Jane suggested that they did n't know what the animals might do to any one who went among them uninvited, he threw it off stoutly.

"Pshaw! They can't do *anything* to us! They're stuffed, Silly!"

And to Dorcas Jane, who was by this time completely under the spell of the adventure, it seemed quite likely that the animals should be stuffed so that they could n't hurt you, and yet not stuffed so much that they could n't come alive again.

It was all of a week before they could begin. There is a kind of feeling you have to have about an adventure without which the affair does n't come off properly. Anybody who has been much by himself in the woods has had it; or sometime, when you are all alone in the house, all at once there comes a kind of pricking of your skin and a tightness in your chest, not at all unpleasant, and a kind of feeling that the furniture has its eye on you, or that some one behind your shoulder is about to speak, and immediately after that something happens. Or you feel sure it would have happened if somebody had n't interrupted.

Dorcas Jane *never* had feelings like that. But about a week after Oliver had proposed to her that they spend a part of the night in the long gallery, he was standing in front of the Buffalo case, wondering what actually did happen when a buffalo caught you. Quite unexpectedly, deep behind the big bull's glassy eye, he caught a gleam as of another eye looking at him, meaningly, and with a great deal of friendliness. Oliver felt prickles come out suddenly all over his body, and without quite knowing why, he began to move away from that place, tip-toe and slippingly, like a wild creature in the woods when it does not know who may be about. He told himself it would never do to have the animals come alive without Dorcas Jane, and before all those stupid, staring folk who might come in at any minute and spoil everything.

That night, after their father had gone off clanking to his furnaces, Dorcas heard her brother tapping on the partition between their rooms, as he did sometimes when they played "prisoner." She knew exactly what he meant by it and tapped back that she was ready.

Everything worked out just as they had planned. They heard the strange, hollow-sounding echoes of the watchman's voice dying down the halls, as stair by stair they dropped the street lamps below them, and saw strange shadows start out of things that were perfectly harmless and familiar by day.

There was no light in the gallery except faint up-and-down glimmers from the glass of the cases, and here and there the little spark of an eye. Outside there was a whole world of light, the milky way of the street with the meteor roar of the Elevated going by, processions of small moons marching below them across the park, and blazing constellations in the high windows opposite. Tucked into one of the window benches between the cases, the children seemed to swing into another world where almost anything might happen. And yet for at least a quarter of an hour nothing did.

"I don't believe nothing ever does," said Dorcas Jane, who was not at all careful of her grammar.

"Sh-sh!" said Oliver. They had sat down directly in front of the Buffalo Trail, though Dorcas would have preferred to be farther away from the Polar Bear. For suppose it had n't been property stuffed! But Oliver had eyes only for the trail.

"I want to see where it begins and where it goes," he insisted.

So they sat and waited, and though the great building was never allowed to grow quite cold, it was cool enough to make it pleasant for them to sit close together and for Dorcas to tuck her hand into the crook of his arm. . . .

All at once the Bull Buffalo shook himself.

II
WHAT THE BUFFALO CHIEF TOLD

"*Wake! Wake!*" said the Bull Buffalo, with a roll to it, as though the word had been shouted in a deep voice down an empty barrel. He shook the dust out of his mane and stamped his fore-foot to set the herd in motion. There were thousands of them feeding as far as the eye could reach, across the prairie, yearlings and cows with their calves of that season, and here and there a bull, tossing his heavy head and sending up light puffs of dust under the pawings of his hoof as he took up the leader's signal.

"Wake! Wa—ake!"

It rolled along the ground like thunder. At the sound the herds gathered themselves from the prairie, they turned back from the licks, they rose up *plop* from the wallows, trotting singly in the trails that rayed out to every part of the pastures and led up toward the high ridges.

"Wa-ak—" began the old bull; then he stopped short, threw up his head, sniffing the wind, and ended with a sharp snort which changed the words to "*What? What?*"

"What's this," said the Bull Buffalo, "Pale Faces?"

"They are very young," said the young cow, the one with the

going look. She had just been taken into the herd that season and had the place of the favorite next to the leader.

"If you please, sir," said Oliver, "we only wished to know where the trail went."

"Why," said the Buffalo Chief, surprised, "to the Buffalo roads, of course. We must be changing pasture." As he pawed contempt upon the short, dry grass, the rattlesnake, that had been sunning himself at the foot of the hummock, slid away under the bleached buffalo skull, and the small, furry things dived everywhere into their burrows.

"That is the way always," said the young cow, "when the Buffalo People begin their travels. Not even a wolf will stay in the midst of the herds; there would be nothing left of him by the time the hooves had passed over."

The children could see how that might be, for as the thin lines began to converge toward the high places, it was as if the whole prairie had turned black and moving. Where the trails drew out of the flat lands to the watersheds, they were wide enough for eight or ten to walk abreast, trodden hard and white as country roads. There was a deep, continuous murmur from the cows like the voice of the earth talking to itself at twilight.

"Come," said the old bull, "we must be moving."

"But what is that?" said Dorcas Jane, as a new sound came from the direction of the river, a long chant stretching itself like a snake across the prairie, and as they listened there were words that lifted and fell with an odd little pony joggle.

"That is the Pawnees, singing their travel song," said the Buffalo Chief.

And as he spoke they could see the eagle bonnets of the tribesmen coming up the hollow, every man mounted, with his round shield and the point of his lance tilted forward. After them came the women on the pack-ponies with the goods, and the children stowed on the travoises of lodge-poles that trailed from the ponies' withers.

"Ha-ah," said the old bull. "One has laid his ear to the ground in their lodges and has heard the earth tremble with the passing of the Buffalo People."

"But where do they go?" said Dorcas.

"They follow the herds," said the old bull, "for the herds are their food and their clothes and their housing. It is the Way Things Are that the Buffalo People should make the trails and men should ride in them. They go up along the watersheds where the floods cannot mire, where the snow is lightest, and there are the best lookouts."

"And, also, there is the easiest going," said a new voice with a snarly running whine in it. It came from a small gray beast with pointed ears and a bushy tail, and the smut-tipped nose that all coyotes have had since their very first father blacked himself bringing fire to Man from the Burning Mountain. He had come up very softly at the heels of the Buffalo Chief, who wheeled suddenly and blew steam from his nostrils.

"That," he said, "is because of the calves. It is not because a buffalo cannot go anywhere it pleases him; down ravines where a horse would stumble and up cliffs where even you, O Smut Nose, cannot follow."

"True, Great Chief," said the Coyote, "but I seem to remember trails that led through the snow to very desirable places."

This was not altogether kind, for it is well known that it is only when snow has lain long enough on the ground to pack and have a hard coating of ice, that the buffaloes dare trust themselves upon it. When it is new-fallen and soft they flounder about helplessly until they die of starvation, and the wolves pull them down, or the Indians come and kill them. But the old bull had the privilege which belongs to greatness, of not being obliged to answer impertinent things that were said to him. He went on just as if nothing had interrupted, telling how the buffalo trails had found the mountain passes and how they were rutted deep into the earth by the migrating herds.

"I have heard," he said, "that when the Pale Faces came into the country they found no better roads anywhere than the buffalo traces—"

"Also," purred Moke-icha, "I have heard that they found trails through lands where no buffalo had been before them." Moke-icha, the Puma, lay on a brown boulder that matched so perfectly with her watered coat that if it had not been for the ruffling of the wind on her short fur and the twitchings of her tail, the children might not have discovered her. "Look," she said, stretching out one of her great pads toward the south, where the trail ran thin and white across a puma-colored land, streaked with black lava and purple shadow. Far at the other end it lifted in red, wall-sided buttes where the homes of the Cliff People stuck like honeycombs in the wind-scoured hollows. "Now I recall a trail in that country," said Moke-icha, "that was older than the oldest father's father of them could remember. Four times a year the People of the Cliffs went down on it to the Sacred Water, and came back with bags of salt on their shoulders."

Even as she spoke they could see the people coming out of the Cliff dwellings and the priests going into the kivas preparing for the journey.

That was how it was; when any animal spoke of the country he knew best, that was what the children saw. And yet all the time there was the beginning of the buffalo trail in front of them, and around them, drawn there by that something of himself which every man puts into the work of his hands, the listening tribesmen. One of these spoke now in answer to Moke-icha.

"Also in my part of the country," he said, "long before there were Pale Faces, there were trade trails and graded ways, and walled ways between village and village. We traded for cherts as far south as Little River in the Tenasas Mountains, and north to the Sky-Blue Water for copper which was melted out of rocks, and there were workings at Flint Ridge that were older than the great mound at Cahokia."

"Oh," cried both the children at once, "Mound-Builders!"—and they stared at him with interest. He was probably not any taller than the other Indians, but seemed so on account of his feather headdress which was built up in front with a curious cut-out copper ornament. They thought they recognized the broad banner stone of greenish slate which he carried, the handle of which was tasseled with turkey beards and tiny tails of ermine. He returned the children's stare in the friendliest possible fashion, twirling his banner stone as a policeman does his night stick.

"Were you? Mound-Builders, you know?" questioned Oliver.

"You could call us that. We called ourselves Tallegewi, and our trails were old before the buffalo had crossed east of the Missi-Sippu, the Father of all Rivers. Then the country was full of the horned people, thick as flies in the Moon of Stopped Waters." As he spoke, he pointed to the moose and wapiti trooping down the shallow hills to the watering-places. They moved with a dancing motion, and the multitude of their horns was like a forest walking, a young forest in the spring before the leaves are out and there is a clicking of antlered bough on bough. "They would come in twenty abreast to the licks where we lay in wait for them," said the Tallega. "They were the true trail-makers."

"Then you must have forgotten what I had to do with it," said a voice that seemed to come from high up in the air, so that they all looked up suddenly and would have been frightened at the huge bulk, if the voice coming from it in a squeaky whisper had not made it seem ridiculous. It was the Mastodon, who had strolled in from the prehistoric room, though it was a wonder to the children how so large a beast could move so silently.

"Hey," said a Lenni-Lenape, who had sat comfortably smoking all this time, "I've heard of you—there was an old Telling of my father's—though I hardly think I believed it. What are you doing here?"

"I've a perfect right to come," said the Mastodon, shuffling embarrassedly from foot to foot. "I was the first of my kind to have a man belonging to me, and it was I that showed him the trail to the sea."

"Oh, please, would you tell us about it?" said Dorcas.

The Mastodon rocked to and fro on his huge feet, embarrassedly.

"If—if it would please the company—"

Everybody looked at the Buffalo Chief, for, after all, it was he who began the party. The old bull pawed dust and blew steam from his nostrils, which was a perfectly safe thing to do in case the story did n't turn out to his liking.

"Tell, tell," he agreed, in a voice like a man shouting down twenty rain barrels at once.

And looking about slyly with his little twinkling eyes at the attentive circle, the Mastodon began.

III
HOW THE MASTODON HAPPENED FIRST TO BELONG TO A MAN, AS TOLD BY ARRUMPA

"In my time, everything, even the shape of the land was different. From Two Rivers it was all marsh, marsh and swamp with squidgy islands, with swamp and marsh again till you came to hills and hard land, beyond which was the sea. Nothing grew then but cane and coarse grass, and the water rotting the land until there was no knowing where it was safe treading from year to year. Not that it mattered to my people. We kept to the hills where there was plenty of good browse, and left the swamp to the Grass-Eaters—bunt-headed, woolly-haired eaters of grass!"

Up came Arrumpa's trunk to trumpet his contempt, and out from the hillslope like a picture on a screen stretched for a moment the flat reed-bed of Two Rivers, with great herds of silly, elephant-looking creatures feeding there, with huge incurving trunks and backs that sloped absurdly from a high fore-hump. They rootled in the tall grass or shouldered in long, snaky lines through the canes, their trunks waggling.

"Mammoths they were called," said Arrumpa, "and they hid in the swamp because their tusks curved in and they were afraid of Saber-Tooth, the Tiger. There were a great many of them, though not so many as our people, and also there was Man. It was the year my tusks began to grow that I first saw him. We were coming up from the river to the bedding-ground and there was a thin rim of the moon like a tusk over the hill's shoulder. I remember the damp smell of the earth and the good smell of the browse after the sun goes down, and between them a thin blue mist curling with a stinging smell that made prickles come along the back of my neck.

" 'What is that?' I said, for I walked yet with my mother.

" 'It is the smell which Man makes so that other people may know where he is and keep away from him,' she said, for my mother had never been friends with Man and she did not know any better.

"Then we came up over the ridge and saw them, about a score, naked and dancing on the naked front of the hill. They had a fire in their midst from which the blue smell went up, and as they danced they sang—

> 'Hail, moon, young moon!
> Hail, hail, young moon!
> Bring me something that I wish,
> Hail, moon, hail!'

—catching up fire-sticks in their hands and tossing them toward the tusk of the moon. That was how they made the moon grow, by working fire into it, so my man told me afterwards. But it was not until I began to walk by myself that he found me.

"I had come up from the lower hills all one day," said the Mastodon. "There was a feel in the air as if the Great Cold had breathed into it. It curdled blue as pond water, and under the blueness the forest color showed like weed under water. I walked by myself and did not care who heard me. Now and then I tore up a young tree, for my tusks had grown fast that year and it was good to feel the tree lug at its roots and struggle with me. Farther up, the wind walked on the dry leaves with a sound like a thousand wapiti trooping down the mountain. Every little while, for want of something to do, I charged it. Then I carried a pine, which I had torn up, on my tusks, until the butt struck a boulder which went down the hill with an avalanche of small stones that set all the echoes shouting.

"In the midst of it I lifted up my voice and said that I was I, Arrumpa, walking by myself,—and just then a dart struck me. The men had come up under cover of the wind on either side so that there was nothing for me to do but to move forward, which I did, somewhat hurriedly.

"I had not come to my full size then, but I was a good weight for my years," said Arrumpa modestly,—"a very good weight, and it was my weight that saved me, for the edge of the ravine that opened suddenly in front of me crumbled, so that I came down into the bottom of it with a great mass of rubbish and broken stone, with a twisted knee, and very much astonished.

"I remember blowing to get the blood and dust out of my eyes,—there was a dart stuck in my forehead,—and seeing the men come swarming over the edge of the ravine, which was all walled in on every side, shaking their spears and singing. That was the way with men; whatever they did they had to sing about it. 'Ha-ahe-ah!' they sang—

'Great Chief, you're about to die,
The Gods have said it.'

"So they came capering, but there was blood in my eyes and my knee hurt me, so when one of them stuck his spear almost up to the haft in my side, I tossed him. I took him up lightly on my tusks and he lay still at the far end of the ravine where I had dropped him. That stopped the shouting; but it broke out again suddenly, for the women had come down the wild vines on the walls, with their young on their shoulders, and the wife of the man I had tossed found him. The noise of the hunters was as nothing to the noise she made at me. Madness overtook her; she left off howling over her man and seizing her son by the hand,—he was no more than half-grown, not up to my shoulder,—she pushed him in front of me. 'Take him! Take my son, Man-Killer!' she screamed. 'After you have taken the best of the tribe, will you stop at a youngling?' Then all the others screeched at her like gulls frightened from their rock, and stopped silent in great fear to see what I would do about it.

"I did not know what to do, for there was no way I could tell her I was sorry I had killed her husband; and the lad stood where she had pushed him, not making any noise at all but a sharp, steady breathing. So I took him up in my trunk, for, indeed, I did not know what to do, and as I held him at the level of my eyes, I saw a strange thing,—that the boy was not afraid. He was not in the least afraid, but very angry.

"'I hate you, Arrumpa,' he said, 'because you have killed my father. I am too little to kill you for it now, but when I am a man I shall kill you.' He struck me with his fists. 'Put me down, Man-Killer!'

"So I put him down. What else was there to do? And there was a sensation in my breast, a sensation as of bending the knees and bowing the neck—not at all unpleasant— He stood where I placed him, between my tusks, and one of the hunters, who was a man in authority, called out to him to come away while they killed me.

"'That you shall not,' said my manling, 'for he has killed my father, therefore he is mine to kill according to the custom of killing.'

"Then the man was angry.

"'Come away, little fool,' he said. 'He is our meat. Have we not followed him for three days and trapped him?'

"The boy looked at him under his brows, drawn level.

"'That was my father's spear that stuck in him, Opata,' he said.

"Now, as the man spoke, I began to see what they had done to me these three days, for there was no way out of the ravine, and the women had brought their fleshing-knives and baskets: but the boy was quicker even than my anger. He reached up a hand to either of my tusks,—he could barely lay hands on them,—and his voice shook, though I do not think it was with anger. 'He is mine to kill,' he said, 'according to custom. He is my Arrumpa, and I call the tribe to witness. Not one of you shall lay hands on him until one of us has killed the other.'

"Then I lifted up my trunk over him, for my heart swelled against the hunters, and I gave voice as a bull should when he walks by himself.

"'Arr-rr-ump!' I said. And the people were all silent with astonishment.

"Finally the man who had first spoken, spoke again, very humbly, 'Great Chief, give us leave to take away your father.' So we gave them leave. They took the hurt man—his back was broken—away by the vine ladders, and my young man went and lay face down where his father had lain, and shook with many strange noises while water came out of his eyes. When he sat up at last and saw me blowing dust on the spear-cut in my side to stop the bleeding, he gathered broad leaves, dipped them in pine gum, and laid them on the cut. Then I blew dust on these, and seeing that I was more comfortable, Taku-Wakin—that was what I learned to call him—saluted with both hands to his head, palms outward. 'Friend,' he said,—'for if you are not my friend I think I have not one other in the world,—besides, I am too little to kill you,—I go to bury my father.'

"For three days I bathed my knee in the spring, and saw faces come to peer about the edge of it and heard the beat of the village drums. The third day my young man came, wearing his father's collar of bear's teeth, with neither fire-stick nor food nor weapon upon him.

"'Now I am all the man my mother has,' he said; 'I must do what is necessary to become a tribesman.'

"I did not know then what he meant, but it seems it was a custom."

All the Indians in the group that had gathered about the Mastodon, nodded at this.

"It was so in my time," said the Mound-Builder. "When a youth has come to the age where he is counted a man, he goes apart and neither eats nor drinks until, in the shape of some living thing, the Great Mystery has revealed itself to him."

"It was so he explained it to me," agreed Arrumpa; "and for three days he ate and drank nothing, but walked by himself talking to his god. Other times he would talk to me, scratching my hurts and taking the ticks out of my ears, until—I do not know what it was, but between me and Taku-Wakin it happened that we understood, each of us, what the other was thinking in his heart as well as if we had words— Is this also a custom?"

A look of intelligence passed between the members of his audience.

"Once to every man," said an Indian who leaned against Moke-icha's boulder, "when he shuts all thought of killing out of his heart and gives himself to the beast as to a brother, knowledge which is different from the knowledge of the chase comes to both of them."

"Oh," said Oliver, "I had a dog once—" But he became very much embarrassed when he discovered that he had drawn the attention of the company. It had always been difficult for him to explain why it was he had felt so certain that his dog and he had always known what the other was thinking; but the Indians and the animals understood him.

"All this Taku explained to me," went on Arrumpa. "The fourth day, when Taku fainted for lack of food, I cradled him in my tusks and was greatly troubled. At last I laid him on the fresh grass by the spring and blew water on him. Then he sat up laughing and spluttering, but faintly.

"'Now am I twice a fool,' he said, 'not to know from the first that you are my Medicine, the voice of the Mystery.'

"Then he shouted for his mother, who came down from the top of the ravine, very timidly, and fed him.

"After that he would come to me every day, sometimes with a bough of wild apples or a basket of acorns, and I would set him on my neck so he could scratch between my ears and tell me all his troubles. His father, he said, had been a strong man who put himself at the head of the five chiefs of the tribe and persuaded them to leave off fighting one another and band together against the enemy tribes. Opata, the man who had wished to kill me, was the man likeliest to be made High Chief in his father's place.

"'And then my bad days will begin,' said Taku-Wakin, 'for he hates me for my father's sake, and also a little for yours, Old Two-Tails, and he will persuade the Council to give my mother to another man and I shall be made subject to him. Worse,' he said,— 'the Great Plan of my father will come to nothing.'

"He was always talking about this Great Plan and fretting over it, but I was too new to the customs of men to ask what he meant by it.

"'If I had but a Sign,' he said, 'then they would give me my father's place in the Council . . . but I am too little, and I have not yet killed anything worth mentioning.'

"So he would sit on my neck and drum with his heels while he thought, and there did not seem to be anything I could do about it. By this time my knee was quite well. I had eaten all the brush in the ravine and was beginning to be lonely. Taku was n't able to visit me so often, for he had his mother and young brothers to kill for.

"So one night when the moon came walking red on the trail of the day, far down by Two Rivers I heard some of my friends trumpeting; therefore I pulled down young trees along the sides of the ravine, with great lumps of earth, and battered the rotten cliffs until they crumbled in a heap by which I scrambled up again.

"I must have traveled a quarter of the moon's course before I heard the patter of bare feet in the trail and a voice calling:—

"'Up! Take me up, Arrumpa!'

"So I took him up, quite spent with running, and yet not so worn out but that he could smack me soundly between the eyes, as no doubt I deserved.

"'Beast of a bad heart,' he said, 'did I not tell you that to-morrow the moon is full and the Five Chiefs hold Council?' So he had, but my thick wits had made nothing of it. 'If you leave me this night,' said Taku, 'then they will say that my Medicine has left me and my father's place will be given to Opata.'

"'Little Chief,' I said, 'I did not know that you had need of me, but it came into my head that I also had need of my own people. Besides, the brush is eaten.'

" 'True, true!' he said, and drummed on my forehead. 'Take me home,' he said at last, 'for I have followed you half the night, and I must not seem wearied at the Council.'

"So I took him back as far as the Arch Rock which springs high over the trail by which the men of Taku's village went out to the hunting. There was a cleft under the wing of the Arch, close to the cliff, and every man going out to the hunt threw a dart at it, as an omen. If it stuck, the omen was good, but if the point of the dart broke against the face of the cliff and fell back, the hunter returned to his hut, and if he hunted at all that day, he went out in another direction. We could see the shafts of the darts fast in the cleft, bristling in the moonlight.

" 'Wait here, under the Arch,' said Taku-Wakin, 'till I see if the arrow of my thought finds a cleft to stick into.'

"So we waited, watching the white, webby moons of the spiders, wet in the grass, and the man huts sleeping on the hill, and felt the Dawn's breath pricking the skin of our shoulders. The huts were mere heaps of brush like rats' nests.

" 'Shall I walk on the huts for a sign, Little Chief?' said I.

" 'Not that, Old Hilltop,' he laughed; 'there are people under the huts, and what good is a Sign without people?'

"Then he told me how his father had become great by thinking, not for his own clan alone, but for all the people—it was because of the long reach of his power that they called him Long-Hand. Now that he was gone there would be nothing but quarrels and petty jealousies. 'They will hunt the same grounds twice over,' said Taku-Wakin; 'they will kill one another when they should be killing their enemies, and in the end the Great Cold will get them.'

"Every year the Great Cold crept nearer. It came like a strong arm and pressed the people west and south so that the tribes bore hard on one another.

" 'Since old time,' said Taku-Wakin, 'my people have been sea people. But the People of the Great Cold came down along the ice-rim and cut them off from it. My father had a plan to get to the sea, and a Talking Stick which he was teaching me to understand, but I cannot find it in any of the places where he used to hide it. If I had the Stick I think they would make me chief in my father's place. But if Opata is made chief, then I must give it to him if I find it, and Opata will have all the glory. If I had but a Sign to keep them from making Opata chief . . .' So he drummed on my head with his heels while I leaned against the Arch Rock—oh, yes, I can sleep very comfortably, standing—and the moon slid down the hill until it shone clear under the rock and touched the feathered butts of the arrows. Then Taku woke me.

"'Up, put me up, Arrumpa! For now I have thought of a Sign that even the Five Chiefs will have respect for.'

"So I put him up until his foot caught in the cleft of the rock and he pried out five of the arrows.

"'Arrows of the Five Chiefs,' he said,—'that the chiefs gave to the gods to keep, and the gods have given to me again!'

"That was the way always with Taku-Wakin, he kept all the god customs of the people, but he never doubted, when he had found what he wanted to do, that the gods would be on his side. He showed me how every arrow was a little different from the others in the way the blood drain was cut or the shaft feathered.

"'No fear,' he said. 'Every man will know his own when I come to the Council.'

"He hugged the arrows to his breast and laughed over them, so I hugged him with my trunk, and we agreed that once in every full moon I was to come to Burnt Woods, and wait until he called me with something that he took from his girdle and twirled on a thong. I do not know what it was called, but it had a voice like young thunder."

"Like this?" The Mound-Builder cut the air with an oddly shaped bit of wood swung on an arm's-length of string, once lightly, like a covey of quail rising, and then loud like a wind in the full-branched forest.

"Just such another. Thrice he swung it so that I might not mistake the sound, and that was the last I saw of him, hugging his five arrows, with the moon gone pale like a meal-cake, and the tame wolves that skulk between the huts for scraps, slinking off as he spoke to them."

"And did they—the Five Chiefs, I mean—have respect for his arrows?" Dorcas Jane wondered.

"So he told me. They came from all the nine villages and sat in a council ring, each with the elders of his village behind him, and in front his favorite weapon, tied with eagle feathers for enemies he had slain, and red marks for battles, and other signs and trophies. At the head of the circle there was the spear of Long-Hand, and a place left for the one who should be elected to sit in it. But before the Council had time to begin, came Taku-Wakin with his arms folded—though he told me it was to hide how his heart jumped in his bosom—and took his father's seat. Around the ring of the chiefs and elders ran a growl like the circling of thunder in sultry weather, and immediately it was turned into coughing; every man trying to eat his own exclamation, for, as he sat, Taku laid out, in place of a trophy, the five arrows.

"'Do we sit at a game of knuckle-bone?' said Opata at last, 'or is this a Council of the Elders?'

"'Game or Council,' said Taku-Wakin, 'I sit in my father's place until I have a Sign from him whom he will have to sit there.'"

"But I don't understand—" began Oliver, looking about the circle of listening Indians. "His father was dead, was n't he?"

"What is 'dead'?" said the Lenni-Lenape; "Indians do not know. Our friends go out of their bodies; where? Into another—or into a beast? When I was still strapped in my basket my father set me on a bear that he had killed and prayed that the bear's cunning and strength should pass into me. Taku-Wakin's people thought that the heart of Long-Hand might have gone into the Mastodon."

"Why not?" agreed Arrumpa gravely. "I remember that Taku would call me Father at times, and—if he was very fond of me—Grandfather. But all he wanted at that time was to keep Opata from being elected in his father's place, and Opata, who understood this perfectly, was very angry.

"'It is the custom,' he said, 'when a chief sleeps in the High

Places,'—he meant the hilltops where they left their dead on poles or tied to the tree branches,—'that we elect another to his place in the Council.'

"'Also it is a custom,' said Taku-Wakin, 'to bring the token of his great exploit into Council and quicken the heart by hearing of it. You have heard, O Chiefs,' he said, 'that my father had a plan for the good of the people, and it has come to me in my heart that that plan was stronger in him than death. For he was a man who finished what he had begun, and it may be that he is long-handed enough to reach back from the place where he has gone. And this is a Sign to me, that he has taken his cut stick, which had the secret of his plan, with him.'

"Taku-Wakin fiddled with the arrows, laying them straight, hardly daring to look up at Opata, for if the chief had his father's cut stick, now would be the time that he would show it. Out of the tail of his eye he could see that the rest of the Council were startled. That was the way with men. Me they would trap, and take the skin of Saber-Tooth to wrap their cubs in, but at the hint of a Sign, or an old custom slighted, they would grow suddenly afraid. Then Taku looked up and saw Opata stroking his face with his hand to hide what he was thinking. He was no fool, and he saw that if the election was pressed, Taku-Wakin, boy as he was, would sit in his father's place because of the five arrows. Taku-Wakin stood up and stretched out his hand to the Council.

"'Is it agreed, O Chiefs, that you keep my father's place until there is a Sign?'—and a deep Hu-hub ran all about the circle. It was sign enough for them that the son of Long-Hand played unhurt with arrows that had been given to the gods. Taku stretched his hand to Opata, 'Is it agreed, O Chief?'

"'So long as the tribe comes to no harm,' said Opata, making the best of a bad business. 'It shall be kept until Long-Hand or his Talking Rod comes back to us.'

"'And,' said Taku-Wakin to me, 'whether Opata or I first sits in it, depends on which one of us can first produce a Sign.'

IV
THE SECOND PART OF THE MASTODON
STORY, CONCERNING THE TRAIL TO THE SEA
AND THE TALKING STICK OF TAKU-WAKIN

"It was the Talking Stick of his father that Taku-Wakin wanted,"
said Arrumpa. "He still thought Opata might have it, for every
now and then Taku would catch him coming back with marsh mud
on his moccasins. That was how I began to understand that the
Great Plan was really a plan to find a way *through* the marsh to the
sea on the other side of it.

"'Opata has the Stick,' said Taku, 'but it will not talk to him;
therefore he goes, as my father did, when the waters are low and
the hummocks of hard ground stand up, to find a safe way for the
tribe to follow. But my father had worked as far as the Grass Flats
and beyond them, to a place of islands.'

"'Squidgy Islands,' I told him. 'The Grass-Eaters go there to
drop their calves every season.' Taku kicked me behind the ears.

"'Said I not you were a beast of a bad heart!' he scolded. But how
should I know he would care to hear about a lot of silly Mammoths. 'Also,' he said, 'you are my Medicine. You shall find me the
trail of the Talking Stick, and I, Taku, son of Long-Hand, shall lead
the people.'

"'In six moons,' I told him, 'the Grass-Eaters go to the Islands to calve—'

"'In which time,' said Taku, 'the chiefs will have quarreled six times, and Opata will have eaten me. Drive them, Arrumpa, drive them!'

"Umph, uh-ump!" chuckled the old beast reminiscently. "We drove; we drove. What else was there to do? Taku-Wakin was my man. Besides, it was great fun. One-Tusk helped me. He was one of our bachelor herd who had lost a tusk in his first fight, which turned out greatly to his advantage. He would come sidling up to a refractory young cow with his eyes twinkling, and before anybody suspected he could give such a prod with his one tusk as sent her squealing. . . . But that came afterward. The Mammoth herd that fed on our edge of the Great Swamp was led by a wrinkled old cow, wise beyond belief. Scrag we called her. She would take the herd in to the bedding-ground by the river, to a landing-point on the opposite side, never twice the same, and drift noiselessly through the canebrake, choosing blowy hours when the swish of cane over woolly backs was like the run of the wind. Days when the marsh would be full of tapirs wallowing and wild pig rooting and fighting, there might be hundreds feeding within sound of you and not a hint of it, except the occasional *toot-toot* of some silly cow calling for Scrag, or a young bull blowing water.

"They bedded at the Grass Flats, but until Scrag herself had a mind to take the trail to the Squidgy Islands, there was nobody but Saber-Tooth could persuade her.

"'Then Saber-Tooth shall help us,' said my man.

"Not for nothing was he called Taku-Wakin, which means 'The Wonderful.' He brought a tiger cub's skin of his father's killing, dried stiff and sewed up with small stones inside it. At one end there was a thong with a loop in it, and it smelled of tiger. I could see the tip of One-Tusk's trunk go up with a start every time he winded it. There was a curled moon high up in the air like a feather, and a moon-white tusk glinting here and there, where the herds drifted across the flats. There was no trouble about our

going among them so long as Scrag did not wind us. *They* claimed
to be kin to us, and they cared nothing for Man even when they
smelled him. We came sidling up to a nervous young cow, and
Taku dropped from my neck long enough to slip the thong over a
hind foot as she lifted it. The thong was wet at first and scarcely
touched her. Presently it tightened. Then the cow shook her foot
to free it and the skin rattled. She squealed nervously and started
out to find Scrag, who was feeding on the far side of the hummock,
and at every step the tiger-skin rattled and bounced against her.
Eyes winked red with alarm and trunks came lifting out of the
tall grass like serpents. One-Tusk moved silently, prod-prodding;
we could hear the click of ivory and the bunting of shoulder
against shoulder. Then some silly cow had a whiff of the skin that
bounded along in their tracks like a cat, and raised the cry of
'Tiger! Tiger!' Far on the side from us, in the direction of the
Squidgy Islands, Scrag trumpeted, followed by frantic splashing as
the frightened herd plunged into the reed-beds. Taku slipped from
my neck, shaking with laughter.

"'Follow, follow,' he said; 'I go to bring up the people.'

"It was two days before Scrag stopped running.

"From the Grass Flats on to the Islands it was all one reed-
bed where the water gathered into runnels between hummocks of
rotten rushes, where no trail would lie and any false step might
plunge you into black bog to the shoulder. About halfway we
found the tiger-skin tramped into the mire, but as soon as we
struck the Islands I turned back, for I was in need of good oak
browse, and I wished to find out what had become of Taku-Wakin.
It was not until one evening when I had come well up into the hills
for a taste of fir, that I saw him, black against the sun with the tribe
behind him. The Five Chiefs walked each in front of his own
village, except that Taku-Wakin's own walked after Opata, and
there were two of the Turtle clan, each with his own head man;
and two under Apunkéwis. Before all walked Taku-Wakin holding
a peeled stick upright and seeing the end of the trail, but not what

lay close in front of him. He did not even see me as I slipped around the procession and left a wet trail for him to follow.

"That was how we crossed to the Islands, village by village, with Taku-Wakin close on my trail, which was the trail of the Grass-Eaters. They swam the sloughs with their children on their shoulders, and made rafts of reeds to push their food bundles over. By night they camped on the hummocks and built fires that burned for days in the thick litter of reeds. Red reflections glanced like fishes along the water. Then there would be the drums and the— the thunder-twirler—"

"But what kept him so long and how did he persuade them?" Dorcas Jane squirmed with curiosity.

"He'd been a long time working out the trail through the cane-brake," said Arrumpa, "making a Talking Stick as his father had taught him; one ring for a day's journey, one straight mark for so many man's paces; notches for turns. When he could not re-member his father's marks he made up others. When he came to his village again he found they had all gone over to Opata's. Apunkéwis, who had the two villages under Black Rock and was a friend of Long-Hand, told him that there would be a Sign.

"'There will,' said Taku-Wakin, 'but I shall bring it.' He knew that Opata meant mischief, but he could not guess what. All the way to Opata's his thought went round and round like a fire-stick in the hearth-hole. When he heard the drums he flared up like a spark in the tinder. Earlier in the evening there had been a Big Eating at Opata's, and now the men were dancing.

"'*Eyah, eyah!*' they sang.

"Taku-Wakin whirled like a spark into the ring. '*Eyah, eyah!*' he shouted,—

> 'Great are the people
> They have found a sign,
> The sign of the Talking Rod!
> Eyah! My people!'

"He planted it full in the firelight where it rocked and beckoned. '*Eyah*, the rod is calling,' he sang.

"The moment he had sight of Opata's face he knew that whatever the chief had meant to do, he did not have his father's Stick. Taku caught up his own and twirled it, and finally he hid it under his coat, for if any one had handled it he could have seen that this was not the Stick of Long-Hand, but fresh-peeled that season. But because Opata wanted the Stick of Long-Hand, he thought any stick of Taku's must be the one he wanted. And what Opata thought, the rest of the tribe thought also. So they rose up by clans and villages and followed after the Sign. That was how we came to the Squidgy Islands. There were willows there and young alders and bare knuckles of rock holding up the land.

"Beyond that the Swamp began; the water gathered itself into bayous that went slinking, wolflike, between the trees, or rose like a wolf *through* the earth and stole it from under your very foot. It doubled into black lagoons to doze, and young snakes coiled on the lily-pads, so that when the sun warmed them you could hear the *shi-shisi-ss* like a wind rising. Also by night there would be greenish lights that followed the trails for a while and went out suddenly in whistling noises. Now and then in broad day the Swamp would fall asleep. There would be the plop of turtles falling into the creek and the slither of alligators in the mud, and all of a sudden not a ripple would start, and between the clacking of one reed and another would come the soundless lift and stir of the Swamp snoring. Then the hair on your neck would rise, and some man caught walking alone in it would go screaming mad with fear.

"Six moons we had to stay in that place, for Scrag had hidden the herd so cleverly that it was not until the week-old calves began to squeak for their mothers that we found them. And from the time they were able to run under their mother's bodies, One-Tusk and I kept watch and watch to see that they did not break back to the Squidgy Islands. It was necessary for Taku-Wakin's plan that they should go out on the other side where there was good land between the Swamp and the Sea, not claimed by the Kooskooski.

We learned to eat grass that summer and squushy reeds with no strength in them—did I say that all the Grass-Eaters were pot-bellied? Also I had to reason with One-Tusk, who had not loved a man, and found that the Swamp bored him. By this time, too, Scrag knew what we were after; she covered her trail and crossed it as many times as a rabbit. Then, just as we thought we had it, the wolf water came and gnawed the trail in two.

"Taku-Wakin would come to me by the Black Lagoon and tell me how Opata worked to make himself chief of the nine villages. He had his own and Taku-Wakin's, for Taku had never dared to ask it back again, and the chief of the Turtle clan was Opata's man.

" 'He tells the people that my Stick will not talk to me any more. But how can it talk, Arrumpa, when you have nothing to tell it?'

" 'Patience,' I said. 'If we press the cows too hard they will break back the way they have come, and that will be worse than waiting.'

" 'And if I do not get them forward soon,' said Taku-Wakin, 'the people will break back, and my father will be proved a fool. I am too little for this thing, Grandfather,' he would say, leaning against my trunk, and I would take him up and comfort him.

"As for Opata, I used to see him sometimes, dancing alone to in-crease his magic power,—I speak but as the people of Taku-Wakin spoke,—and once at the edge of the lagoon, catching snakes. Opata had made a noose of hair at the end of a peeled switch, and he would snare them as they darted like streaks through the water. I saw him cast away some that he caught, and others he dropped into a wicker basket, one with a narrow neck such as women used for water. How was I to guess what he wanted with them? But the man smelled of mischief. It lay in the thick air like the smell of the lagoons; by night you could hear it throbbing with the drums that scared away the wandering lights from the nine villages.

"Scrag was beginning to get the cows together again; but by that time the people had made up their minds to stay where they were. They built themselves huts on platforms above the water and caught turtles in the bayous.

" 'Opata has called a Council,' Taku told me, 'to say that I must

make my Stick talk, or they will know me for a deceiver, a maker of
short life for them.'

" 'Short life to him,' I said. 'In three nights or four, the Grass-
Eaters will be moving.'

" 'And my people are fast in the mud,' said Taku-Wakin. 'I am a
mud-head myself to think a crooked rod could save them.' He
took it from his girdle warped by the wet and the warmth of his
body. 'My heart is sick, Arrumpa, and Opata makes them a better
chief than I, for I have only tried to find them their sea again. But
Opata understands them. This is a foolish tale that will never be
finished.'

"He loosed the stick from his hand over the black water like a
boy skipping stones, but—this is a marvel—it turned as it flew and
came back to Taku-Wakin so that he had to take it in his hand or it
would have struck him. He stood looking at it astonished, while
the moon came up and made dart-shaped ripples of light behind
the swimming snakes in the black water. For he saw that if the
Stick would not leave him, neither could he forsake—Is this also
known to you?" For he saw the children smiling.

The Indian who leaned against Moke-icha's boulder drew a
crooked stick, shaped something like an elbow, from under his
blanket. Twice he tossed it lightly and twice it flew over the heads
of the circle and back like a homing pigeon as he lightly caught it.

"Boomerangs!" cried the children, delighted.

"We called it the Stick-which-kills-flying," said the Indian, and
hid it again under his blanket.

"Taku-Wakin thought it Magic Medicine," said the Mastodon.
"It was a Sign to him. Two or three times he threw the stick and
always it came back to him. He was very quiet, considering what it
might mean, as I took him back between the trees that stood knee-
deep in the smelly water. We saw the huts at last, built about in a
circle and the sacred fire winking in the middle. I remembered the
time I had watched with Taku under the Arch Rock.

" 'Give me leave,' I said, 'to walk among the huts, and see what
will come of it.'

"Taku-Wakin slapped my trunk.

"'Now by the oath of my people, you shall walk,' he said. 'If the herds begin to move, and if no hurt comes to anybody by it, you shall walk; for as long as they are comfortable, even though the Rod should speak, they would not listen.'

"The very next night Scrag began to move her cows out toward the hard land, and when I had marked her trail for five man journeys, I came back to look for Taku-Wakin. There was a great noise of singing a little back from the huts at the Dancing-Place, and all the drums going, and the smoke that drifted along the trails had the smell of a Big Eating. I stole up in the dark till I could look over the heads of the villagers squatted about the fire. Opata was making a speech to them. He was working himself into a rage over the wickedness of Taku-Wakin. He would strike the earth with his stone-headed spear as he talked, and the tribe would yelp after him like wolves closing in on a buck. If the Talking Stick which had led them there was not a liar, let it talk again and show them the way to their sea. Let it talk! And at last, when they had screeched themselves hoarse, they were quiet long enough to hear it.

"Little and young, Taku-Wakin looked, standing up with his Stick in his hand, and the words coming slowly as if he waited for them to reach him from far off. The Stick was no liar, he said; it was he who had lied to them; he had let them think that this was his father's Stick. It was a new stick much more powerful, as he would yet show them. And who was he to make it talk when it would not? Yet it would talk soon . . . very soon . . . he had heard it whispering. . . . Let them not vex the Stick lest it speak strange and unthought-of things. . . .

"Oh, but he was well called 'The Wonderful.' I could see the heads of the tribesmen lifting like wolves taking a new scent, and mothers tighten their clutch on their children. Also I saw Opata. Him I watched, for he smelt of mischief. His water-basket was beside him, and as the people turned from baiting Taku-Wakin to believing him, I saw Opata push the bottle secretly with his spear-butt. It rolled into the cleared space toward Taku-Wakin, and the grass ball which stopped its mouth fell out unnoticed. *But no water came out!*

"Many of the waters of the Swamp were bitter and caused sickness, so it was no new thing for a man to have his own water-bottle at Council. But why should he carry a stopped bottle and no water in it? Thus I watched, while Taku-Wakin played for his life with the people's minds, and Opata watched neither the people nor him, but the unstopped mouth of the water-bottle.

"I looked where Opata looked, for I said to myself, from that point comes the mischief, and looking I saw a streak of silver pour out of the mouth of the bottle and coil and lift and make as a snake will for the nearest shadow. It was the shadow of Taku-Wakin's bare legs. Then I knew why Opata smelled of mischief when he had caught snakes in the lagoon. But I was afraid to speak, for I saw that if Taku moved the snake would strike, and there is no cure for the bite of the snake called Silver Moccasin.

"Everybody's eyes were on the rod but mine and Opata's, and as I saw Taku straighten to throw, I lifted my voice in the dark and trumpeted, 'Snake! Snake!' Taku leaped, but he knew my voice and he was not so frightened as the rest of them, who began falling on their faces. Taku leaped as the Silver Moccasin lifted to strike, and the stick as it flew out of his hand, low down like a skimming bird, came back in a circle—he must have practiced many times with it—and dropped the snake with its back broken. The people put their hands over their mouths. They had not seen the snake at all, but a stick that came back to the thrower's hand was magic. They waited to see what Opata would do about it.

"Opata stood up. He was a brave man, I think, for the Stick was Magic to him, also, and yet he stood out against it. Black Magic he said it was, and no wonder it had not led them out of the Swamp, since it was a false stick and Taku-Wakin a Two-Talker. Taku-Wakin could no more lead them out of the Swamp than his stick would leave him. Like it, they would be thrown and come back to the hand of Taku-Wakin for his own purposes.

"He was a clever man, was Opata. He was a fine tall man,

beaked like an eagle, and as he moved about in the clear space by the fire, making a pantomime of all he said, as their way is in speech-making, he began to take hold on the minds of the people. Taku-Wakin watched sidewise; he saw the snake writhing on the ground and the unstopped water-bottle with the ground dry under it. I think he suspected. I saw a little ripple go over his naked body as if a thought had struck him. He stepped aside once, and as Opata came at him, threatening and accusing, he changed his place again, ever so slightly. The people yelped as they thought they saw Taku fall back before him. Opata was shaking his spear, and I began to wonder if I had not waited too long to come to Taku-Wakin's rescue, when suddenly Opata stopped still in his tracks and shuddered. He went gray in the firelight, and—he was a brave man who knew his death when he had met it—from beside his foot he lifted up the broken-backed snake on his spear-point. Even as he held it up for all of them to see, his limbs began to jerk and stiffen.

"I went back to look for One-Tusk. The end of those who are bitten by the moccasin is not pretty to see, and besides, I had business. One-Tusk and I walked through all nine villages . . . and when we had come out on the other side there were not two sticks of them laid together. Then the people came and looked and were afraid, and Taku-Wakin came and made a sound as when a man drops a ripe paw-paw on the ground. 'Pr-r-utt!' he said, as though it were no more matter than that. 'Now we shall have the less to carry.' But the mother of Taku-Wakin made a terrible outcry. In the place where her hut had been she had found the Talking Stick of Taku's father, trampled to splinters.

"She had had it all the time hidden in her bundle. Long-Hand had told her it was Magic Medicine and she must never let any one have it. *She* thought it was the only thing that had kept her and her children safe on this journey. But Taku told them that it was his father's Rod which had bewitched them and kept them from going any farther because it had come to the end of its knowledge. Now they would be free to follow his own Stick, which was so much wiser. So he caught their minds as he had caught the Stick, swinging back from disaster. For this is the way with men, if they have reason which suits them they do not care whether it is reasonable or not. It was sufficient for them, one crooked stick being broken, that they should rise up with a shout and follow another."

Arrumpa was silent so long that the children fidgeted.

"But it could n't have been just as easy as that," Dorcas insisted. "And what did they do when they got to the sea finally?"

"They complained of the fishy taste of everything," said Arrumpa; "also they suffered on the way for lack of food, and Apunkéwis was eaten by an alligator. Then they were afraid again when they came to the place beyond the Swamp where the water went to and fro as the sea pushed it, until some of the old men remembered they had heard it was the sea's custom. Twice daily the water came in as if to feed on the marsh grass. Great clouds of gulls flew inland, screaming down the wind, and across the salt flats they had their first sight of the low, hard land.

"We lost them there, for we could not eat the salt grass, and Scrag had turned north by a mud slough where the waters were bitter, and red moss grew on the roots of the willows. We ate for a quarter of the moon's course before we went back around the hard land to see what had become of Taku-Wakin. We fed as far as there was any browse between the sea and the marsh, and at last we saw them come, across the salt pastures. They were sleek as otters with the black slime of the sloughs, and there was not a garment left on them which had not become water-soaked and useless. Some of the women had made slips of sea-birds' skins and nets of marsh grass for carrying their young. It was only by these things that you could tell that they were Man. They came out where the hard land thinned to a tusk, thrust far out into the white froth and the thunder. We saw them naked on the rocks, and then with a great shout join hands as they ran all together down the naked sand to worship the sea. But Taku-Wakin walked by himself . . ."

"And did you stay there with him?" asked Oliver when he saw by the stir in the audience that the story was quite finished.

"We went back that winter—One-Tusk and I; in time they all went," said Arrumpa. "It was too cold by the sea in winter. And the land changed. Even in Taku-Wakin's time it changed greatly. The earth shook and the water ran out of the marsh into the sea again, and there was hard ground most of the way to Two Rivers. Every year the tribes used to go down by it to gather sea food."

The Indians nodded.

"It was so in our time," they said. "There were great heaps of shells by the sea where we came and dried fish and feasted."

"Shell Mounds," said Oliver. "I've heard of those, too. But I never thought they had stories about them."

"There is a story about everything," said the Buffalo Chief; and by this time the children were quite ready to believe him.

V

HOW HOWKAWANDA AND FRIEND-AT-THE-BACK FOUND THE TRAIL TO THE BUFFALO COUNTRY; TOLD BY THE COYOTE

"Concerning that Talking Stick of Taku-Wakin's,"—said the Coyote, as the company settled back after Arrumpa's story,—"there is a Telling of *my* people . . . not of a Rod, but a Skin, a hide of thy people, Great Chief,"—he bowed to the Bull Buffalo,—"that talked of Tamal-Pyweack and a Dead Man's Journey—" The little beast stood with lifted paw and nose delicately pointed toward the Bighorn's country as it lifted from the prairie, drawing the earth after it in great folds, high crest beyond high crest flung against the sun; light and color like the inside of a shell playing in its snow-filled hollows.

Up sprang every Plainsman, painted shield dropped to the shoulder, right hand lifted, palm outward, and straight as an arrow out of every throat, the "Heya-heya-huh!" of the Indian salutation.

"Backbone of the World!" cried the Blackfoot. "Did you come over that, Little Brother?"

"Not I, but my father's father's first father. By the Crooked Horn,"—he indicated a peak like a buffalo horn, and a sag in the crest below it.

"Then that," said Bighorn, dropping with one bound from his

aerial lookout, "should be *my* story, for my people made that trail, and it was long before any other trod in it."

"It was of that first treading that the Skin talked," agreed the Coyote. He looked about the company for permission to begin, and then addressed himself to Arrumpa. "You spoke, Chief Two-Tails, of the 'tame wolves' of Taku-Wakin; *were* they wolves, or—"

"Very like you, Wolfling, now that I think of it," agreed the Mastodon, "and they were not tame exactly; they ran at the heels of the hunters for what they could pick up, and sometimes they drove up game for him."

"Why should a coyote, who is the least of all wolves, hunt for himself when he can find a man to follow?" said the Blackfoot, who sat smoking a great calumet out of the west corridor. "Man is the wolf's Medicine. In him he hears the voice of the Great Mystery, and becomes a dog, which is great gain to him."

Pleased as if his master had patted him, without any further introduction the Coyote began his story.

"Thus and so thought the First Father of all the Dogs in the year when he was called Friend-at-the-Back, and Pathfinder. That was the time of the Great Hunger, nearly two years after he joined the man pack at Hidden-under-the-Mountain and was still known by his lair name of Younger Brother. He followed a youth who was the quickest afoot and the readiest laugher. He would skulk about the camp at Hidden-under-the-Mountain watching until the hunters went out. Sometimes Howkawanda—that was the young man he followed—would give a coyote cry of warning, and sometimes Younger Brother would trot off in the direction where he knew the game to be, looking back and pointing until the young men caught the idea; after which, when they had killed, the hunters would laugh and throw him pieces of liver.

"The Country of Dry Washes lies between the Cinoave on the south and the People of the Bow who possessed the Salmon Rivers, a great gray land cut across by deep gullies where the wild waters come down from the Wall-of-Shining-Rocks and worry the bone-white boulders. The People of the Dry Washes live meanly, and are meanly spoken of by the People of the Coast who drove them inland from the sea borders. After the Rains, when the quick grass sprang up, vast herds of deer and pronghorn come down from the mountains; and when there were no rains the people ate lizards and roots. In the moon of the Frost-Touching-Mildly clouds came up from the south with a great trampling of thunder, and flung out over the Dry Washes as a man flings his blanket over a maiden. But if the Rains were scant for two or three seasons, then there was Hunger, and the dust devils took the mesas for their dancing-places.

"Now, Man tribe and Wolf tribe are alike in one thing. When there is scarcity the packs increase to make surer of bringing down the quarry, but when the pinch begins they hunt scattering and avoid one another. That was how it happened that the First Father, who was still called Younger Brother, was alone with Howkawanda when he was thrown by a buck at Talking Water in the moon of the Frost-Touching-Mildly. Howkawanda had caught the buck by the antlers in a blind gully at the foot of the Tamal-Pyweack, trying for the throw back and to the left which drops a buck running, with his neck broken. But his feet slipped on the grass which grows sleek with dryness, and by the time the First Father came up the buck had him down, scoring the ground on either side of the man's body with his sharp antlers, lifting and trampling. Younger Brother leaped at the throat. The toss of the antlers to meet the stroke drew the man up standing. Throwing his whole weight to the right he drove home with his hunting-knife and the buck toppled and fell as a tree falls of its own weight in windless weather.

"'Now, for this,' said Howkawanda to my First Father, when they had breathed a little, 'you are become my very brother.' Then he marked the coyote with the blood of his own hurts, as the custom is when men are not born of one mother, and Younger Brother, who had never been touched by a man, trembled. That night, though it made the hair on his neck rise with strangeness, he went into the hut of Howkawanda at Hidden-under-the-Mountain and the villagers wagged their heads over it. 'Hunger must be hard on our trail,' they said, 'when the wolves come to house with us.'

"But Howkawanda only laughed, for that year he had found a maiden who was more than meat to him. He made a flute of four notes which he would play, lying out in the long grass, over and over, until she came out to him. Then they would talk, or the maiden would pull grass and pile it in little heaps while Howkawanda looked at her and the First Father looked at his master, and none of them cared where the Rains were.

"But when no rain fell at all, the camp was moved far up the shrunken creek, and Younger Brother learned to catch grasshoppers, and ate juniper berries, while the men sat about the fire hugging their lean bellies and talking of Dead Man's Journey. This they would do whenever there was a Hunger in the Country of the Dry Washes, and when they were fed they forgot it."

The Coyote interrupted his own story long enough to explain that though there were no buffaloes in the Country of the Dry Washes, on the other side of the Wall-of-Shining-Rocks the land was black with them. "Now and then stray herds broke through by passes far to the north in the Land of the Salmon Rivers, but the people of that country would not let Howkawanda's people hunt them. Every year, when they went up by tribes and villages to the Tamal-Pyweack to gather pine nuts, the People of the Dry Washes looked for a possible trail through the Wall to the Buffalo Country. There was such a trail. Once a man of strange dress and speech had found his way over it, but he was already starved when they picked him up at the place called Trap-of-the-Winds, and died before he could tell anything. The most that was known of this trail at Hidden-under-the-Mountain was that it led through Knife-Cut Cañon; but at the Wind Trap they lost it.

"'I have heard of that trail,' said the First Father of all the Dogs to Howkawanda, one day, when they had hunted too far for returning and spent the night under a juniper: 'a place where the wind tramples between the mountains like a trapped beast. But there is a trail beyond it. I have not walked in it. All my people went that way at the beginning of the Hunger.'

"'For your people there may be a way,' said Howkawanda, 'but for mine—they are all dead who have looked for it. Nevertheless, Younger Brother, if we be not dead men ourselves when this Hunger is past, you and I will go on this Dead Man's Journey. Just now we have other business.'

"It is the law of the Hunger that the strongest must be fed first, so that there shall always be one strong enough to hunt for the others. But Howkawanda gave the greater part of his portion to his maiden.

"So it happened that sickness laid hold on Howkawanda between two days. In the morning he called to Younger Brother. 'Lie outside,' he said, 'lest the sickness take you also, but come to me every day with your kill, and let no man prevent you.'

"So Younger Brother, who was able to live on juniper berries, hunted alone for the camp of Hidden-under-the-Mountain, and Howkawanda held back Death with one hand and gripped the heart of the First Father of all the Dogs with the other. For he was afraid that if he died, Younger Brother would turn wolf again, and the tribe would perish. Every day he would divide what Younger Brother brought in, and after the villagers were gone he would inquire anxiously and say, 'Do you smell the Rain, Friend and Brother?'

"But at last he was too weak for asking, and then quite suddenly his voice was changed and he said, 'I smell the Rain, Little Brother!' For in those days men could smell weather quite as well as the other animals. But the dust of his own running was in Younger Brother's nose, and he thought that his master's mind wandered. The sick man counted on his fingers. 'In three days,' he said, 'if the Rains come, the back of the Hunger is broken. Therefore I will not die for three days. Go, hunt, Friend and Brother.'

"The sickness must have sharpened Howkawanda's senses, for the next day the coyote brought him word that the water had come back in the gully where they threw the buck, which was a sign that rain was falling somewhere on the high ridges. And the next day he brought word, 'The tent of the sky is building.' This was the tentlike cloud that would stretch from peak to peak of the Tamal-Pyweack at the beginning of the Rainy Season.

"Howkawanda rose up in his bed and called the people. 'Go, hunt! go, hunt!' he said; 'the deer have come back to Talking Water.' Then he lay still and heard them, as many as were able, going out joyfully. 'Stay you here, Friend and Brother,' he said, 'for now I can sleep a little.'

"So the First Father of all the Dogs lay at his master's feet and whined a little for sympathy while the people hunted for themselves, and the myriad-footed Rain danced on the dry thatch of the hut and the baked mesa. Later the creek rose in its withered banks and began to talk to itself in a new voice, the voice of Raining-on-the-Mountain.

"'Now I shall sleep well,' said the sick man. So he fell into deeper and deeper pits of slumber while the rain came down in torrents, the grass sprouted, and far away Younger Brother could hear the snapping of the brush as the Horned People came down the mountain.

"It was about the first streak of the next morning that the people waked in their huts to hear a long, throaty howl from Younger Brother. Howkawanda lay cold, and there was no breath in him. They thought the coyote howled for grief, but it was really because, though his master lay like one dead, there was no smell of death about him, and the First Father was frightened. The more he howled, however, the more certain the villagers were that Howkawanda was dead, and they made haste to dispose of the body. Now that the back of the Hunger was broken, they wished to go back to Hidden-under-the-Mountain.

"They drove Younger Brother away with sticks and wrapped the young man in fine deerskins, binding them about and about with thongs, with his knife and his fire-stick and his hunting-gear beside him. Then they made ready brush, the dryest they could find, for it was the custom of the Dry Washes to burn the dead. They thought of the Earth as their mother and would not put anything into it to defile it. The Head Man made a speech, putting in all the virtues of Howkawanda, and those that he might have had if he had been spared to them longer, while the women cast dust on their hair and rocked to and fro howling. Younger Brother crept as close to the pyre as he dared, and whined in his throat as the fire took hold of the brush and ran crackling up the open spaces.

"It took hold of the wrapped deerskins, ran in sparks like little deer in the short hair, and bit through to Howkawanda. But no sooner had he felt the teeth of the flame than the young man came back from the place where he had been, and sat up in the midst of the burning. He leaped out of the fire, and the people scattered like embers and put their hands over their mouths, as is the way with men when they are astonished. Howkawanda, wrapped as he was, rolled on the damp sand till the fires were out, while Younger Brother gnawed him free of the death-wrappings, and the people's hands were still at their mouths. But the first step he took toward them they caught up sticks and stones to threaten.

"It was a fearful thing to them that he should come back from being dead. Besides, the hair was burned half off his head, and he was streaked raw all down one side where the fire had bitten him. He stood blinking, trying to pick up their meaning with his eyes. His maiden looked up from her mother's lap where she wept for him, and fled shrieking.

"'Dead, go back to the dead!' cried the Head Man, but he did not stop to see whether Howkawanda obeyed him, for by this time the whole pack was squealing down the creek to Hidden-under-the-Mountain. Howkawanda looked at his maiden running fast with the strength of the portion he had saved for her; looked at the empty camp and the bare hillside; looked once at the high Wall of the Pyweack, and laughed as much as his burns would let him.

"'If we two be dead men, Brother,' he said, 'it may be we shall have luck on a Dead Man's Journey.'

"It would have been better if they could have set out at once, for rain in the Country of Dry Washes means snow on the Mountain. But they had to wait for the healing of Howkawanda's burns, and to plump themselves out a little on the meat—none too fat—that came down on its own feet before the Rains. They lay in the half-ruined huts and heard, in the intervals of the storm, the beating of tom-toms at Hidden-under-the-Mountain to keep off the evil influences of one who had been taken for dead and was alive again.

"By the time they were able to climb to the top of Knife-Cut Cañon the snow lay over the mountains like a fleece, and at every turn of the wind it shifted. From the Pass they dropped down into a pit between the ranges, where, long before they came to it, they could hear the wind beating about like a trapped creature. Here great mountain-heads had run together like bucks in autumn, digging with shining granite hooves deep into the floor of the Cañon. Into this the winds would drop from the high places like broken-winged birds, dashing themselves against the polished walls of the Pyweack, dashing and falling back and crying woundedly. There was no other way into this Wind Trap than the way Howkawanda and Younger Brother had come. If there was any way out only the Four-Footed People knew it.

"But over all their trails snow lay, deepening daily, and great rivers of water that fell into the Trap in summer stood frozen stiff like ice vines climbing the Pyweack.

"The two travelers made them a hut in broad branches of a great fir, for the snow was more than man-deep already, and crusted over. They laid sticks on the five-branched whorl and cut away the boughs above them until they could stand. Here they nested, with the snow on the upper branches like thatch to keep them safe against the wind. They ran on the surface of the snow, which was packed firm in the bottom of the Trap, and caught birds and small game wintering in runways under the snow where the stiff brush arched and upheld it. When the wind, worn out with its struggles, would lie still in the bottom of the Trap, the two would race over the snow-crust whose whiteness cut the eye like a knife, working into every winding of the Cañon for some clue to the Dead Man's Journey.

"On one of these occasions, caught by a sudden storm, they hugged themselves for three days and ate what food they had, mouthful by mouthful, while the snow slid past them straight and sodden. It closed smooth over the tree where their house was, to the middle branches. Two days more they waited until the sun by day and the cold at night had made a crust over the fresh fall. On the second day they saw something moving in the middle of the Cañon. Half a dozen wild geese had been caught in one of the wind currents that race like rivers about the High Places of the World, and dropped exhausted into the Trap. Now they rose heavily; but, starved and blinded, they could not pitch their flight to that great height. Round and round they beat, and back they dropped from the huge mountain-heads, bewildered. Finally, the leader rose alone higher and higher in that thin atmosphere until the watchers almost lost him, and then, exhausted, shot downward to the ledge where Howkawanda and Younger Brother hugged themselves in the shelter of a wind-driven drift. They could see the gander's body shaken all over with the pumping of his heart as Younger Brother took him hungrily by the neck.

"'Nay, Brother,' said Howkawanda, 'but I also have been counted dead, and it is in my heart that this one shall serve us better living than dead.' He nursed the great white bird in his bosom and fed it with the last of their food and a little snow-water melted in his palm. In an hour, rested and strengthened, the bird rose again, beating a wide circle slowly and steadily upward, until, with one faint honk of farewell, it sailed slowly out of sight between the peaks, sure of its direction.

"'That way,' said Howkawanda, 'lies Dead Man's Journey.'

"When they came back over the same trail a year later, they were frightened to see what steeps and crevices they had covered.

"Shot downward to the ledge where Howkawanda and Younger Brother hugged themselves."

But for that first trip the snow-crust held firm while they made straight for the gap in the peaks through which the wild goose had disappeared. They traveled as long as the light lasted, though their hearts sobbed and shook with the thin air and the cold.

"The drifts were thinner, and the rocks came through with clusters of wind-slanted cedars. By nightfall snow began again, and they moved, touching, for they could not see an arm's length and dared not stop lest the snow cover them. And the hair along the back of Younger Brother began to prick.

"'Here I die, indeed,' said Howkawanda at last, for he suffered most because of his naked skin. He sank down in the soft snow at Younger Brother's shoulder.

"'Up, Master,' said Younger Brother, 'I hear something.'

"'It is the Storm Spirit singing my death song,' said Howkawanda.

But the coyote took him by the neck of his deerskin shirt and dragged him a little.

"'Now,' he said, 'I smell something.'

"Presently they stumbled into brush and knew it for red cedar. Patches of it grew thick on the high ridges, matted close for cover. As the travelers crept under it they heard the rustle of shoulder against shoulder, the moving click of horns, and the bleat of yearlings for their mothers. They had stumbled in the dark on the bedding-place of a flock of Bighorn.

"'Now we shall also eat,' said Younger Brother, for he was quite empty.

"The hand of Howkawanda came out and took him firmly by the loose skin between the shoulders.

"'There was a coyote once who became brother to a man,' he said, 'and men, when they enter a strange house in search of shelter and direction, do not first think of killing.'

"'One blood we are,' said the First Father of Dogs, remembering how Howkawanda had marked him, 'but we are not of one smell and the rams may trample me.'

"Howkawanda took off his deerskin and put around the coyote so that he should have man smell about him, for at that time the Bighorn had not learned to fear man.

"They could hear little bleats of alarm from the ewes and the huddling of the flock away from them, and the bunting of the Chief Ram's horns on the cedars as he came to smell them over. Younger Brother quivered, for he could think of nothing but the ram's throat, the warm blood and the tender meat, but the finger of Howkawanda felt along his shoulders for the scar of the Blood-Mixing, the time they had killed the buck at Talking Water. Then the First Father of all the Dogs understood that Man was his Medicine and his spirit leaped up to lick the face of the man's spirit. He lay still and felt the blowing in and out of Howkawanda's long hair on the ram's breath, as he nuzzled them from head to heel. Finally the Bighorn stamped twice with all his four feet together, as a sign that he had found no harm in the strangers. They could feel the flock huddling back, and the warmth of the packed fleeces. In the midst of it the two lay down and slept till morning.

"They were alone in the cedar shelter when they woke, but the track of the flock in the fresh-fallen snow led straight over the crest under the Crooked Horn to protected slopes, where there was still some browse and open going.

"Toward nightfall they found an ancient wether the weight of whose horns had sunk him deep in the soft snow, so that he could neither go forward nor back. Him they took. It was pure kindness, for he would have died slowly otherwise of starvation. That is the Way Things Are," said the Coyote; "when one *must* kill, killing is allowed. But before they killed him they said certain words.

"Later," the Coyote went on, "they found a deer occasionally and mountain hares. Their worst trouble was with the cold. Snow lay deep over the dropped timber and the pine would not burn. Howkawanda would scrape together moss and a few twigs for a little fire to warm the front of him and Younger Brother would snuggle at his back, so between two friends the man saved himself."

The Blackfoot nodded. "Fire is a very old friend of Man," he said; "so old that the mere sight of it comforts him; they have come a long way together."

"Now I know," said Oliver, "why you called the first dog Friend-at-the-Back."

"Oh, but there was more to it than that," said the Coyote, "for the next difficulty they had was to carry their food when they found it. Howkawanda had never had good use of his shoulder since the fire bit it, and even a buck's quarter weights a man too much in loose snow. So he took a bough of fir, thick-set with little twigs, and tied the kill on that. This he would drag behind him, and it rode lightly over the surface of the drifts. When the going was bad, Younger Brother would try to tug a little over his shoulder, so at last Howkawanda made a harness for him to pull straight ahead. Hours when they would lie storm-bound under the cedars, he whittled at the bough and platted the twigs together till it rode easily.

"In the moon of Tender Leaves, the people of the Buffalo Country, when they came up the hills for the spring kill, met a very curious procession coming down. They saw a man with no clothes but a few tatters of deerskin, all scarred down one side of his body, and following at his back a coyote who dragged a curiously plaited platform, by means of two poles harnessed across his shoulders. It was the first travoise. The men of the Buffalo Country put their hands over their mouths, for they had never seen anything like it."

The Coyote waited for the deep "huh-huh" of approval which circled the attentive audience at the end of the story.

"Fire and a dog!" said the Blackfoot, adding a little pinch of sweet-grass to his smoke as a sign of thankfulness,—"Friend-on-the-Hearth and Friend-at-the-Back! Man may go far with them."

Moke-icha turned her long flanks to the sun. "Now I thought the tale began with a mention of a Talking Skin—"

"Oh, that!" The Coyote recalled himself. "After he had been a year in the Buffalo Country, Howkawanda went back to carry news of the trail to the Dry Washes. All that summer he worked over it while his dogs hunted for him—for Friend-at-the-Back had taken a mate and there were four cubs to run with them. Every day, as Howkawanda worked out the trail, he marked it with stone and tree-blazes. With colored earth he marked it on a buffalo skin, from the Wind Trap to the Buffalo Country.

"When he came to Hidden-under-the-Mountain he left his dogs behind, for he said, 'Howkawanda is a dead man to them.' In the Buffalo Country he was known as Two-Friended, and that was his name afterward. He was dressed after the fashion of that country, with a great buffalo robe that covered him, and his face was painted. So he came to Hidden-under-the-Mountain as a stranger and made signs to them. And when they had fed him, and sat him in the chief place as was the custom with strangers, he took the writing from under his robe to give it to the People of the Dry Washes. There was a young woman near by nursing her child, and she gave a sudden sharp cry, for she was the one that had been his maiden, and under the edge of his robe she saw his scars. But when Howkawanda looked hard at her she pretended that the child had bitten her."

Dorcas Jane and Oliver drew a long breath when they saw that, so far as the rest of the audience was concerned, the story was finished. There were a great many questions they wished to ask,— as to what became of Howkawanda after that, and whether the People of the Dry Washes ever found their way into the Buffalo Country,—but before they could begin on them, the Bull Buffalo stamped twice with his fore-foot for a sign of danger. Far down at the other end of the gallery they could hear the watchman coming.

VI
DORCAS JANE HEARS HOW THE CORN CAME
TO THE VALLEY OF THE MISSI-SIPPU;
TOLD BY THE CORN WOMAN

It was one of those holidays, when there isn't any school and the Museum is only opened for a few hours in the afternoon, that Dorcas Jane had come into the north gallery of the Indian room where her father was at work mending the radiators. This was about a week after the children's first adventure on the Buffalo Trail, but it was before the holes had been cut in the Museum wall to let you look straight across the bend in the Colorado and into the Hopi pueblo. Dorcas looked at all the wall cases and wondered how it was the Indians seemed to have so much corn and so many kinds of it, for she had always thought of corn as a civilized sort of thing to have. She sat on a bench against the wall wondering, for the lovely clean stillness of the room encouraged thinking, and the clink of her father's hammers on the pipes fell presently into the regular *tink-tink-a-tink* of tortoise-shell rattles, keeping time to the shuffle and beat of bare feet on the dancing-place by the river. The path to it led across a clearing between little hillocks of freshly turned earth, and the high forest overhead was bursting into tiny green darts of growth like flame. The rattles were sewed to the leggings of the women—little yellow and black land-tortoise shells filled with pebbles—who sang as they danced and cut themselves with flints until they bled.

"Oh," said Dorcas, without waiting to be introduced, "what makes you do that?"

"To make the corn grow," said the tallest and the handsomest of the women, motioning to the others to leave off their dancing while she answered. "Listen! You can hear the men doing their part."

From the forest came a sudden wild whoop, followed by the sound of a drum, little and far off like a heart beating. "They are scaring off the enemies of the corn," said the Corn Woman, for Dorcas could see by her headdress, which was of dried corn tassels dyed in colors, and by a kind of kilt she wore, woven of corn husks, that that was what she represented.

"Oh!" said Dorcas; and then, after a moment, "It sounds as if you were sorry, you know."

"When the seed corn goes into the ground it dies," said the Corn Woman; "the tribe might die also if it never came alive again. Also we lament for the Giver-of-the-Corn who died giving."

"I thought corn just grew," said Dorcas; "I did n't know it came from any place."

"From the People of the Seed, from the Country of Stone Houses. It was bought for us by Given-to-the-Sun. Our people came from the East, from the place where the Earth opened, from the place where the Noise was, where the Mountain thundered. . . . This is what I have heard; this is what the Old Ones have said," finished the Corn Woman, as though it were some sort of song.

She looked about to the others as if asking their consent to tell the story. As they nodded, sitting down to loosen their heavy leggings, Dorcas could see that what she had taken to be a shock of last year's cornstalks, standing in the middle of the dancing-place, was really tied into a rude resemblance to a woman. Around its neck was one of the Indian's sacred bundles; Dorcas thought it might have something to do with the story, but decided to wait and see.

"There was a trail in those days," said the Corn Woman, "from the buffalo pastures to the Country of the Stone House. We used to travel it as far as the ledge where there was red earth for face-painting, and to trade with the Blanket People for salt. But no far-ther. Hunting-parties that crossed into Chihuahua returned some-times; more often they were given to the Sun.—On the tops of the hills where their god-houses were," explained the Corn Woman seeing that Dorcas was puzzled. "The Sun was their god to them. Every year they gave captives on the hills they built to the Sun."

Dorcas had heard the guard explaining to visitors in the Aztec room. "Teocales," she suggested.

"That was one of their words," agreed the Corn Woman. "They called themselves Children of the Sun. This much we knew; that there was a Seed. The People of the Cliffs, who came to the edge of the Windswept Plain to trade, would give us cakes sometimes for dried buffalo tongues. This we understood was *mahiz*, but it was not until Given-to-the-Sun came to us that we thought of having it for ours. Our men were hunters. They thought it shame to dig in the ground.

"Shungakela, of the Three Feather band, found her at the fork of the Turtle River, half starved and as fierce as she was hungry, but *he* called her 'Waits-by-the-Fire' when he brought her back to his tipi, and it was a long time before we knew that she had any other name. She belonged to one of the mountain tribes whose villages were raided by the People of the Sun, and because she had been a child at the time, she was made a servant. But in the end, when she had shot up like a red lily and her mistress had grown fond of her, she was taken by the priests of the Sun.

"At first the girl did not know what to make of being dressed so handsomely and fed upon the best of everything, but when they painted her with the sign of the Sun she knew. Over her heart they painted it. Then they put about her neck the Eye of the Sun, and the same day the woman who had been her mistress and was fond of her, slipped her a seed which she said should be eaten as she went up the Hill of the Sun, so she would feel nothing. Given-to-the-Sun hid it in her bosom.

"There was a custom that, in the last days, those who were to go up the Hill of the Sun could have anything they asked for. So the girl asked to walk by the river and hear the birds sing. When they had walked out of sight of the Stone Houses, she gave her watchers the seed in their food and floated down the river on a piece of bark until she came ashore in the thick woods and escaped. She came north, avoiding the trails, and after a year Shungakela found her. Between her breasts there was the sign of the Sun."

The Corn Woman stooped and traced in the dust the ancient sign of the intertwined four corners of the Earth with the Sun in the middle. "Around her neck in a buckskin bag was the charm that is known as the Eye of the Sun. She never showed it to any of us, but when she was in trouble or doubt, she would put her hand over it. It was her Medicine."

"It was good Medicine, too," spoke up the oldest of the dancing women.

"We had need of it," agreed the Corn Woman. "In those days the Earth was too full of people. The tribes swarmed, new chiefs arose, kin hunted against kin. Many hunters made the game shy, and it removed to new pastures. Strong people drove out weaker and took away their hunting-grounds. We had our share of both fighting and starving, but our tribe fared better than most because of the Medicine of Waits-by-the-Fire, the Medicine of the Sun. She was a wise woman. She was made Shaman. When she spoke, even the chiefs listened. But what could the chiefs do except hunt farther and fight harder? So Waits-by-the-Fire talked to the women. She talked of corn, how it was planted and harvested, with what rites and festivals.

"There was a God of the Seed, a woman god who was served by women. When the women of our tribe heard that, they took heart. The men had been afraid that the God of the Corn would not be friendly to us. I think, too, they did not like the idea of leaving off the long season of hunting and roving, for corn is a town-maker. For the tending and harvesting there must be one place, and for the guarding of the winter stores there must be a safe place. So said Waits-by-the-Fire to the women digging roots or boiling old bones in the long winter. She was a wise woman.

"It was the fight we had with the Tenasas that decided us. That was a year of great scarcity and the Tenasas took to sending their young men, two or three at a time, creeping into our hunting-grounds to start the game, and turn it in the direction of their own country. When our young men were sure of this, they went in force and killed inside the borders of the Tenasas. They had sur-prised a herd of buffaloes at Two Kettle Licks and were cutting up the meat when the Tenasas fell upon them. Waits-by-the-Fire lost her last son by that battle. One she had lost in the fight at Red Buttes and one in a year of Hunger while he was little. This one was swift of foot and was called Last Arrow, for Shungakela had said, 'Once I had a quiver full.' Waits-by-the-Fire brought him back on her shoulders from the place where the fight was. She walked with him into the Council.

"'The quiver is empty,' she said; 'the food bags, also; will you wait for us to fill one again before you fill the other?'

"Mad Wolf, who was chief at the time, threw up his hand as a man does when he is down and craves a mercy he is too proud to ask for. 'We have fought the Tenasas,' he said; 'shall we fight our women also?'

"Waits-by-the-Fire did not wait after that for long speeches in the Council. She gathered her company quickly, seven women well seasoned and not comely,—'The God of the Corn is a woman god,' she said, sharp smiling,—and seven men, keen and hard run-ners. The rest she appointed to meet her at Painted Rock ten moons from their going."

"So long as that!" said Dorcas Jane. "Was it so far from where you lived to Mex—to the Country of Stone Houses?"

"Not so far, but they had to stay from planting to harvest. Of what use was the seed without knowledge. Traveling hard they crossed the River of the White Rocks and reached, by the end of that moon, the mountain overlooking the Country of Stone Houses. Here the men stayed. Waits-by-the-Fire arranged everything. She thought the people of the towns might hesitate to admit so many men strangers. Also she had the women put on worn moccasins with holes, and old food from the year before in their food bags."

"I should think," began Dorcas Jane, "they would have wanted to put on the best they had to make a good impression."

"She was a wise woman," said the Corn Woman; "she said that if they came from near, the people of the towns might take them for spies, but they would not fear travelers from so far off that their moccasins had holes in them."

The Corn Woman had forgotten that she was telling a story older than the oaks they sat under. When she came to the exciting parts she said "we" and "us" as though it were something that had happened to them all yesterday.

"It was a high white range that looked on the Country of Stone Houses," she said, "with peaks that glittered, dropping down ridge by ridge to where the trees left off at the edge of a wide, basket-colored valley. It hollowed like a meal basket and had a green pattern woven through it by a river. Shungakela went with the women to the foot of the mountain, and then, all at once, he would not let them go until Waits-by-the-Fire promised to come back to the foot of the mountain once in every moon to tell him how things went with us. We thought it very childish of him, but afterward we were glad we had not made any objection.

"It was mid-morning when the Seven walked between the fields, with little food in their bags and none whatever in their stomachs, all in rags except Waits-by-the-Fire, who had put on her Shaman's dress, and around her neck, tied in a bag with feathers, the Medicine of the Sun. People stood up in the fields to stare, and we would have stared back again, but we were afraid. Behind the stone house we saw the Hill of the Sun and the priests moving up and down as Waits-by-the-Fire had described it.

"Below the hill, where the ground was made high, at one side of the steps that went up to the Place of Giving, stood the house of the Corn Goddess, which was served by women. There the Seven laid up their offering of poor food before the altar and stood on the steps of the god-house until the head priestess noticed them. Wisps of incense smoke floated out of the carved doorways and the drone of the priestess like bees in a hollow log. All the people came out on their flat roofs to watch—Did I say that they had two and even three houses, one on top of the other, each one smaller than the others, and ladders that went up and down to them?—They stood on the roofs and gathered in the open square between the houses as still and as curious as antelopes, and at last the priestess of the Corn came out and spoke to us. Talk went between her and Waits-by-the-Fire, purring, spitting talk like water stumbling among stones. Not one word did our women understand, but they saw wonder grow among the Corn Women, respect and amazement.

"Finally, we were taken into the god-house, where in the half dark, we could make out the Goddess of the Corn, cut in stone, with green stones on her forehead. There were long councils between Waits-by-the-Fire and the Corn Woman and the priests that came running from the Temple of the Sun. Outside the rumor and the wonder swelled around the god-house like a sudden flood. Faces bobbed up like rubbish in the flood into the bright blocks of light that fell through the doorway, and were shifted and shunted by other faces peering in. After a long time the note of wonder outside changed to a deep, busy hum; the crowd separated and let through women bearing food in pots and baskets. Then we knew that Waits-by-the-Fire had won."

"But what?" insisted Dorcas; "what was it that she had told them?"

"That she had had a dream which was sent by the Corn Spirit

and that she and those with her were under a vow to serve the Corn
for the space of one growing year. And to prove that her dream was
true the Goddess of the Corn had revealed to her the speech of the
Stone House tribe and also many hidden things. These were things
which she remembered from her captivity which she told them."

"What sort of things?"

"Why, that in such a year they had had a pestilence and that the
father of the Corn Woman had died of eating over-ripe melons.
The Corn Women were greatly impressed. But she carried it almost too far . . . perhaps . . . and perhaps it was appointed from the
beginning that that was the way the Corn was to come. It was
while we were eating that we realized how wise she was to make us
come fasting, for first the people pitied us, and then they were
pleased with themselves for making us comfortable. But in the
middle of it there was a great stir and a man in chief's dress came
pushing through. He was the Cacique of the Sun and he was vexed
because he had not been called earlier. He was that kind of a man.

"He spoke sharply to the Chief Corn Woman to know why
strangers were received within the town without his knowledge.

"Waits-by-the-Fire answered quickly. 'We are guests of the
Corn, O Cacique, and in my dream I seem to have heard of your
hospitality to women of the Corn.' You see there had been an old
story when he was young, how one of the Corn Maidens had gone
to his house and had been kept there against her will, which was a
discredit to him. He was so astonished to hear the strange woman
speak of it that he turned and went out of the god-house without
another word. The people took up the incident and whispered it
from mouth to mouth to prove that the strange Shaman was a
great prophet. So we were appointed a house to live in and were
permitted to serve the Corn."

"But what did you do?" Dorcas insisted on knowing.

"We dug and planted. All this was new to us. When there was
no work in the fields we learned the ways of cooking corn, and to
make pots. Hunting-tribes do not make pots. How should we
carry them from place to place on our backs? We cooked in bas-

kets with hot stones, and sometimes when the basket was old we plastered it with mud and set it on the fire. But the People of the Corn made pots of coiled clay and burned it hard in the open fires between the houses. Then there was the ceremony of the Corn to learn, the prayers and the dances. Oh, we had work enough! And if ever anything was ever said or done to us which was not pleasant, Waits-by-the-Fire would say to the one who had offended, 'We are only the servants of the Corn, but it would be a pity if the same thing happened to you that happened to the grandfather of your next-door neighbor!'

"And what happened to him?"

"Oh, a plague of sores, a scolding wife, or anything that she chanced to remember from the time she had been Given-to-the-Sun. *That* stopped them. But most of them held us to be under the protection of the Corn Spirit, and when our Shaman would disappear for two or three days—that was when she went to the mountain to visit Shungakela—*we* said that she had gone to pray to her own gods, and they accepted that also."

"And all this time no one recognized her?"

"She had painted her face for a Shaman," said the Corn Woman slowly, "and besides it was nearly forty years. The woman who had been kind to her was dead and there was a new Priest of the Sun. Only the one who had painted her with the sign of the Sun was left, and he was doddering." She seemed about to go on with her story, but the oldest dancing woman interrupted her.

"Those things helped," said the dancing woman, "but it was her thought which hid her. She put on the thought of a Shaman as a man puts on the thought of a deer or a buffalo when he goes to look for them. That which one fears, that it is which betrays one. She was a Shaman in her heart and as a Shaman she appeared to them."

"She certainly had no fear," said the Corn Woman, "though from the first she must have known—

"It was when the seed corn was gathered that we had the first hint of trouble," she went on. "When it was ripe the priests and

Caciques went into the fields to select the seed for next year. Then it was laid up in the god-houses for the priestess of the Corn to keep. That was in case of an enemy or a famine when the people might be tempted to eat it. After it was once taken charge of by the priestess of the Corn they would have died rather than give it up. Our women did not know how they should get the seed to bring away from the Stone House except to ask for it as the price of their year's labor."

"But could n't you have just taken some from the field?" inquired Dorcas. "Would n't it have grown just the same?"

"That we were not sure of; and we were afraid to take it without the good-will of the Corn Goddess. Centeotli her name was. Waits-by-the-Fire made up her mind to ask for it on the first day of the Feast of the Corn Harvest, which lasts four days, and is a time of present-giving and good-willing. She would have got it, too, if it had been left to the Corn Women to decide. But the Cacique of the Sun, who was always watching out for a chance to make himself important, insisted that it was a grave matter and should be taken to Council. He had never forgiven the Shaman, you see, for that old story about the Corn Maiden.

"As soon as the townspeople found that the Caciques were considering whether it was proper to give seed corn to the strangers, they began to consider it, too, turning it over in their minds together with a great many things that had nothing to do with it. There had been smut in the corn that year; there was a little every year, but this season there was more of it, and a good many of the bean pods had not filled out. I forgot," said the Corn Woman, "to speak of the beans and squashes. They were the younger sisters of the corn; they grew with the corn and twined about it. Now, every man who was a handful or two short of his crop began to look at us doubtfully. Then they would crowd around the Cacique of the Sun to argue the matter. They remembered how our Shaman had gone apart to pray to her own gods and they thought the Spirit of the Corn might have been offended. And the Cacique would inquire of every one who had a toothache or any such matter, in such a

way as to make them think of it in connection with the Shaman.—
In every village," the Corn Woman interrupted herself to say,
"there is evil enough, if laid at the door of one person, to get her
burned for a witch!"

"Was she?" Dorcas Jane squirmed with anxiety.

"She was standing on the steps at the foot of the Hill of the Sun,
the last we saw of her," said the Corn Woman. "Of course, our
women, not understanding the speech of the Stone Houses, did
not know exactly what was going on, but they felt the changed
looks of the people. They thought, perhaps, they could steal away
from the town unnoticed. Two of them hid in their clothing as
much Seed as they could lay hands on and went down toward the
river. They were watched and followed. So they came back to the
house where Waits-by-the-Fire prayed daily with her hand on
the Medicine of the Sun.

"So came the last day of the feast when the sacred seed would
be sealed up in the god-house. 'Have no fear,' said Waits-by-the-
Fire, 'for my dream has been good. Make yourselves ready for the
trail. Take food in your food bags and your carriers empty on your
backs.' She put on her Shaman's dress and about the middle of the
day the Cacique of the Sun sent for them. He was on the platform
in front of the god-house where the steps go up to the Hill of
the Sun, and the elders of the town were behind him. Priests of the
Sun stood on the steps and the Corn Women came out from the
temple of the Corn. As Waits-by-the-Fire went up with the Seven,
the people closed in solidly behind them. The Cacique looked at
the carriers on their backs and frowned.

"'Why do you come to the god-house with baskets, like la-
borers of the fields?' he demanded.

"'For the price of our labor, O Cacique,' said the Shaman. 'The
gods are not so poor that they accept labor for nothing.'

"'Now, it is come into my heart,' said the Cacique sourly, 'that
the gods are not always pleased to be served by strangers. There
are signs that this is so.'

"'It may be,' said Waits-by-the-Fire, 'that the gods are not pleased. They have long memories.' She looked at him very straight and somebody in the crowd snickered."

"But was n't it awfully risky to keep making him mad like that?" asked Dorcas. "They could have just done anything to her!"

"She was a wise woman; she knew what she had to do. The Cacique *was* angry. He began making a long speech at her, about how the smut had come in the corn and the bean crop was a failure,—but that was because there had not been water enough,—and how there had been sickness. And when Waits-by-the-Fire asked him if it were only in that year they had misfortune, the people thought she was trying to prove that she had n't had anything to do with it. She kept reminding them of things that had happened the year before, and the year before. The Cacique kept growing more and more angry, admitting everything she said, until it showed plainly that the town had had about forty years of bad luck, which the Cacique tried to prove was all because the gods had known in advance that they were going to be foolish and let strangers in to serve the Corn. At first the people grew excited and came crowding against the edge of the platform, shouting, 'Kill her! Kill the witch!' as one and then another of their past misfortunes were recalled to them.

"But, as the Shaman kept on prodding the Cacique, as hunters stir up a bear before killing him, they began to see that there was something more coming, and they stood still, packed solidly in the square to listen. On all the housetops roundabout the women and the children were as still as images. A young priest from the steps of the Hill, who thought he must back up the Cacique, threw up his arms and shouted, 'Give her to the Sun!' and a kind of quiver went over the people like the shiver of still water when the wind smites it. It was only at the time of the New Fire, between harvest and planting, that they give to the Sun, or in great times of war or pestilence. Waits-by-the-Fire moved out to the edge of the platform.

" 'It is not, O People of the Sun, for what is given, that the gods grow angry, but for what is withheld,' she said. 'Is there nothing, priests of the Sun, which was given to the Sun and let go again? Think, O priests. Nothing?'

"The priests, huddled on the stairs, began to question among themselves, and Waits-by-the-Fire turned to the people. 'Nothing, O Offspring of the Sun?'

"Then she put off the Shaman's thought which had been a shield to her. 'Nothing, Toto?' she called to a man in the crowd by a name none knew him by except those that had grown up with him. She was Given-to-the-Sun, and she stood by the carved stone corn of the god-house and laughed at them, shuffling and shouldering like buffaloes in the stamping-ground, and not knowing what to think. Voices began to call for the man she had spoken to, 'Toto, O Toto!'

"The crowd swarmed upon itself, parted and gave up the figure of the ancient Priest of the Sun, for they remembered in his day how a girl who was given to the Sun had been snatched away by the gods out of sight of the people. They pushed him forward, doddering and peering. They saw the woman put back her Shaman's bonnet from her head, and the old priest clap his hand to his mouth like one suddenly astonished.

"Over the Cacique's face came a cold glint like the coming of ice on water. 'You,' he said, 'you are Given-to-the-Sun?' And he made a gesture to the guard to close in on her.

"'Given-to-the-Sun,' she said. 'Take care how you touch that which belongs to the gods, O Cacique!'

"And though he still smiled, he took a step backward.

"'So,' he said, 'you are that woman and this is the meaning of those prophecies!'

"'I am that woman and that prophet,' she said with her hand at her throat and looked from priests to people. 'O People of the Sun, I have heard you have a charm,' she said,—'a Medicine of the Sun called the Eye of the Sun, strong Medicine.'

"No one answered for a while, but they began to murmur among themselves, and at last one shouted that they had such a charm, but it was not for witches or for runaway slave women.

"'You *bad* such a charm,' she said, for she knew well enough that the sacred charm was kept in the god-house and never shown to the people except on very great occasions. She was sure that the priests had never dared to tell the people that their Sacred Stone had disappeared with the escaped captive.

"Given-to-the-Sun took the Medicine bag from her neck and swung it in her fingers. '*Had!*' she said mockingly. The people gave a growl; another time they would have been furious with fright and anger, but they did not wish to miss a syllable of what was about to happen. The priests whispered angrily with the guard, but Given-to-the-Sun did not care what the priests did so long as she had the people. She signed to the Seven, and they came huddling to her like quail; she put them behind her.

"'Is it not true, Children of the Sun, that the favor of the Sun goes with the Eye of the Sun and it will come back to you when the Stone comes back?'

"They muttered and said that it was so.

"'Then, will your priests show you the Eye of the Sun or shall I show you?'

"There was a shout raised at that, and some called to the priests to show the Stone, and others that the woman would bring trouble on them all with her offenses. But by this time they knew very well where the Stone was, and the priests were too astonished to think of anything. Slowly the Shaman drew it out of the Medicine bag—"

The Corn Woman waited until one of the women handed her the sacred bundle from the neck of the Corn image. Out of it, after a little rummaging, she produced a clear crystal of quartz about the size of a pigeon's egg. It gave back the rays of the Sun in a dazzle that, to any one who had never seen a diamond, would have seemed wonderfully brilliant. Where it lay in the Corn Woman's hand it scattered little flecks of reflected light in rainbow splashes. The Indian women made the sign of the Sun on their foreheads and Dorcas felt a prickle of solemnity along the back of her neck as she looked at it. Nobody spoke until it was back again in the Medicine bundle.

"Given-to-the-Sun held it up to them," the story went on, "and there was a noise in the square like a noise of the stamping-ground at twilight. Some bellowed one thing and some another, and at last a priest of the Sun moved sharply and spoke:—

"'The Eye of the Sun is not for the eyes of the vulgar. Will you let this false Shaman impose on you, O Children of the Sun, with a common pebble?'

"Given-to-the-Sun stooped and picked up a mealing-stone that was used for grinding the sacred meal in the temple of the Corn.

"'If your Stone is in the temple and this is a common pebble,' said she, 'it does not matter what I do with it.' And she seemed about to crush it on the top of the stone balustrade at the edge of the platform. The people groaned. They knew very well that this was their Sacred Stone and that the priests had deceived them. Given-to-the-Sun stood resting one stone upon the other.

"'The Sun has been angry with you,' she said, 'but the Goddess of the Corn saves you. She has brought back the Stone and the Sacrifice. Do not show yourselves ungrateful to the Corn by denying her servants their wages. What! will you have all the gods against you? Priestess of the Corn,' she called toward the temple, 'do you also mislead the people?'

"At that the Corn Women came hurrying, for they saw that the people were both frightened and angry; they brought armsful of corn and seeds for the carriers, they took bracelets from their arms and put them for gifts in the baskets. The priests of the Sun did not say anything. One of the women's headbands slipped and the basket swung sideways. Given-to-the-Sun whipped off her belt and tucked it under the basket rim to make it ride more evenly. The woman felt something hard in the belt pressing her shoulder, but she knew better than to say anything. In silence the crowd parted and let the Seven pass. They went swiftly with their eyes on the ground by the north gate to the mountain. The priests of the Sun stood still on the steps of the Hill of the Sun and their eyes glittered. The Sacrifice of the Sun had come back to them.

"When our women passed the gate, the crowd saw Given-to-the-Sun restore what was in her hand to the Medicine bag; she lifted her arms above her head and began the prayer to the Sun."

"I see," said Dorcas after a long pause; "she stayed to keep the People of the Sun pacified while the women got away with the seed. That was splendid. But, the Eye of the Sun, I thought you saw her put that in the buckskin bag again?"

"She must have had ready another stone of shape and size like it," said the Corn Woman. "She thought of everything. She was a wise woman, and so long as she was called Given-to-the-Sun the Eye of the Sun was hers to give. Shungakela was not surprised to find that his wife had stayed at the Hill of the Sun; so I suppose she must have told him. He asked if there was a token, and the woman whose basket she had propped with her girdle gave it to him with the hard lump that pressed her shoulder. So the Medicine of the Sun came back to us.

"Our men had met the women at the foot of the mountain and they fled all that day to a safe place the men had made for them. It was for that they had stayed, to prepare food for flight, and safe places for hiding in case they were followed. If the pursuit pressed too hard, the men were to stay and fight while the women escaped with the corn. That was how Given-to-the-Sun arranged it.

"Next day as we climbed, we saw smoke rising from the Hill of the Sun, and Shungakela went apart on the mountain, saying, 'Let me alone, for I make a fire to light the feet of my wife's spirit. . . .' They had been married twenty years.

"We found the tribe at Painted Rock, but we thought it safer to come on east beyond the Staked Plains as Given-to-the-Sun had advised us. At Red River we stopped for a whole season to plant corn. But there was not rain enough there, and if we left off watching the fields for a day the buffaloes came and cropped them. So for the sake of the corn we came still north and made friends with the Tenasas. We bought help of them with the half of our seed, and they brought us over the river, the Missi-Sippu, the Father of all Rivers. The Tenasas had boats, round like baskets, covered with buffalo hide, and they floated us over, two swimmers to every boat to keep us from drifting downstream.

"Here we made a town and a god-house, to keep the corn contented. Every year when the seed is gathered seven ears are laid up in the god-house in memory of the Seven, and for the seed which must be kept for next year's crop there are seven watchers"—the Corn Woman included the dancers and herself in a gesture of pride. "We are the keepers of the Seed," she said, "and no man of the tribe knows where it is hidden. For no matter how hungry the people may become the seed corn must not be eaten. But with us there is never any hunger, for every year from planting time till the green corn is ready for picking, we keep all the ceremonies of the corn, so that our cribs are filled to bursting. Look!"

The Corn Woman stood up and the dancers getting up with her shook the rattles of their leggings with a sound very like the noise a radiator makes when some one is hammering on the other end of it. And when Dorcas turned to look for the Indian cribs there was nothing there but the familiar wall cases and her father mending the steam heater.

SIGN OF THE SUN AND THE FOUR QUARTERS

VII
A TELLING OF THE SALT TRAIL,
OF TSE-TSE-YOTE AND THE DELIGHT-MAKERS;
TOLD BY MOKE-ICHA

Oliver was so interested in his sister's account of how the corn
came into the country, that that very evening he dragged out a
tattered old atlas which he had rescued from the Museum waste,
and began to look for the places named by the Corn Woman.
They found the old Chihuahua Trail sagging south across the Rio
Grande, which, on the atlas map, carried its ancient name of River
of the White Rocks. Then they found the Red River, but there was
no trace of the Tenasas, unless it might be, as they suspected from
the sound, in the Country of the Tennessee. It was all very dis-
appointing.

"I suppose," suggested Dorcas Jane, "they don't put down the
interesting places. It's only the ones that are too dull to be remembered that have to be printed."

Oliver, who did not believe this was quite the principle on
which atlases were constructed, had made a discovery. Close to
the Rio Grande, and not far from the point where the Chihuahua
Trail crossed it, there was a cluster of triangular dots, marked Cliff
Dwellings. "There was corn there," he insisted. "You can see it in

the wall cases, and Cliff Dwellings are the oldest old places in the United States. If they were here when the Corn Woman passed, I don't see why she had to go to the Stone Houses for seed." And when they had talked it over they decided to go that very night and ask the Buffalo Chief about it.

"There was always corn, as I remember it," said the old bull, "growing tall about the tipis. But touching the People of the Cliffs—that would be Moke-icha's story."

The great yellow cat came slipping out from the over-weighted thickets of wild plum, and settled herself on her boulder with a bound. Stretching forth one of her steel-tipped pads toward the south she seemed to draw the purple distance as one draws a lady by her scarf. The thin lilac-tinted haze parted on the gorge of the Rio Grande, between the white ranges. The walls of the cañon were scored with deep perpendicular gashes as though the river had ripped its way through them with its claws. Yellow pines balanced on the edge of the cliffs, and smaller, tributary cañons, that opened into it, widened here and there to let in tall, solitary trees, with patches of sycamore and wild cherry and linked pools for trout.

"That was a country!" purred Moke-icha. "What was it you wished to know about it?"

"Ever so many things," said Oliver promptly—"if there were people there, and if they had corn—"

"Queres they were called," said Moke-icha, "and they were already a people, with corn of four colors for the four corners of the earth, and many kinds of beans and squashes, when they came to Ty-uonyi."

"Where were they when the Corn Woman passed? Who were the Blanket People, and what—"

"Softly," said Moke-icha. "Though I slept in the kivas and am called Kabeyde, Chief of the Four-Footed, I did not know all the tales of the Queres. They were a very ancient people. On the Salt Trail, where it passed by Split Rock, the trail was bitten deep into the granite. I think they could not have been more than three or four hundred years in Ty-uonyi when I knew them. They came from farther up the river where they had cities built into the rock. And before that? How should I know? They *said* they came from a hole in the ground, from Shipapu. They traded to the south with salt which they brought from the Crawling Water for green stones and a kind of white wool which grew on bushes, from which they made their clothes. There were no wandering tribes about except the Diné and they were all devils."

"Devils they may have been," said the Navajo, "but they did not say their prayers to a yellow cat, O Kabeyde."

"I speak but as the People of the Cliffs," said Moke-icha soothingly. "If they called the Diné devils, doubtless they had reason; and if they made prayers and images to me, it was not without a reason: not without good reason." Her tail bristled a little as it curled at the tip like a snake. Deep yellow glints swam at the backs of her half-shut eyes.

"It was because of the Diné, who were not friendly to the Queres, that the towns were built as you see, with the solid outer wall and the doors all opening on a court, at the foot of the cliff. It was hot and quiet there with always something friendly going on, children tumbling about among the dogs and the turkeys, an old man rattling a gourd and singing the evil away from his eyes, or the *plump, plump* of the mealing-stone from the doorways. Now and then a maiden going by, with a tray of her best cooking which she carried to her young man as a sign that she had accepted him, would throw me a morsel, and at evenings the priests would come out of the kivas and strike with a clapper of deer's shoulder on a flint gong to call the people to the dancing-places."

The children turned to look once more at the narrow rift of Ty-uonyi as it opened from the cañon of the Rio Grande between two basalt columns to allow the sparkling Rito to pass where barely two men could walk abreast. Back from the stream the pale amber cliffs swept in smooth laps and folds like ribbons. Crowded against its sheer northern face the irregularly terraced heaps of the communal houses looked little as ant heaps at the foot of a garden wall.

Tiers and tiers of the T-shaped openings of the cave dwellings spotted the smooth cliff, but along the single two-mile street, except for an occasional obscure doorway, ran the blank, mud-plastered wall of the kivas.

Where the floor of the cañon widened, the water of the Rito was led out in tiny dikes and ditches to water the garden patches. A bowshot on the opposite side rose the high south wall, wind and rain washed into tents and pinnacles, spotted with pale scrub and blood-red flowers of nopal. Trails spidered up its broken steep, and were lost in the cloud-drift or dipped out of sight over the edge of the timbered mesa.

"We would go over the trail to hunt," said Moke-icha. "There were no buffaloes, but blacktail and mule deer that fattened on the bunch grass, and bands of pronghorn flashing their white rumps. Quail ran in droves and rose among the mesas like young thunder.

"That was my cave," said the Puma, nodding toward a hole high up like a speck on the five-hundred-foot cliff, close up under the great ceremonial Cave which was painted with the sign of the Morning and the Evening Star, and the round, bright House of the Sun Father. "But at first I slept in the kiva with Tse-tse-yote. Speaking of devils—there was no one who had the making of a livelier devil in him than my young master. Slim as an arrow, he would come up from his morning dip in the Rito, glittering like the dark stone of which knives are made, and his hair in the sun gave back the light like a raven. And there was no man's way of walking or standing, nor any cry of bird or beast, that he could not slip into as easily as a snake slips into a shadow. He would never mock when he was asked, but let him alone, and some evening, when the people smoked and rested, he would come stepping across the court in the likeness of some young man whose maiden had just smiled on him. Or if some hunter prided himself too openly on a buck he had killed, the first thing he knew there would be Tse-tse-yote walking like an ancient spavined wether prodded by a blunt arrow, until the whole court roared with laughter.

"Still, Kokomo should have known better than to try to make

him one of the Koshare, for though laughter followed my master as ripples follow a skipping stone, he laughed little himself.

"Who were the Koshare? They were the Delight-Makers; one of their secret societies. They daubed themselves with mud and white paint to make laughter by jokes and tumbling. They had their kiva between us and the Gourd People, but Tse-tse-yote, who had set his heart on being elected to the Warrior Band, the Uakanyi, made no secret of thinking small of the Koshare.

"There was no war at that time, but the Uakanyi went down with the Salt-Gatherers to Crawling Water, once in every year between the corn-planting and the first hoeing, and as escort on the trading trips. They would go south till they could see the blue wooded slope below the white-veiled mountain, and would make smoke for a trade signal, three smokes close together and one farther off, till the Men of the South came to deal with them. But it was the Salt-Gathering that made Tse-tse-yote prefer the Warrior Band to the Koshare, for all that country through which the trail lay was disputed by the Diné. It is true there was a treaty, but there was also a saying at Ty-uonyi, 'a sieve for water and a treaty for the Diné.'"

The Navajo broke in angrily, "The Tellings were to be of the trails, O Kabeyde, and not of the virtues of my ancestors!" The children looked at him, round-eyed.

"Are you the Diné?" they exclaimed both at once. It seemed to bring the Cliff People so much nearer.

"So we were named, though we were called devils by those who feared us, and Blanket People by the Plainsmen. We were a tree whose roots were in the desert and whose branches were over all the north, and there is no Telling of the Queres, Cochiti, or Ty-uonyi, O Kabeyde,"—he turned to the puma,—"which I cannot match with a better of those same Diné."

"There were Diné in this Telling," purred Moke-icha, "and one puma. There was also Pitahaya, the chief, who was so old that he spent most of the time singing the evil out of his eyes. There was Kokomo, who wished to be chief in his stead, and there was

Tse-tse-yote and Moke-icha

Willow-in-the-Wind, the turkey girl, who had no one belonging to her. She had a wind-blown way of walking, and her long hair, which she washed almost every day in the Rito, streamed behind her like the tips of young willows. Finally, there was Tse-tse-yote. But one must pick up the trail before one settles to the Telling," said Moke-icha.

"Tse-tse-yote took me, a nine days' cub, from the lair in Shut Cañon and brought me up in his mother's house, the fifth one on the right from the gate that was called, because of a great hump of arrow-stone which was built into it, Rock-Overhanging. When he was old enough to leave his mother and sleep in the kiva of his clan, he took me with him, where I have no doubt we made a great deal of trouble. Nights when the moon called me, I would creep out of Tse-tse's arms to the top of the ladder. The kivas opened downward from a hole in the roof in memory of Shipapu. Half-awake, Tse-tse would come groping to find me until he trod on one of the others by mistake, who would dream that the Diné were after him and wake the kiva with his howls. Or somebody would pinch my tail and Tse-tse would hit right and left with his pillows—"

"Pillows?" said Oliver.

"Mats of reed or deerskin. They would slap at one another, or snatch at any convenient ankle or hair, until Kokomo, the master of the kiva, would have to come and cuff them apart. Always he made believe that Tse-tse or I had started it, and one night he tried to throw me out by the skin of my neck, and I turned in his hand— How was I to know that the skin of man is so tender?—and his smell was the smell of a man who nurses grudges.

"After that, even Tse-tse-yote saw that I was too old for the kiva, so he made me a cave for myself, high up under the House of the Sun Father, and afterward he widened it so that he could sit there tying prayer plumes and feathering his arrows. By day I hunted with Tse-tse-yote on the mesa, or lay up in a corner of the terrace above the court of the Gourd Clan, and by night—to say the truth, by night I did very much as it pleased me. There was a broken place in the wall-plaster by the gate of the Rock-Overhanging, by which I could go up and down, and if I was caught walking on the terrace, nobody minded me. I was Kabeyde, and the hunters thought I brought them luck."

Thus having picked up the trail to her satisfaction, Moke-icha tucked her paws under her comfortably and settled to her story.

"When Tse-tse-yote took me to sleep with him in the kiva of his clan, Kokomo, who was head of the kiva, objected. So Tse-tse-yote spent the three nights following in a corner of the terrace with me curled up for warmth beside him. Tse-tse's father heard of it and carried the matter to Council. Tse-tse had taken me with his own hands from the lair, knowing very well what my mother would have done to him had she come back and found him there; and Tse-tse's father was afraid, if they took away the first fruits of his son's courage, the courage would go with it. The Council agreed with him. Kokomo was furious at having the management of his kiva taken out of his hands, and Tse-tse knew it. Later, when even Tse-tse's father agreed that I was too old for the kiva, Tse-tse taught me to curl my tail under my legs and slink on my belly when I saw Kokomo. Then he would scold me for being afraid of the kind man, and the other boys would giggle, for they knew very well that Tse-tse had to beat me over the head with a firebrand to teach me that trick.

"It was a day or two after I had learned it, that we met Willow-in-the-Wind feeding her turkey flock by the Rito as we came from hunting, and she scolded Tse-tse for making fun of Kokomo.

"'It is plain,' she said, 'that you are trying to get yourself elected to the Delight-Makers.'

"'You know very well it is no such thing,' he answered her roughly, for it was not permitted a young man to make a choice of the society he would belong to. He had to wait until he was elected by his elders. The turkey girl paddled her toes in the Rito.

"'There is only one way,' she said, 'that a man can be kept from making fun of the Koshare, and that is by electing him a member.

Now, *I* thought you would have preferred the Uakanyi,'—just as if she did not know that there was little else he thought of.

"Tse-tse pulled up the dry grass and tossed it into the water. 'In the old days,' he said, 'I have heard that Those Above sent the Delight-Makers to make the people laugh so that the way should not seem long, and the Earth be fruitful. But now the jests of the Koshare are scorpions, each one with a sting in its tail for the enemies of the Delight-Makers. I had sooner strike mine with a knife or an arrow.'

"'Enemies, yes,' said Willow-in-the-Wind, 'but you cannot use a knife on those who sit with you in Council. You know very well that Kokomo wishes to be chief in place of Pitahaya.'

"Tse-tse looked right and left to see who listened. 'Kokomo is a strong man in Ty-uonyi,' he said; 'it was he who made the treaty with the Diné. And Pitahaya is blind.'

"'Aye,' said the turkey girl; 'when you are a Delight-Maker you can make a fine jest of it.'

"She had been brought up a foundling in the house of the old chief and was fond of him. Tse-tse, who had heard and said more than became a young man, was both angry and frightened; therefore he boasted.

"'Kokomo shall not make me a Koshare,' he said; 'it will not be the first time I have carried the Council against him.'

"At that time I did not know so much of the Diné as that they were men. But the day after Willow-in-the-Wind told Tse-tse that Kokomo meant to have him elected to the Koshare if only to keep him from making a mock of Kokomo, we went up over the south wall hunting.

"It was all flat country from there to the roots of the mountains; great pines stood wide apart, with here and there a dwarf cedar steeping in the strong sun. We hunted all the morning and lay up under a dark oak watching the young winds stalk one another among the lupins. Lifting myself to catch the upper scent, I winded a man that was not of Ty-uonyi. A moment later we saw him with a buck on his shoulders, working his way cautiously toward the head of Dripping Spring Cañon. 'Diné!' said Tse-tse; 'fighting man.' And he signed to me that we must stalk him.

"For an hour we slunk and crawled through the black rock that broke through the mesa like a twisty root of the mountain. At the head of Dripping Spring we smelled wood smoke. We crept along the cañon rim and saw our man at the bottom of it. He had hung up his buck at the camp and was cutting strips from it for his supper.

"'Look well, Kabeyde,' said my master; 'smell and remember. This man is my enemy.' I did not like the smell in any case. The Queres smell of the earth in which they dig and house, but the Diné smelled of himself and the smoke of sagebrush. Tse-tse's hand was on the back of my neck. 'Wait,' he said; 'one Diné has not two blankets.' We could see them lying in a little heap not far from the camp. Presently in the dusk another man came up the cañon from the direction of the river and joined him.

"We cast back and forth between Dripping Spring and the mouth of the Ty-uonyi most of the night, but no more Diné showed themselves. At sunrise Willow-in-the-Wind met us coming up the Rito.

"'Feed farther up,' Tse-tse told her; 'the Diné are abroad.'

"Her face changed, but she did not squeal as the other women did when they heard it. Therefore I respected her. That was the way it was with me. Every face I searched, to see if there was fear in it, and if there was none I myself was a little afraid; but where there was fear the back of my neck bristled. I know that the hair rose on it when we came to tell our story to the Council. That was when Kokomo was called; he came rubbing the sleep out of his eyes, pretending that Tse-tse had made a tale out of nothing.

"'We have a treaty with the Diné,' he said. 'Besides, I was out rehearsing with the Koshare last night toward Shut Cañon; if there had been Diné I should have seen them.'

"It was then that I was aware of Tse-tse's hand creeping along my shoulders to hide the bristling.

"'He is afraid,' said Tse-tse to me in the cave; 'you saw it. Yet he is not afraid of the Diné. Sometimes I think he is afraid of me. That is why he wished me to join the Koshare, for then he will be my Head, and without his leave I can do nothing.'

"This was a true saying. Only a few days after that, I found one of their little wooden images, painted and feathered like a Delight-Maker, in my cave. It was an invitation. It smelled of Kokomo and I scratched dirt on it. Then came Tse-tse, and as he turned the little Koshare over in his hand, I saw that there were many things had come into his head which would never come into mine. Presently I heard him laugh as he did when he had hit upon some new trick for splitting the people's sides, like the bubble of a wicker bottle held under water. He took my chin in his hand. 'Without doubt,' he said, 'this is Kokomo's; he would be very pleased if you returned it to him.' I understood it as an order.

"I carried the little Delight-Maker to Kokomo that night in the inner court, when the evening meal was over and the old men smoked while the younger sat on the housetops and moaned together melodiously. Tse-tse looked up from a game of cherry stones. 'Hey, Kokomo, have you been inviting Kabeyde to join the Koshare? A good shot!' he said, and before Kokomo could answer it, he began putting me through my tricks.

"Tricks?" cried the children.

"Jumping over a stick, you know, and showing what I would do if I met the Diné." The great cat flattened herself along the ground to spring, put back her ears, and showed her teeth with a snarly whine, almost too wicked to be pretended. "I was very good at that," said Moke-icha.

" 'The Delight-Maker was for you, Tse-tse,' said thc turkey girl next morning. 'Kokomo cannot prove that you gave it to Kabeyde, but he will never forgive you.'

"True enough, at the next festival the Koshare set the whole of Ty-uonyi shouting with a sort of play that showed Tse-tse scared by rabbits in the brush, and thinking the Diné were after them. Tse-tse was furious and the turkey girl was so angry on his account that she scolded *him*, which is the way with women.

"You see," explained Moke-icha to the children, "if he wanted to be made a member of the Warrior Band, it would n't help him any to be proved a bad scout, and a bringer of false alarms. And if he could be elected to the Uakanyi that spring, he would probably be allowed to go on the salt expedition between corn-planting and the first hoeing. But after I had carried back the little Delight-Maker to Kokomo, there were no signs of the four-colored arrow, which was the invitation to the Uakanyi, and young men whom Tse-tse had mimicked too often went about pretending to discover Diné wherever a rabbit ran or the leaves rustled.

"Tse-tse behaved very badly. He was sharp with the turkey girl because she had warned him, and when we hunted on the mesa he would forget me altogether, running like a man afraid of himself until I was too winded to keep up with him. I am not built for running," said Moke-icha, "my part was to pick up the trail of the game, and then to lie up while Tse-tse drove it past and spring for the throat and shoulder. But when I found myself neglected I went back to Willow-in-the-Wind who wove wreaths for my neck, which tickled my chin, and made Tse-tse furious.

"The day that the names of those who would go on the Salt Trail were given out—Tse-tse's was not among them—was two or three before the feast of the corn-planting and the last of the winter rains. Tse-tse-yote was off on one of his wild runnings, but I lay in the back of the cave and heard the myriad-footed Rain on the mesa. Between showers there was a soft foot on the ladder outside, and Willow-in-the-Wind pushed a tray of her best cooking into the door of the cave and ran away without looking. That was the fashion of a love-giving. I was much pleased with it."

"Oh!—" Dorcas Jane began to say and broke off. "Tell us what it was!" she finished.

Moke-icha considered.

"Breast of turkey roasted, and rabbit stew with pieces of squash and chia, and beans cooked in fat,—very good eating; and of course thin, folded cakes of maize; though I do not care much for corn cakes unless they are well greased. But because it was a love-gift I ate all of it and was licking the basket-tray when Tse-tse came back. He knew the fashion of her weaving,—every woman's baskets had her own mark,—and as he took it from me his face changed as though something inside him had turned to water. Without a word he went down the hill to the chief's house and I after him.

"'Moke-icha liked your cooking so well,' he said to the turkey girl, 'that she was eating the basket also. I have brought it back to you.' There he stood shifting from one foot to another and Willow-in-the-Wind turned taut as a bowstring.

"'Oh,' she said, 'Moke-icha has eaten it! I am very glad to hear it.' And with that she marched into an inner room and did not come out again all that evening, and Tse-tse went hunting next day without me.

"The next night, which was the third before the feast of planting, being lonely, I went out for a walk on the mesa. It was a clear night of wind and moving shadow; I went on a little way and smelled man. Two men I smelled, Diné and Queresan, and the Queresan was Kokomo. They were together in the shadow of a juniper where no man could have seen them. Where I stood no man could have heard them.

"'It is settled, then,' said Kokomo. 'You send the old man to Shipapu, for which he has long been ready, and take the girl for your trouble.'

"'Good,' said the Diné. 'But will not the Koshare know if an extra man goes in with them?'

"'We go in three bands, and we have taken in so many new members that no one knows exactly.'

"'It is a risk,' said the Diné.

"And as he moved into the wind I knew the smell of him, and it was the man we had seen at Dripping Spring; not the hunter, but the one who had joined him.

"'Not so much risk as the chance of not finding the right house in the dark,' said Kokomo; 'and the girl has no one belonging to her. Who shall say that she did not go of her own accord?'

" 'At any rate,' the Diné laughed, 'I know she must be as beautiful as you say she is, since you are willing to run the risk of my seeing her.'

"They moved off, and the wind walking on the pine needles covered what they said, but I remembered what I had heard because they smelled of mischief.

"Two nights later I remembered it again when the Delight-Makers came out of the dark in three bands and split the people's sides with laughter. They were disguised in black-and-white paint and daubings of mud and feathers, but there was a Diné among them. By the smell I knew him. He was a tall man who tumbled well and kept close to Kokomo. But a Diné is an enemy. Tse-tse-yote had told me. Therefore I kept close at his heels as they worked around toward the house of Pitahaya, and my neck bristled. I could see that the Diné had noticed me. He grew a little frightened, I think, and whipped at me with the whip of feathers which the Koshare carried to tickle the tribesmen. I laid back my ears—I am Kabeyde, and it is not for the Diné to flick whips at me. All at once there rose a shouting for Tse-tse, who came running and beat me over the head with his bow-case.

" 'They will think I set you on to threaten the Koshare because they mocked me,' he said. 'Have you not done me mischief enough already?'

"That was when we were back in the cave, where he penned me till morning. There was no way I could tell him that there was a Diné among the Koshare."

"But I thought—" began Oliver, he looked over to where Arrumpa stood drawing young boughs of maple through his mouth like a boy stripping currants. "Could n't you just have told him?"

"In the old days," said Moke-icha, 'men spoke with beasts as brothers. The Queres had come too far on the Man Trail. I had no words, but I remembered the trick he had taught me, about what to do when I met a Diné. I laid back my ears and snarled at him.

" 'What!' he said; 'will you make a Diné of *me*?' I saw him frown, and suddenly he slapped his thigh as a man does when thought overtakes him. Being but a lad he would not have dared say what he thought, but he took to spending the night on top of the kiva. I would look out of my cave and see him there curled up in a corner, or pacing to and fro with the dew on his blanket and his face turned to the souls of the prayer plumes drifting in a wide band across the middle heaven.

"I would have been glad to keep him company, but as neither Tse-tse nor Willow-in-the-Wind paid any attention to me in those days, I decided that I might as well go with the men and see for myself what lay at the other end of the Salt Trail.

"I gave them a day's start, so that I might not be turned back; but it was not necessary, since no man looked back or turned around on that journey, and no one spoke except those who had been over the trail at least two times. They ate little,—fine meal of parched corn mixed with water,—and what was left in the cup was put into the earth for a thank offering. No one drank except as the leader said they could, and at night they made prayers and songs.

"The trail leaves the mesa at the Place of the Gap, a dry gully snaking its way between puma-colored hills and boulders big as kivas. Lasting Water is at the end of the second day's journey; rainwater that slips down into a black basin with rock overhanging, cool as an olla. The rocks in that place when struck give out a pleasant sound. Beyond the Gap there is white sand in waves like water, wild hills and raw, red cañons. Around a split rock the trail dips suddenly to Sacred Water, shallow and white-bordered like a great dead eye."

"I know that place," said the Navajo, "and I think this must be true, for there is a trail there which bites deep into the granite."

"It was deep and polished even in my day," said Moke-icha, "but that did not interest me. There was no kill there larger than rabbits, and when I had seen the men cast prayer plumes on the Sacred Water and begin to scrape up the salt for their packs, I went back to Ty-uonyi. It was not until I got back to Lasting Water that I picked up the trail of the Diné. I followed it half a day before it occurred to me that they were going to Ty-uonyi. One of the smells—there were three of them—was the Diné who had come in with the Koshare. I remembered the broken plaster on the wall and Tse-tse asleep on the housetops. *Then* I hurried.

"It was blue midnight and the scent fresh on the grass as I came up the Rito. I heard a dog bark behind the first kiva, and, as I came opposite Rock-Overhanging, the sound of feet running. I smelled Diné going up the wall and slipped back in my hurry, but as I came over the roof of the kiva a tumult broke out in the direction of Pitahaya's house. There was a scream and a scuffle. I saw Tse-tse running and sent him the puma cry at which does asleep with their fawns tremble. Down in the long passage between Pitahaya's court and the gate of Rock-Overhanging, Tse-tse answered with the hunting-whistle.

"There was a fight going on in the passage. I could feel the cool draught from the open gate,—they must have opened it from the inside after scaling the wall by the broken plaster,—and smelled rather than saw that one man held the passage against Tse-tse. He was armed with a stone hammer, which is no sort of weapon for a narrow passage. Tse-tse had caught bow and quiver from the arms that hung always at the inner entrance of the passage, but made no attempt to draw. He was crouched against the wall, knife in hand, watching for an opening, when he heard me padding up behind him in the darkness.

"'Good! Kabeyde,' he cried softly; 'go for him.'

"I sprang straight for the opening I could see behind the Diné, and felt him go down as I cleared the entrance. Tse-tse panted behind me,—'Follow, follow!' I could hear the men my cry had waked, pouring out of the kivas, and knew that the Diné we had knocked over would be taken care of. We picked up the trail of those who had escaped, straight across the Rito and over the south wall, but it was an hour before I realized that they had taken Willow-in-the-Wind with them. Old Pitahaya was dead without doubt, and the man who had taken Willow-in-the-Wind was, by the smell, the same that had come in with Kokomo and the Koshare.

"We were hot on their trail, and by afternoon of the next day I was certain that they were making for Lasting Water. So I took Tse-tse over the rim of the Gap by a short cut which I had discovered, which would drop us back into the trail before they had done drinking. Tse-tse, who trusted me to keep the scent, was watching ahead for a sight of the quarry. Thus he saw the Diné before I winded them. I don't know whether they were just a hunting-party, or friends of those we followed. We dropped behind a boulder and Tse-tse counted while I lifted every scent.

"'Five,' he said, 'and the Finisher of the Paths of Our Lives knows how many more between us and Lasting Water!'

"We did not know yet whether they had seen us, but as we began to move again cautiously, a fox barked in the scrub that was not a fox. Off to our left another answered him. So now we were no longer hunters, but hunted.

"Tse-tse slipped his tunic down to his middle and, unbinding his queue, wound his long hair about his head to make himself look as much like a Diné as possible. I could see thought rippling in him as he worked, like wind on water. We began to snake between the cactus and the black rock toward the place where the fox had last barked."

"But *toward* them—" Oliver began.

"They were between us and Lasting Water,"—Moke-icha looked about the listening circle and the Indians nodded, agreeing. "When a fox barked again, Tse-tse answered with the impudent folly of a young kit talking back to his betters. Evidently the man on our left was fooled by it, for he sheered off, but within a bowshot they began to close on us again.

"We had come to a thicket of mesquite from which a man might slip unnoticed to the head of the gully, provided no one watched that particular spot too steadily. There we lay among the thorns and the shadows were long in the low sun. Close on our right a twig snapped and I began to gather myself for the spring. The ground sloped a little before us and gave the advantage. The hand of Tse-tse-yote came along the back of my neck and rested there.

'If a puma lay up here during the sun,' he whispered, 'this is the hour he would go forth to his hunting. He would go stretching himself after sleep and having no fear of man, for where Kabeyde lies up, who expects to find man also.' His hand came under my chin as his custom was in giving orders. This was how I understood it; this I did—"

The great cat bounded lightly to the ground, took two or three stretchy steps, shaking the sleep from her flanks, yawned prodigiously, and trotted off toward a thicket of wild plums into which she slipped like a beam of yellow light into water. A moment later she reappeared on the opposite side, bounded back and settled herself on the boulder. Around the circle ran the short "Huh! Huh!" of Indian approval. The Navajo shifted his blanket.

"A Diné could have done no more for a friend," he admitted.

"I see," said Oliver. "When the Diné saw you coming out of the mesquite they would have been perfectly sure there was no man there. But anyway, they might have taken a shot at you."

"And the twang of the bowstring and the thrashing about of the kill in the thicket would have told Tse-tse exactly where *they* were," said the Navajo. "The Diné when they hunt man do not turn aside for a puma."

"The hardest part of it all," said Moke-icha, "was to keep from showing I winded him. I heard the Diné move off, fox-calling to one another, and at last I smelled Tse-tse working down the gully. He paid no attention to me whatever; his eyes were fixed on the Diné who stood by the spring with his back to him looking down on the turkey girl who was huddled against the rocks with her hands tied behind her. The Diné looked down with his arms folded, evil-smiling. She looked up and I saw her spit at him. The man took her by the shoulder, laughing still, and spun her up standing. Half a bowshot away I heard Tse-tse-yote. 'Down! Down!' he shouted. The girl dropped like a quail. The Diné, whirling on his heel, met the arrow with his throat, and pitched choking. I came as fast as I could between the boulders—I am not built for running— Tse-tse had unbound the girl's hands and she leaned against him.

"Breathing myself before drinking, I caught a new scent up the Gap where the wind came from, but before I had placed it there came a little scrape on the rocks under the roof of Lasting Water, small, like the rasp of a snake coiling. I had forgot there were three Diné at Ty-uonyi; the third had been under the rock drinking. He came crawling now with his knife in his teeth toward Tse-tse. Me he had not seen until he came round the singing rock, face to face with me . . .

"When it was over," said Moke-icha, "I climbed up the black roof of Lasting Water to lick a knife cut in my shoulder. Tse-tse talked to the girl, of all things, about the love-gift she had put in the cave for me. 'Moke-icha had eaten it before I found her,' he insisted, which was unnecessary. I lay looking at the Diné I had killed and licking my wound till I heard, around the bend of the Gap, the travel song of the Queres.

"It was the Salt Pack coming back, every man with his load on his shoulders. They put their hands in their mouths when they saw Tse-tse. There was talk; Willow-in-the-Wind told them something. Tse-tse turned the man he had shot face upward. There was black-and-white paint on his body; the stripes of the Koshare do not come off easily. I saw Tse-tse look from the man to Kokomo and the face of the Koshare turned grayish. I had lived with man, and man-thoughts came to me. I had tasted blood of my master's enemies; also Kokomo was afraid, and that is an offense to me. I dropped from where I lay . . . I had come to my full weight . . . I think his back was broken.

"It is the Way Things Are," said Moke-icha. "Kokomo had let in the Diné to kill Pitahaya to make himself chief, and he would have killed Tse-tse for finding out about it. That I saw and smelled in him. But I did not wait this time to be beaten with my master's bow-case. I went back to Shut Cañon, for now that I had killed one of them, it was not good for me to live with the Queres. Nevertheless, in the rocks above Ty-uonyi you can still see the image they made of me."

VIII
YOUNG-MAN-WHO-NEVER-TURNS-BACK: A TELLING OF THE TALLEGEWI, BY ONE OF THEM

It could only have been for a few moments at the end of Moke-icha's story, before the cliff picture split like a thin film before the dancing circles of the watchmen's lanterns, and curled into the shadows between the cases. A thousand echoes broke out in the empty halls and muffled the voices as the rings of light withdrew down the long gallery in glimmering reflections. When they passed to the floor below a very remarkable change had come over the landscape.

The Buffalo Chief and Moke-icha had disappeared. A little way ahead the trail plunged down the leafy tunnel of an ancient wood, along which the children saw the great elk trotting leisurely with his cows behind him, flattening his antlers over his back out of the way of the low-branching maples. The switching of the brush against the elk's dun sides startled the little black bear, who was still riffling his bee tree. The children watched him rise inquiringly to his haunches before he scrambled down the trail out of sight.

"Lots of those fellows about in my day," said the Mound-Builder. "We used to go for them in the fall when they grew fat on the dropping nuts and acorns. Elk, too. I remember a ten-pronged buck that I shot one winter on the Elk's-Eye River . . ."

"The Muskingum!" exclaimed an Iroquois, who had listened in silence to the puma's story. "Did you call it that too? Elk's-Eye! Clear brown and smooth-flowing. That's the Scioto Trail, is n't it?" he asked of the Mound-Builder.

"You could call it that. There was a cut-off at Beaver Dam to Flint Ridge and the crossing of the Muskingum, and another that led to the mouth of the Kanawha where it meets the River of White-Flashing."

"He means the Ohio," explained the Iroquois to the children. "At flood the whole surface of the river would run to white riffles like the flash of a water-bird's wings. But the French called it La Belle Rivière. I'm an Onondaga myself," he added, "and in my time the Five Nations held all the territory, after we had driven out the Tallegewi, between the Lakes and the O-hey-yo." He stretched the word out, giving it a little different turn. "Indians' names talk little," he laughed, "but they say much."

"Like the trails," agreed the Mound-Builder, who was one of the Tallegewi himself, "every word is the expression of a need. We had a trade route over this one for copper which we fetched from the Land of the Sky-Blue Water and exchanged for sea-shells out of the south. At the mouth of the Scioto it connected with the Kaskaskia Trace to the Missi-Sippu, where we went once a year to shoot buffaloes on the plains."

"When the Five Nations possessed the country, the buffaloes came to us," said the Onondaga.

"Then the Long Knives came on the sea in the East and there was neither buffaloes nor Mengwe," answered the Mound-Builder, who did not like these interruptions. He went on describing the Kaskaskia Trail. "It led along the highlands around the upper waters of the Miami and the drowned lands of the Wabash. It was a wonderful trip in the month of the Moon Halting, when there was a sound of dropping nuts and the woods were all one red and yellow rain. But in summer . . . I should know," said the Mound-Builder; "I carried a pipe as far as Little Miami once . . ."

He broke off as though the recollection was not altogether a happy one and began to walk away from the wood, along the trail, which broadened quickly to a graded way, and led up the slope of a high green mound.

The children followed him without a word. They understood that they had come to the place in the Story of the Trails, which is known in the schoolbooks as "History." From the top of the mound they could see strange shapes of earthworks stretching between them and the shore of Erie. Lakeward the sand and the standing grass was the pale color of the moon that floated above it in the midday sky. Between them the blue of the lake melted into the blue horizon; the turf over the mounds was thick and wilted.

"I suppose I must remember it like this," said the Tallega, "because this is the way I saw it when I came back, an old man, after the fall of Cahokia. But when this mound was built there were towns here, busy and crowded. The forest came close up on one side, and along the lake front, field touched field for a day's journey. My town was the middle one of three of the Eagle Clan. Our Town House stood here, on the top of this mound, and on that other, the tallest, stood the god-house, with the Sacred Fire, and the four old men watchers to keep it burning."

"I thought," said Oliver, trying to remember what he had read about it, "that the mounds were for burials. People dig into them, you know."

"They might think that," agreed the Tallega, "if all they know comes from what they find by digging. They were for every purpose that buildings are used for, but we always thought it a good omen if we could start a Town Mound with the bones of some one we had loved and respected. First, we laid a circle of stones and an altar with a burnt offering, then the bones of the chief, or some of our heroes who were killed in battle. Then the women brought earth in baskets. And if a chief had served us well, we sometimes buried him on top and raised the mound higher over him, and the mound would be known by his name until another chief arose who surpassed him.

"Then there were earthworks for forts and signal stations. You'll find those on the high places overlooking the principal trails; there were always heaps of wood piled up for smoke signals. The circles were for meeting-places and for games."

"What sort of games?" demanded Oliver.

"Ball-play and races; all that sort of thing. There was a game we played with racquets between goals. Village played against village. The people would sit on the earthworks and clap and shout when the game pleased them, and gambled everything they had on their home-town players.

"I suppose," he added, looking around on the green tumuli, "I remember it like this, because when I lived here I was so full of what was going on that I had no time for noticing how it looked to me."

"What did go on?" both the children wished immediately to know.

"Something different every time the moon changed. Ice-fishing, corn-husking. We did everything together; that was what made it so interesting. The men let us go to the fur traps to carry home the pelts, and we hung up the birch-bark buckets for our mothers at the sugar-boiling. Maple sugar, you know. Then we would persuade them to ladle out a little of the boiling sap into plates that we patted out of the snow, which could always be found lingering in the hollows, at sugar-makings. When it was still waxy and warm, we rolled up the cooled syrup and ate it out of hand.

"In summer whole families would go to the bottom lands paw-paw gathering. Winter nights there was story-telling in the huts. We had a kind of corn, very small, that burst out white like a flower when it was parched . . ."

"Pop-corn!" cried both the children at once. It seemed strange that anything they liked so much should have belonged to the Mound-Builders.

"Why, that was what *we* called it!" he agreed, smiling. "Our mothers used to stir it in the pot with pounded hickory nuts and bears' grease. Good eating! And the trading trips! Some of our men used to go as far as Little River for chert which they liked better for arrow-points than our own flints, being less brittle and more easily worked. That was a canoe trip, down the Scioto, down the O-hey-yo, up the Little Tenasa as far as Little River. There was adventure enough to please everybody.

"That bird-shaped mound," he pointed, "was built the time we won the Eagle-Dancing against all the other villages."

The Mound-Builder drew out from under his feather robe a gorget of pearl shell, beautifully engraved with the figure of a young man dancing in an eagle-beaked mask, with eagles' wings fastened to his shoulders.

"Most of the effigy mounds," he said, taking the gorget from his neck to let the children examine it, "were built that way to celebrate a treaty or a victory. Sometimes," he added, after a pause, looking off across the wide flat mounds between the two taller ones, "they were built like these, to celebrate a defeat. It was there we buried the Tallegewi who fell in our first battle with the Lenni-Lenape."

"Were they Mound-Builders, too?" the children asked respectfully, for though the man's voice was sad, it was not as though he spoke of an enemy.

"People of the North," he said, "hunting-people, good foes and good fighters. But afterward, they joined with the Mengwe and drove us from the country. *That* was a Mingo,"—he pointed to the Iroquois who had called himself an Onondaga, disappearing down the forest tunnel. They saw him a moment, with arrow laid to bow, the sunlight making tawny splotches on his dark body, as on the trunk of a pine tree, and then they lost him.

"We were planters and builders," said the Tallega, "and they were fighters, so they took our lands from us. But look, now, how time changes all. Of the Lenni-Lenape and the Mengwe there is only a name, and the mounds are still standing."

"You said," Oliver hinted, "that you carried a pipe once. Was that—anything particular?"

"It might be peace or war," said the Mound-Builder. "In my case it was an order for Council, from which war came, bloody and terrible. A Pipe-Bearer's life was always safe where he was recognized, though when there is war one is very likely to let fly an arrow at anything moving in the trails. That reminds me . . ." The Tallega put back his feathered robe carefully as he leaned upon his elbow, and the children snuggled into a little depression at the top of the mound where the fire-hole had been, to listen.

"There was a boy in our town," he began, "who was the captain of all our plays from the time we first stole melons and roasting-ears from the town gardens. He got us into no end of trouble, but no matter what came of it, we always stood up for him before the elders. There was nothing *they* could say which seemed half so important to us as praise or blame from Ongyatasse. I don't know why, unless it was because he could out-run and out-wrestle the best of us; and yet he was never pleased with himself unless the rest of us were satisfied to have it that way.

"Ongyatasse was what his mother called him. It means something very pretty about the colored light of evening, but the name that he earned for himself, when he was old enough to be Name-Seeking, was Young-Man-Who-Never-Turns-Back. He was the arrow laid to the bow, and he could no more take himself back from the adventure he had begun than the shaft can come back to the bowstring.

"Before we were old enough to go up to the god-house and hear the sacred Tellings, he had half the boys in our village bound to him in an unbreakable vow never to turn back from anything we had started. It got us into a great many difficulties, some of which were ridiculous, but it had its advantages. The time we chased a young elk we had raised, across the squash and bean vines of Three Towns, we escaped punishment on the ground of our vow. Any Tallega parent would think a long time before he expected his son to break a promise."

Oliver kept to the main point of interest. "Did you get the elk?"

"*Of course.* You see we were never allowed to carry a man's hunting outfit until we had run down some big game, and brought it in alive to prove ourselves proper sportsmen. So partly for that and partly because Ongyatasse always knew the right words to say to everybody, we were forgiven the damage to the gardens.

"That was the year the Lenni-Lenape came to the Grand Council, which was held here at Sandusky, asking permission to cross our territory toward the Sea on the East. They came out of Shinaki, the Fir-Land, as far as Namae-sippu, and stood crowded between the lakes north of the river. For the last year or two, hunting-parties of theirs had been warned back from trespass, but this was the first time we youngsters had seen anything of them.

"They were fine-looking fellows, fierce, and tall appearing, with their hair cropped up about their ears, and a long hanging scalp-lock tied with eagle feathers. At the same time they seemed savage to us, for they wore no clothing but twisty skins about their middles, ankle-cut moccasins, and the Peace Mark on their foreheads.

"Because of the Mark they bore no weapons but the short hunting-bow and wolfskin quivers, with the tails hanging down, and painted breastbands. They were chiefs, by their way of walking, and one of them had brought his son with him. He was about Ongyatasse's age, as handsome as a young fir. Probably he had a name in his own tongue, but we called him White Quiver. Few of us had won ours yet, and his was man's size, of white deerskin and colored quill-work.

"Our mothers, to keep us out of the way of the Big Eating which they made ready for the visiting chiefs, had given us some strips of venison. We were toasting them at a fire we had made close to a creek, to stay our appetites. My father, who was Keeper of the Smoke for that occasion,—I was immensely proud of him,— saw the Lenape boy watching us out of the tail of his eye, and motioned to me with his hand that I should make him welcome. My father spoke with his hand so that White Quiver should understand—" The Mound-Builder made with his own thumb and forefinger the round sign of the Sun Father, and then the upturned palm to signify that all things should be as between brothers. "I was

perfectly willing to do as my father said, for, except Ongyatasse, I
had never seen any one who pleased me so much as the young
stranger. But either because he thought the invitation should have
come from himself as the leader of the band, or because he was a
little jealous of our interest in White Quiver, Ongyatasse tossed me
a word over his shoulder, 'We play with no crop-heads.'

"That was not a true word, for the Lenni-Lenape do not crop
the head until they go on the war-path, and White Quiver's hair
lay along his shoulders, well oiled, with bright bits of shell tied in
it, glittering as he walked. Also it is the rule of the Tellings that one
must feed the stranger. But me, I was never a Name-Seeker. I was
happy to stand fourth from Ongyatasse in the order of our running. For the rest, my brothers used to say that I was the tail and
Ongyatasse wagged me.

"Whether he had heard the words or not, the young Lenape
saw me stutter in my invitation. There might have been a quiver in
his face,—at my father's gesture he had turned toward me,—but
there was none in his walking. He came straight on toward our fire
and *through* it. Three strides beyond it he drank at the creek as
though that had been his only object, and back through the fire to
his father. I could see red marks on his ankles where the fire had
bitten him, but he never so much as looked at them, nor at us any
more than if we had been trail-grass. He stood at his father's side
and the drums were beginning. Around the great mound came the
Grand Council with their feather robes and the tall headdresses,
up the graded way to the Town House, as though all the gay weeds
in Big Meadow were walking. It was the great spectacle of the year,
but it was spoiled for all our young band by the sight of a slim
youth shaking off our fire, as if it had been dew, from his reddened
ankles.

"You see," said the Mound-Builder, "it was much worse for us
because we admired him immensely, and Ongyatasse, who liked
nothing better than being kind to people, could n't help seeing
that he could have made a much better point for himself by doing the honors of the village to this chief's son, instead of their

both going around with their chins in the air pretending not to see one another.

"The Lenni-Lenape won the permission they had come to ask for, to pass through the territory of the Tallegewi, under conditions that were made by Well-Praised, our war-chief, a fat man, a wonderful orator, who never took a straight course where he could find a cunning one. What those conditions were you shall hear presently. At the time, we boys were scarcely interested. That very summer we began to meet small parties of strangers drifting through the woods, as silent and as much at home in them as foxes. But the year had come around to the Moon of Sap Beginning before we met White Quiver again.

"A warm spell had rotted the ice on the rivers, followed by two or three days of sharp cold and a tracking snow. We had been out with Ongyatasse to look at our traps, and then the skin-smooth surface of the river beguiled us.

"We came racing home close under the high west bank where the ice was thickest, but as we neared Bent Bar, Young-Man-Who-Never-Turns-Back turned toward the trail that cut down to the ford between the points of Hanging Wood. The ice must have rotted more than we guessed, for halfway across, Ongyatasse dropped through it like a pebble into a pot-hole. Next to him was Tiakens, grandson of Well-Praised, and between me and Tiakens a new boy from Painted Turtle. I heard the splash and shout of Tiakens following Ongyatasse,—of course, he said afterward that he would have gone to the bottom with him rather than turn back, but I doubt if he could have stopped himself,—and the next thing I knew the Painted Turtle boy was hitting me in the nose for stopping him, and Kills Quickly, who had not seen what was happening, had crashed into us from behind. We lay all sprawled in a heap while the others hugged the banks, afraid to add their weight to the creaking ice, and Ongyatasse was beating about in the rotten sludge, trying to find a place firm enough to climb out on.

"We had seen both boys disappear for an instant as the ice gave under them, but even when we saw them come to the surface, with

Ongyatasse holding Tiakens by the hair, we hardly grasped what had happened. The edge of the ice-cake had taken Tiakens under the chin and he was unconscious. If Ongyatasse had let go of him he would have been carried under the ice by the current, and that would have been the last any one would have seen of him until the spring thaw. But as fast as Ongyatasse tried to drag their double weight onto the ice, it broke, and before the rest of us had thought of anything to do the cold would have cramped him. I saw Ongyatasse stuffing Tiakens's hair into his mouth so as to leave both his hands free, and then there was a running gasp of astonishment from the rest of the band, as a slim figure shot out of Dark Woods, skimming and circling like a swallow. We had heard of the snowshoes of the Lenni-Lenape, but this was the first time we had seen them. For a moment we were so taken up with the wonder of his darting pace, that it was not until we saw him reaching his long shoeing-pole to Ongyatasse across the ice, that we realized what he was doing. He had circled about until he had found ice that held, and kicking off his snowshoes, he stretched himself flat on it. I knew enough to catch him by the ankles—even then I could n't help wondering if the scar was still there, for we knew instantly who he was—and somebody caught my feet, spreading our weight as much as possible. Over the bridge we made, Ongyatasse and Tiakens, who had come to himself by this time, crawled out on firm ice. In a very few minutes we had stripped them of their wet clothing and were rubbing the cramp out of their legs.

"Ongyatasse, dripping as he was, pushed us aside and went over to White Quiver, who was stooping over, fastening his snowshoes. It seemed to give him a great deal of trouble, but at last he raised his head.

" 'This day I take my life at your hands,' said Ongyatasse.

" 'Does Young-Man-Who-Never-Turns-Back take so much from a Crop-Head?' said the Lenni-Lenape in good Tallegewi, which shows how much they knew of us already and how they began to hate us.

"But when he was touched, Ongyatasse had no equal for highness.

"'Along with my life I would take friendship too, if it were offered,' he said, and smiled, shivering as he was, in a way we knew so well who had never resisted it. We could see the smile working on White Quiver like a spell. Ongyatasse put an arm over the Lenape's shoulders.

"'Where the life is, the heart is also,' he said, 'and if the feet of Ongyatasse do not turn back from the trail they have taken, neither does his heart.' From his neck he slipped off his amulet of white deer's horn which brought him his luck in hunting, and threw it around the other's neck.

"'Ongyatasse, you have given away your luck!' cried Tiakens, whose head was a little light with the blow the ice-cake had given him.

"'Both the luck and the life of Young-Man-Who-Never-Turns-Back are safe in the hands of a Lenni-Lenape,' said White Quiver, as high as one of his own fir trees, but he loosed a little smile at the corner of his mouth as he turned to Tiakens, chattering like a squirrel. 'Unless you find a fire soon, Young-Man-Who-Never-Turns-Back will have need of another friend,' he said; and picking up his shoeing-pole, he was off in the wood again like a weasel darting to cover. We heard the swish of the boughs, heavy with new snow, and then silence.

"But if we had not been able to forget him after the first meeting, you can guess how often we talked of him in the little time that was left us. It was not long. Tiakens nearly died of the chill he got, and the elders were stirred up at last to break up our band before it led to more serious folly. Ongyatasse was hurried off with a hunting-party to Maumee, and I was sent to my mother's brother at Flint Ridge to learn stone-working.

"Not that I objected," said the Tallega. "I have the arrow-maker's hand." He showed the children his thumb set close to the wrist, the long fingers and the deep-cupped palm with the callus running down the middle. "All my family were clever craftsmen," said the

Tallega. "You could tell my uncle's points anywhere you found them by the fine, even flaking, and my mother was the best feather-worker in Three Towns,"—he ran his hands under the folds of his mantle and held it out for the children to admire the pattern. "Uncle gave me this banner stone as the wage of my summer's work with him, and I thought myself overpaid at the time."

"But what did you do?" asked both children at once.

"Everything, from knocking out the crude flakes with a stone hammer to shaping points with a fire-hardened tip of deer's horn. The ridge was miles long and free to any one who chose to work it, but most people preferred to buy the finished points and blades. There was a good trade, too, in turtle-backs." The Tallega poked about in the loose earth at the top of the mound and brought up a round, flattish flint about the size of a man's hand, that showed disk-shaped flakings arranged like the marking of a turtle-shell. "They were kept workable by being buried in the earth, and made into knives or razors or whatever was needed," he explained.

"That summer we had a tremendous trade in broad arrow-points, such as are used for war or big game. We sold to all the towns along the north from Maumee to the headwaters of the Susquehanna, and we sold to the Lenni-Lenape. They would ap-pear suddenly on the trails with bundles of furs or copper, of which they had a great quantity, and when they were satisfied with what was offered for it, they would melt into the woods again like quail. My uncle used to ask me a great many questions about them which I remembered afterward. But at the time—you see there was a girl, the daughter of my uncle's partner. She was all dusky red like the tall lilies at Big Meadow, and when she ran in the village races with her long hair streaming, they called her Flying Star.

"She used to bring our food to us when we opened up a new working, a wolf's cry from the old,—sizzling hot deer meat and piles of boiled corn on bark platters, and meal cakes dipped in maple syrup. I stayed on till the time of tall weeds as my father had ordered, and then for a while longer for the new working, which interested me tremendously. First we brought hickory wood and built a fire on the exposed surface of the ridge. Then we splintered the hot stone by throwing water on it, and dug out the splinters. In two or three days we had worked clean through the ledge of flint to the limestone underneath. This we also burnt with fire, after we had protected the fresh flint by plastering it with clay. When we had cleared a good piece of the ledge, we could hammer it off with the stone sledges and break it up small for working. It was as good sport to me as moose-hunting or battle.

"We had worked a man's length under the ledge, and one day I looked up with the sun in my eyes, as it reddened toward the west, and saw Ongyatasse standing under a hickory tree. He was dressed for running, and around his mouth and on both his cheeks was the white Peace Mark. I made the proper sign to him as to one carrying orders.

" 'You are to come with me,' he said. 'We carry a pipe to Miami.' "

IX
HOW THE LENNI-LENAPE CAME FROM
SHINAKI AND THE TALLEGEWI FOUGHT THEM:
THE SECOND PART
OF THE MOUND-BUILDER'S STORY

"Two things I thought as I looked at Never-Turns-Back, black against the sun. First, that it could be no very great errand that he ran upon, or they would never have trusted it to a youth without honors; and next, that affairs at Three Towns must be serious, indeed, if they could spare no older man for pipe-carrying. A third came to me in the night as I considered how little agreement there was between these two, which was that there must be more behind this sending than a plain call to Council.

"Ongyatasse told me all he knew as we lay up the next night at Pigeon Roost. There had not been time earlier, for he had hurried off to carry his pipe to the village of Flint Ridge as soon as he had called me, and we had padded out on the Scioto Cut-off at daybreak.

"What he said went back to the conditions that were made by Well-Praised for the passing of the Lenni-Lenape through our territory. They were to go in small parties, not more than twenty

fighting men to any one of them. They were to change none of our
landmarks, enter none of our towns without permission from the
Town Council, and to keep between the lake and the great bend
of the river, which the Lenni-Lenape called Allegheny, but was
known to us as the River of the Tallegewi.

"Thus they had begun to come, few at first, like the trickle of
melting ice in the moon of the Sun Returning, and at the last, like
grasshoppers in the standing corn. They fished out our rivers and
swept up the game like fire in the forest. Three Towns sent scouts
toward Fish River who reported that the Lenape swarmed in the
Dark Wood, that they came on from Shinaki thick as their own
firs. Then the Three Towns took council and sent a pipe to the
Eagle villages, to the Wolverines and the Painted Turtles. These
three kept the country of the Tallegewi on the north from Maumee to the headwaters of the Allegheny, and Well-Praised was
their war leader.

"Still," said the Mound-Builder, "except that he was the swiftest
runner, I could n't understand why they had chosen an untried
youth for pipe-carrying."

He felt in a pouch of kit fox with the tail attached, which hung
from the front of his girdle like the sporran of a Scotch High-
lander. Out of it he drew a roll of birch bark painted with juice of
pokeberries. The Tallega spread it on the grass, weighting one end
with the turtle-back, as he read, with the children looking over his
shoulder.

Well-Praised, war-chief of the Eagle Clan to the Painted
Turtles;—Greeting.

Come to the Council House at Three Towns.

On the fifth day of the Moon Halting.

🧍🧍

We meet as Brothers.

"An easy scroll to read," said the Tallega, as the released edges of the birch-bark roll clipped together. "But there was more to it than that. There was an arrow play; also a question that had to be answered in a certain way. Ongyatasse did not tell me what they were, but I learned at the first village where we stopped.

"This is the custom of pipe-carrying. When we approached a settlement we would show ourselves to the women working in the fields or to children playing, anybody who would go and carry word to the Head Man that the Pipe was coming. It was in order to be easily recognized that Ongyatasse wore the Peace Mark."

The Mound-Builder felt in his pouch for a lump of chalky white clay with which he drew a wide mark around his mouth, and two cheek-marks like a parenthesis. It would have been plain as far as one could see him.

"That was so the villages would know that one came with Peace words in his mouth, and make up their minds quickly whether they wanted to speak with him. Sometimes when there was quarreling between the clans they would not receive a messenger. But even in war-times a man's life was safe as long as he wore the White Mark."

"Ours is a white flag," said Oliver.

The Mound-Builder nodded.

"All civilized peoples have much the same customs," he agreed, "but the Lenni-Lenape were savages.

"We lay that night at Pigeon Roost in the Scioto Bottoms with wild pigeons above us thick as blackberries on the vines. They woke us going out at dawn like thunder, and at mid-morning they still darkened the sun. We cut into the Kaskaskia Trail by a hunting-trace my uncle had told us of, and by the middle of the second day we had made the first Eagle village. When we were sure we had been seen, we sat down and waited until the women came bringing food. Then the Head Man came in full dress and smoked with us."

Out of his pouch the Tallega drew the eagle-shaped ceremonial pipe of red pipestone, and when he had fitted it to the feathered stem, blew a salutatory whiff of smoke to the Great Spirit.

"Thus we did, and later in the Council House there were ceremonies and exchange of messages. It was there, when all seemed finished, that I saw the arrow play and heard the question.

"Ongyatasse drew an arrow from his quiver and scraped it. There was dried blood on the point, which makes an arrow untrue to its aim, but it was no business for a youth to be cleaning his arrows before the elders of the Town House; therefore, I took notice that this was the meat of his message. Ongyatasse scraped and the Head Man watched him.

"'There are many horned heads in the forest this season,' he said at last.

"'Very many,' said Ongyatasse; 'they come into the fields and eat up the harvest.'

"'In that case,' said the Head Man, 'what should a man do?'

"'What can he do but let fly at them with a broad arrow?' said Ongyatasse, putting up his own arrow, as a man puts up his work when it is finished.

"But as the arrow was not clean, and as the Lenni-Lenape had shot all the deer, if I had not known that Well-Praised had devised both question and answer, it would have seemed all foolishness. There had been no General Council since the one at which the treaty of passage was made with the Lenni-Lenape; therefore I knew that the War-Chief had planned this sending of dark messages in advance, messages which no Young-Man-Who-Never-Turns-Back had any right to understand.

"'But why the Painted Scroll?' I said to Ongyatasse; for if, as I supposed, the real message was in the question and answer, I could not see why there should still be a Council called.

" 'The scroll,' said my friend, 'is for those who are meant to be fooled by it.'

" 'But who should be fooled?'

" 'Whoever should stop us on the trail.'

" 'My thoughts do not move so fast as my feet, O my friend,' said I. 'Who would stop a pipe-carrier of the Tallegewi?'

" 'What if it should be the Horned Heads?' said Ongyatasse.

"That was a name we had given the Lenni-Lenape on account of the feathers they tied to the top of their hair, straight up like horns sprouting. Of course, they could have had no possible excuse for stopping us, being at peace, but I began to put this together with things Ongyatasse had told me, particularly the reason why no older man than he could be spared from Three Towns. He said the men were rebuilding the stockade and getting in the harvest.

"The middle one of Three Towns was walled, a circling wall of earth half man high, and on top of that, a stockade of planted posts and wattles. It was the custom in war-times to bring the women and the corn into the walled towns from the open villages. But there had been peace so long in Tallega that our stockade was in great need of rebuilding, and so were the corn bins. Well-Praised was expecting trouble with the Lenni-Lenape, I concluded; but I did not take it very seriously. The Moon of Stopped Waters was still young in the sky, and the fifth day of the Moon Halting seemed very far away to me.

"We were eleven days in all carrying the Pipe to the Miami villages, and though they fed us well at the towns where we stopped, we were as thin as snipe at the end of it. It was our first important running, you see, and we wished to make a record. We followed the main trails which followed the watersheds. Between these, we plunged down close-leaved, sweating tunnels of underbrush, through tormenting clouds of flies. In the bottoms the slither of our moccasins in the black mud would wake clumps of water snakes, big as a man's head, that knotted themselves together in the sun. There is a certain herb which snakes do not love which we rubbed on our ankles, but we could hear them rustle and hiss as we ran, and the hot air was all a-click and a-glitter with insects' wings; . . . also there were trumpet flowers, dusky-throated, that made me think of my girl at Flint Ridge. . . . Then we would come out on long ridges where oak and hickory shouldered one another like the round-backed billows of the lake after the storm. We made our record. And for all that we were not so pressed nor so over-come with the dignity of our errand that we could not spare one afternoon to climb up to the Wabashiki Beacon. It lies on the watershed between the headwaters of the Maumee and the Wabash, a cone-shaped mound and a circling wall within which there was always wood piled for the beacon light, the Great Gleam, the Wabashiki, which could be seen the country round for a two days' journey. The Light-Keeper was very pleased with our company and told us old tales half the night long, about how the Beacon had been built and how it was taken by turns by the Round Heads and the Painted Turtles. He asked us also if we had seen anything of a party of Lenni-Lenape which he had noted the day before, crossing the bottoms about an hour after he had sighted us. He thought they must have gone around by Crow Creek, avoiding the village, and that we should probably come up with them the next morning, which proved to be the case.

"They rose upon us suddenly as we dropped down to the east fork of the Maumee, and asked us rudely where we were going. They had no right, of course, but they were our elders, to whom it is necessary to be respectful, and they were rather terrifying, with their great bows, tall as they were, stark naked except for a strip of deerskin, and their feathers on end like the quills of an angry porcupine. We had no weapons ourselves, except short hunting-bows,—one does not travel with peace on his mouth and a war weapon at his back,—so we answered truly, and Ongyatasse read the scroll to them, which I thought unnecessary.

"'Now, I think,' said my friend, when the Lenape had left us with some question about a hunting-party, which they had evidently invented to excuse their rudeness, 'that it was for such as these that the scroll was written.' But we could not understand why Well-Praised should have gone to all that trouble to let the Lenni-Lenape know that he had called a Council.

"When we had smoked our last pipe, we were still two or three days from Three Towns, and we decided to try for a cut-off by a hunting-trail which Ongyatasse had been over once, years ago, with his father. These hunting-traces go everywhere through the Tallegewi Country. You can tell them by the way they fork from the main trails and, after a day or two, thin into nothing. We traveled well into the night from the place that Ongyatasse remembered, so as to steer by the stars, and awoke to the pleasant pricking of adventure. But we had gone half the morning before we began to be sure that we were followed.

"Jays that squawked and fell silent as we passed, called the alarm again a few minutes later. A porcupine which we saw, asleep upon a log, woke up and came running from behind us. We thought of the Lenni-Lenape. Where a bare surface of rock across our path made it possible to turn out without leaving a track, we stole back a few paces and waited. Presently we made out, through the thick leaves, a youth, about our age we supposed, for his head was not cropped and he was about the height of Ongyatasse. When we had satisfied ourselves that he was alone, we took pleasure in puzzling him. As soon as he missed our tracks in the trail, he knew that he was discovered and played quarry to our fox very craftily. For an hour or two we stalked one another between the buckeye boles, and then I stepped on a rotten log which crumbled and threw me noisily. The Lenape let fly an arrow in our direction. We were nearing a crest of a ridge where the underbrush thinned out, and as soon as we had a glimpse of his naked legs slipping from tree to tree, Ongyatasse made a dash for him. We raced like deer through the still woods, Ongyatasse gaining on the flying figure, and I about four laps behind him. A low branch swished blindingly across my eyes for a moment, and when I could look again, the woods were suddenly still and empty.

"I dropped instantly, for I did not know what this might mean, and creeping cautiously to the spot where I had last seen them, I saw the earth opening in a sharp, deep ravine, at the bottom of which lay Ongyatasse with one leg crumpled under him. I guessed that the Lenape must have led him to the edge and then slipped aside just in time to let the force of Ongyatasse's running carry him over. Without waiting to plan, I began to climb down the steep side of the ravine. About halfway down I was startled by a rustling below, and, creeping along the bottom of the bluff, I saw the Lenni-Lenape with his knife between his teeth, within an arm's length of my friend. I cried out, and in a foolish effort to save him, I must have let go of the ledge to which I clung. The next thing I knew I was lying half-stunned, with a great many pains in different parts of me, at the bottom of the ravine, almost within touch of Ongyatasse and a young Lenape with an amulet of white deer's horn about his neck and, across his back, what had once been a white quiver. He was pouring water from a birch-bark cup upon my friend, and as soon as he saw that my eyes were opened he came and offered me a drink. There did not seem to be anything to say, so we said nothing, but presently, when I could sit up, he washed the cut on the back of my head, and then he showed me that Ongyatasse's knee was out of place, and said that we ought to pull it back before he came to himself.

"I crawled over—I had saved myself by falling squarely on top of White Quiver so that nothing worse happened to me than sore ribs and a finger broken—and took my friend around the body while our enemy pulled the knee, and Ongyatasse groaned aloud and came back. Then White Quiver tied up my finger in a splint of bark, and we endured our pains and said nothing.

"We were both prisoners of the Lenape. So we considered ourselves; we waited to see what he would do about it. Toward evening he went off for an hour and returned with a deer which he dressed very skillfully and gave us to eat. Then, of the wet hide, he made a bandage for Ongyatasse's knee, which shrunk as it dried and kept down the swelling.

"'Now I shall owe you my name as well as my life,' said Ongya-tasse, for if his knee had not been properly attended, that would have been the end of his running.

"'Then your new name would be Well-Friended,' said the Len-ape, and he made a very good story of how I had come tumbling down on both of them. We laughed, but Ongyatasse had another question.

"'There was peace on my mouth and peace between Lenni-Lenape and Tallegewi. Why should you chase us?'

"'The Tallegewi send a Pipe to the Three Clans. Will you swear that the message that went with it had nothing to do with the Lenni-Lenape?'

"'What should two boys know of a call to Council?' said Ong-yatasse, and showed him the birch-bark scroll, to which White Quiver paid no attention.

"'There is peace between us, and a treaty, the terms of which were made by the Tallegewi, all of which we have kept. We have entered no town without invitation. When one of our young men stole a maiden of yours we returned her to her village.' He went on telling many things, new to us, of the highness of the Lenni-Lenape. 'All this was agreed at the Three Towns by Cool Waters,' said he. 'Now comes a new order. We may not enter the towns at all. The treaty was for camping privileges in any one place for the space of one moon. Now, if we are three days in one place, we are told that we must move on. The Lenni-Lenape are not Two-Talkers. If we wear peace on our mouths we wear it in our hearts also.'

"'There is peace between your people and mine, and among the Tallegewi, peace.'

"'So,' said White Quiver. 'Then why do they rebuild their stockades and fetch arrow-stone from far quarries? And why do they call a Council in the Moon of the Harvest?'

"I remembered the good trade my uncle, the arrow-maker, had had that summer, and was amazed at his knowledge of it, so I answered as I had been taught. 'If I were a Lenape,' said I, 'and thought that the Councils of the Tallegewi threatened my people, I would know what those Councils were if I made myself a worm in the roof-tree to overhear it.'

" 'Aye,' he said, 'but you are only a Tallega.'

"He was like that with us, proud and humble by turns. Though he was a naked savage, traveling through our land on sufferance, he could make us crawl in our hearts for the Tallegewi. He suspected us of much evil, most of which was true as it turned out; yet all the time we lay at the bottom of the ravine, for the most part helpless, he killed every day for us, and gathered dry grass to make a bed for Ongyatasse.

"We talked no more of the Council or of our errand, but as youths will, we talked of highness, and of big game in Shinaki, and of the ways of the Tallegewi, of which for the most part he was scornful.

"Corn he allowed us as a great advantage, but of our towns he doubted whether they did not make us fat and Two-Talkers.

" 'Town is a trade-maker,' he said; 'men who trade much for things, will also trade for honor.'

" 'The Lenni-Lenape carry their honor in their hands,' said Ongyatasse, 'but the Tallegewi carry theirs in their forehead.'

"He meant," said the Mound-Builder, turning to the children, "that the Lenni-Lenape fought for what they held most dear, and the Tallegewi schemed and plotted for it. That was as we were taught. With us, the hand is not lifted until the head has spoken. But as it turned out, between Tallegewi and Lenape, the fighters had the best of it."

He sighed, making the salutation to the dead as he looked off, across the burial-grounds, to the crumbling heap of the god-house.

"But I don't understand," said Dorcas; "were Ongyatasse and White Quiver friends or enemies?"

"They were two foes who loved one another, and though their tribes fell into long and bloody war, between these two there was highness and, at the end, most wonderful kindness. The first time that we got Ongyatasse to his feet and he found that his knee, though feeble, was as good as ever, he said to White Quiver, leaning on his shoulder,—

"'Concerning the call to Council, there was more to it than was written on the scroll, the meaning of which was hidden from me who carried it.'

"'Which is no news to me,' said the Lenni-Lenape; 'also,' he said, 'the message was arranged beforehand, for it required no answer.'

"I asked him how he knew that, and he mocked at me.

"'Any time these five days you could have gone forward with the answer had it been important for you to get back to Cool Waters!'

"That was true. I could have left Ongyatasse and gone on alone, but nothing that had happened so far had made us think that we must get back quickly. White Quiver asked us one day what reason Well-Praised had given for requiring that the Lenni-Lenape should pass through the country with not more than twenty fighting men in the party. To save the game, we told him, which seemed to us reasonable; though I think from that hour we began to feel that the Tallegewi, with all their walled towns and monuments, had been put somehow in the wrong by the wild tribes of Shinaki.

"We stayed on in the ravine, waiting on Ongyatasse's knee, until we saw the new rim of the Halting Moon curled up like a feather. The leaves of the buckeye turned clear yellow and the first flock of wild geese went over. We waited one more day for White Quiver to show us a short cut to the Maumee Trail, and just when we had given him up, we were aware of a strange Lenape in war-paint moving among the shadows. He stood off from us with his arms folded and his face was as bleak as a winter-bitten wood.

"'Wash the lie from your mouth,' he said, 'and follow.'

"Without a word he turned and began to move from us through the smoky light with which the wood was filling. His head was cropped for war—that was why we did not know him—and along the shoulder he turned toward us was the long scrape of a spear-point. That was why we followed, saying nothing. Toward daylight the lame knee began to give trouble. White Quiver came back and put his shoulder under Ongyatasse's, so we moved forward, wordlessly. Birds awoke in the woods, and hoarfrost lay white on the crisped grasses.

"On a headland from which the lake glinted white as a blade of flint on the horizon, we waited the sunrise. Smoke arose, from Wabashiki, from the direction of the Maumee settlements, from the lake shore towns; tall plumes of smoke shook and threatened. Curtly, while we ate, White Quiver told us what had happened; how the Tallegewi, in violation of the treaty, had fallen suddenly on scattered bands of the Lenni-Lenape and all but exterminated them. The Tallegewi said that it was because they had discovered that the Lenni-Lenape had plotted to fall upon our towns, as soon as the corn was harvested, and take them. But White Quiver thought that the whole thing was a plan of Well-Praised from the beginning. He had been afraid to refuse passage to the Lenape, on account of their great numbers, and had arranged to have them broken up in small parties so that they could be dealt with separately."

"And which was it?" Oliver wished to know.

"It was a thousand years ago," said the Mound-Builder. "Who remembers? But we were ashamed, my friend and I, for we understood now that the secret meaning of our message about the Horned Heads had been that the Tallegewi should fall upon the Lenape wherever they found them. You remember that it was part of the question and answer that they 'came into the fields and ate up the harvest.'

"There might have been a plot, but, on the other hand, we knew that the painted scroll had been a blind to make the Lenni-Lenape think that the Tallegewi would do nothing until they had taken counsel. But we had carried a war message with peace upon our mouths and we were ashamed before White Quiver. We had talked much highness with him, and besides, we loved him. As it turned out we were not wrong in thinking he loved us. As we stood making out the points of direction for the trail, Ongyatasse's knee gave under him, and as White Quiver put out his arm without thinking, a tremor passed over them. They stood so leaning each on each for a moment. 'Your trail lies thus . . . and thus . . .' said the Lenape, 'but I do not know what you will find at the end of it.' Then he loosed his arm from my friend's shoulder, took a step back, and the forest closed about him.

"We were two days more on the trail, though we did not go directly to Cool Waters. Some men of the Painted Turtles that we met, told us the fight had passed from the neighborhood of the towns and gathered at Bent Bar Crossing. Our fathers were both there, which we made an excuse for joining them. At several places we saw evidences of fighting. All the bands of Lenni-Lenape that were not too far in our territory had come hurrying back toward Fish River, and other bands, as the rumor of fighting spread, came down out of Shinaki like buzzards to a carcass. From Cool Waters to Namae-sippu, the Dark Wood was full of war-cries and groaning. At Fish River the Tallegewi fell in hundreds . . . there is a mound there . . . at Bent Bar the Lenni-Lenape held the ford, keeping a passage open for flying bands that were pressed up from the south by the Painted Turtles. Ongyatasse went about getting together his old band from the Three Towns, fretting because we were not allowed to take the front of the battle.

"Three days the fight raged about the crossing. The Lenni-Lenape were the better bowmen; their long arrows carried heavier points. Some that I found in the breasts of my friends, I had made, and it made my own heart hot within me. The third day, men from the farther lake towns came up the river in their canoes, and the Lenape, afraid of being cut off from their friends in the Dark Wood, broke across the river. As soon as they began to go, our young men, who feared the fight would be over without them, could not be held back. Ongyatasse at our head, we plunged into the river after them.

"Even in flight the Lenni-Lenape were most glorious fighters. They dived among the canoes to hack holes in the bottoms, and rising from under the sides they pulled the paddlers bodily into the river. We were mad with our first fight, we youngsters, for we let them lead us up over the bank and straight into ambush. We were the Young-Men-Who-Never-Turned-Back.

"That was a true name for many of us," said the Mound-Builder. "I remember Ongyatasse's shrill eagle cry above the 'G'we! G'we!' of the Lenni-Lenape, and the next thing I knew I was struggling in the river, bleeding freely from a knife wound, and somebody was pulling me into a canoe and safety."

"And Ongyatasse—?" The children looked at the low mound between the Council Place and the God-House.

The Mound-Builder nodded.

"We put our spears together to make a tent over him before the earth was piled," he said, "and it was good to be able to do even so much as that for him. For we thought at first we should never find him. He was not on the river, nor in our side of the Dark Wood, and the elders would not permit us to go across in search of him. But at daylight the gatherers of the dead saw something moving from under the mist that hid the opposite bank of the river. We waited, arrow on bowstring, not knowing if it were one of our own coming back to us or a Lenape asking for parley. But as it drew near we saw it was a cropped head, and he towed a dead Tallega by the hair. Ripples that spread out from his quiet wake took the sun, and the measured dip of the swimmer's arm was no louder than the wing of the cooter that paddled in the shallows.

"It had been a true word that Ongyatasse had given his life and his luck to White Quiver; the Lenape had done his best to give them back again. As he came ashore with the stiffened form, we saw him take the white deer amulet from his own neck and fasten it around the neck of Ongyatasse. Then, disdaining even to make the Peace sign for his own safe returning, he plunged into the river again, swimming steadily without haste until the fog hid him."

The Mound-Builder stood up, wrapping his feather mantle about him and began to move down the slope of the Town Mound, the children following. There were ever so many things they wished to hear about, which they hoped he might be going to tell them, but halfway down he turned and pointed. Over south and east a thin blue film of smoke rose up straight from the dark forest.

"That's for you, I think. Your friend, the Onondaga, is signaling you; he knows the end of the story."

Taking hands, the children ran straight in the direction of the smoke signal, along the trail which opened before them.

X
THE MAKING OF A SHAMAN: A TELLING OF
THE IROQUOIS TRAIL, BY THE ONONDAGA

Down the Mound-Builder's graded way the children ran looking
for the Onondaga. Like all the trail in the Museum Country it covered a vast tract of country in a very little while, so that it was no
time at all before they came out among high, pine-covered swells,
that broke along the water-courses into knuckly granite headlands.
From one of these, steady puffs of smoke arose, and a moment later
they could make out the figure of an Indian turning his head from
side to side as he searched the surrounding country with the look of
eagles. They knew him at once, by the Medicine bundle at his belt
and the slanting Iroquois feather, for their friend the Onondaga.

"I was looking for you by the lake shore trail," he explained as
Oliver and Dorcas Jane climbed up to him. "You must have come
by the Muskingham-Mahoning; it drops into the Trade Trail of the
Iroquois yonder,"—he pointed south and east,—"the Great Trail,
from the Mohican-ittuck to the House of Thunder." He meant the
Hudson River and the Falls of Niagara. "Even at our village, which
was at the head of the lake here, we could hear the Young Thun-
ders, shouting from behind the falls," he told them.

A crooked lake lay below them like a splinter of broken glass between the headlands. From the far end of it the children could see smoke rising. "We used to signal our village from here when we went on the war-trail," said the Onondaga; "we would cut our mark on a tree as we went out, and as we came back we added the war count. I was looking for an old score of mine to-day."

"Had it anything to do with the Mound-Builders?" Dorcas wished to know. "He said you knew the end of that story."

The Onondaga shook his head.

"That was a hundred years before my time, and is a Telling of the Lenni-Lenape. In the Red Score it is written, the Red Score of the Lenni-Lenape. When my home was in the village there, the Five Nations held all the country between the lakes and the Mohican-ittuck. But there were many small friendly tribes along the borders, Algonquian mostly."

He squatted on his heels beside the fire and felt in his belt for the pipe and tobacco pouch without which no Telling proceeds properly.

"In my youth," said the Onondaga, "I was very unhappy because I had no Vision. When my time came I walked in the forest and ate nothing, but the Mystery would not speak to me. Nine days I walked fasting, and then my father came to find me under a pine tree, with my eyes sunk in my head and my ribs like a basket. But because I was ashamed I told him my Mystery was something that could not be talked about, and so I told the Shaman.

"My father was pleased because he thought it meant that I was to be a very great Shaman myself, and the other boys envied me. But in my heart I was uneasy. I did not know what to make of my life because the Holder of the Heavens had not revealed himself to me. To one of my friends he had appeared as an eagle, which meant that he was to be a warrior, keen and victorious; and to another as a fox, so that he studied cunning; but without any vision I did not know what to make of myself. My heart was slack as a wetted bowstring. My father reproached me.

" 'The old women had smoke in their eyes,' he said; 'they told me I had a son, now I see it is a woman child.'

"My mother was kinder. 'Tell me,' she said, 'what evil dream unknots the cords of your heart?'

"So at last I told her.

"My mother was a wise woman. 'To a dog or a child,' she said, 'one speaks the first word on the lips, but before a great Shaman one considers carefully. What is a year of your life to the Holder of the Heavens? Go into the forest and wait until his message is ripe for you.' She was a wise woman.

"So I put aside my bow and quiver, and with them all desire of meat and all thought of killing. With my tomahawk I cut a mark in that chestnut yonder and buried my weapon at the foot of it. I had my knife, my pipe, and my fire-stick. Also I felt happy and important because my mother had made me believe that the Holder of the Heavens thought well of me. I was giving him a year in which to tell me what to do with my life.

"I turned east, for, I said, from the east light comes. It was an old trail even in those days. It follows the watershed from the lake to Oneida, and clears the Mohawk Valley northward. It was the Moon of Tender Leaves when I set out, and by the time nuts began to ripen I had come to the lowest hills of the Adirondacks.

"Sometimes I met hunting-parties or women gathering berries, and bought corn and beans from them, but for the most part I lived on seeds and roots and wild apples.

"By the time I had been a month or two without killing, the smell of meat left me. Rabbits ran into my hands, and the mink, stealing along the edge of the marsh to look for frogs, did not start from me. Deer came at night to feed on the lily buds on the lake borders. They would come stealing among the alders and swim far out to soak their coats. When they had made themselves mosquito-proof, they would come back to the lily beds and I would swim among them stilly, steering by the red reflection of my camp-fire in their eyes. When my thought that was not the thought of killing touched them, they would snort a little and return to the munching of lilies, and the trout would rise in bubbly rings under my arms as I floated. But though I was a brother to all the Earth, the Holder of the Heavens would not speak to me.

"Sometimes, when I had floated half the night between the hollow sky of stars and its hollow reflection, the Vision seemed to gather on the surface of the water. It would take shape and turn to the flash of a loon's wet wing in the dawning. Or I would sit still in the woods until my thought was as a tree, and the squirrels would take me for a tree and run over me. Then there would come a strange stir, and the creeping of my flesh along my spine until the Forest seemed about to speak . . . and suddenly a twig would snap or a jay squawk, and I would be I again, and the tree a tree . . .

"It was the first quarter of the Moon of Falling Leaves," said the Onondaga filling his pipe again and taking a fresh start on his story. "There was a feel in the air that comes before the snow, but I was very happy in my camp by a singing creek far up on the Adirondacks, and kept putting off moving the camp from day to day. And one evening when I came in from gathering acorns, I discovered that I had had a visitor. Mush of acorn meal which I had left in my pot had been eaten. That is right, of course, if the visitor is hungry; but this one had wiped out his tracks with a leafy bough, which looked like trickery.

"It came into my mind that it might have been one of the Gahonga, the spirits that dwell in rocks and rivers and make the season fruitful."

"Oh!" cried Dorcas, "Indian fairies! Did you have those?"

"There are spirits in all things," said the Onondaga gravely. "There are Odowas, who live in the underworld and keep back the evil airs that bring sickness. You can see the bare places under the pines where they have their dancing-places. And there are the Gandaiyah who loose wild things from the traps and bring dew on the strawberry blossoms. But all these are friendly to man. So I cooked another pot of food and lay down in my blanket. I sleep as light as a wild thing myself. In the middle of the night I was wakened by the sound of eating. Presently I heard something scrape the bottom of the pot, and though I was afraid, I could not bear to have man or spirit go from my camp hungry. So I spoke to the sound.

"'There is food hanging in the tree,' I said. I had hung it up to keep the ants from it. But as soon as I finished speaking I heard the Thing creeping away. In the morning I found it had left the track of one small torn moccasin and a strange misshapen lump. It came up from and disappeared into the creek, so I was sure it must have been a Gahonga. But that evening as I sat by my fire I was aware of it behind me. No, I heard nothing; I felt the thought of that creature touching my thought. Without looking round I said, 'What is mine is yours, brother.' Then I laid dry wood on the fire, and getting up I walked away without looking back. But when I was out of the circle of light I looked and I saw the Thing come out of the brush and warm its hands.

"Then I knew that it was human, so I dropped my blanket over it from behind and it lay without moving. I thought I had killed it, but when I lifted the blanket I saw that it was a girl, and she was all but dead with fright. She lay looking at me like a deer that I had shot, waiting for me to plunge in the knife. It is a shame to any man to have a girl look at him as that one looked at me. I made the sign of friendship and set food before her, and water in a cup of bark. Then I saw what had made the clumsy track; it was her foot which she had cut on the rocks and bound up with strips of bark. Also she was sick with fright and starvation.

"For two days she lay on my bed and ate what I gave her and looked at me as a trapped thing looks at the owner of the trap. I tried her with all the dialects I knew, and even with a few words I had picked up from a summer camp of Wabaniki. I had met them a week or two before at Owenunga, at the foot of the mountains.

"She put her hand over her mouth and looked sideways to find a way out of the trap.

"I was sorry for her, but she was a great nuisance. I was so busy getting food for her that I had no time to listen for the Holder of the Heavens, and besides, there was a thickening of the air, what we call the Breath of the Great Moose, which comes before a storm. If we did not wish to be snowed in, we had to get down out of the mountain, and on account of her injured foot we had to go slowly.

"I had it in mind to take her to the camp of the Wabaniki at Owenunga, but when she found out where we were going she tried to run away. After that I carried her, for the cut in her foot opened and bled.

"She lay in my arms like a hurt fawn, but what could I do? There was a tent of cloud all across the Adirondack, and besides, it is not proper for a young girl to be alone in the woods with a strange man," said the Onondaga, but he smiled to himself as he said it.

"It was supper-time when we came to Crooked Water. There was a smell of cooking, and the people gathering between the huts.

"There was peace between the Five Nations and the Wabaniki, so I walked boldly into the circle of summer huts and put the girl down, while I made the stranger's sign for food and lodging. But while my hand was still in the air, there was a shout and a murmur and the women began snatching their children back. I could see them huddling together like buffalo cows when their calves are tender, and the men pushing to the front with caught-up weapons in their hands.

"I held up my own to show that they were weaponless.

"'I want nothing but food and shelter for this poor girl,' I said. I had let her go in order to make the sign language, for I had but a few words of their tongue. She crouched at my feet covering her face with her long hair. The people stood off without answering, and somebody raised a cry for Waba-mooin. It was tossed about from mouth to mouth until it reached the principal hut, and presently a man came swaggering out in the dress of a Medicine Man. He was older than I, but he was also fat, and for all his Shaman's dress I was not frightened. I knew by the way the girl stopped crying that she both knew and feared him.

"The moment Waba-mooin saw her he turned black as a thunderhead. He scattered words as a man scatters seeds with his hand. I was too far to hear him, but the people broke out with a shower of sticks and stones. At that the girl sprang up and spread her arms between me and the people, crying something in her own tongue, but a stone struck her on the point of the shoulder. She would have dropped, but I caught her. I held her in my arms and looked across at the angry villagers and Waba-mooin. Suddenly power came upon me . . .

"It is something all Indian," said the Onondaga,—"something White Men do not understand. It is Magic Medicine, the power of the Shaman, the power of my thought meeting the evil thought of the Wabaniki and turning it back as a buffalo shield turns arrows. I gathered up the girl and walked away from that place slowly as becomes a Shaman. No more stones struck me; the arrow of Waba-mooin went past me and stuck in an oak. My power was upon me.

"I must have walked half the night, hearing the drums at Crooked Water scaring away evil influences. I would feel the girl warm and soft in my arms as a fawn, and then after a time she would seem to be a part of me. The trail found itself under my feet; I was not in the least wearied. The girl was asleep when I laid her down, but toward morning she woke, and the moment I looked in her eyes, I knew that whatever they had stoned her for at Owenunga, her eyes were friendly.

"'M'toulin,' she said, which is the word in her language for Shaman, 'what will you do with me?'

"There was nothing I could do but take her to my mother as quickly as possible. There was a wilderness of hills to cross before we struck the trail through Mohawk Valley. That afternoon the snow began to fall in great dry flakes, thickening steadily. The girl walked when she could, but most of the time I carried her. I had the power of a Shaman, though the Holder of the Heavens had not yet spoken to me.

"We pushed to the top of the range before resting, and all night we could hear the click and crash of deer and moose going down before the snow. All the next day there was one old bull moose kept just ahead of us. We knew he was old because of his size and his being alone. Two or three times we passed other bulls with two or three cows and their calves of that season yarding among the young spruce, but the old bull kept on steadily down the mountain. His years had made him weather-wise. The third day the wind shifted the snow, and we saw him on the round crown of a hill below us, tracking."

The Onondaga let his pipe go out while he explained the winter habits of moose.

"When the snow is too deep for yarding," he said, "they look for the lower hills that have been burnt over, so that the growth is young and tender. When the snow is soft, after a thaw, they will track steadily back and forth until the hill is laced with paths. They will work as long as the thaw lasts, pushing the soft snow with their shoulders to release the young pine and the birches. Then, when the snow crusts, they can browse all along the paths for weeks, tunneling far under.

"We saw our bull the last afternoon as we came down from the cloud cap, and then the white blast cut us off and we had only his trail to follow. When we came to the hill we could still hear him thrashing about in his trails, so I drew down the boughs of a hemlock and made us a shelter and a fire. For two days more the storm held, with cold wind and driven snow. About the middle of the second day I heard a heavy breathing above our hut, and presently the head of the moose came through the hemlock thatch, and his eyes were the eyes of a brother. So I knew my thought was still good, and I made room for him in the warmth of the hut. He moved out once or twice to feed, and I crept after him to gather grass seeds and whatever could be found that the girl could eat. We had had nothing much since leaving the camp at Crooked Water.

"And by and by with the hunger and anxiety about Nukēwis, which was the name she said she should be called by, my thought was not good any more. I would look at the throat of the moose as he crowded under the hemlock and think how easily I could slit it with my knife and how good moose meat toasted on the coals would taste. I was glad when the storm cleared and left the world all white and trackless. I went out and prayed to the Holder of the Heavens that he would strengthen me in the keeping of my vow and also that he would not let the girl die.

"While I prayed a rabbit that had been huddling under the brush and the snow, came hopping into my trail; it hopped twice and died with the cold. I took it for a sign; but when I had cooked it and was feeding it to the girl she said:—

" 'Why do you not eat, M'toulin,' for we had taught one another a few words of our own speech.

" 'I am not hungry,' I told her.

" 'While I eat I can see that your throat is working with hunger,' she insisted. And it was true I could have snatched the meat from her like a wolf, but because of my vow I would not.

" 'M'toulin, there is a knife at your belt; why have you not killed the moose to make meat for us?'

" 'Eight moons I have done no killing, seeking the Vision and the Voice,' I told her. 'It is more than my life to me.'

"When I had finished, she reached over with the last piece of rabbit and laid it on the fire. It was a sacrifice. As we watched the flame lick it up, all thought of killing went out of my head like the smoke of sacrifice, and my thought was good again.

"When the meat she had eaten had made her strong, Nukēwis sat up and crossed her hands on her bosom.

" 'M'toulin,' she said, 'the evil that has come on you belongs to me. I will go away with it. I am a witch and bring evil on those who are kind to me.'

" 'Who says you are a witch?'

" 'All my village, and especially Waba-mooin. I brought sickness on the village, and on you hunger and the breaking of your vow.'

" 'I have seen Waba-mooin,' I said. 'I do not think too much of his opinions.'

" 'He is the Shaman of my village,' said Nukēwis. 'My father was

Shaman before him, a much greater Shaman than Waba-mooin will ever be. He wanted my father's Medicine bundle which hung over the door to protect me; my father left it to me when he died. But afterward there was a sickness in the village, and Waba-mooin said it was because the powerful Medicine bundle was left in the hands of an ignorant girl. He said for the good of the village it ought to be taken away from me. But *I* thought it was because so many people came to my house with their sick, because of my Medicine bundle, and Waba-mooin missed their gifts. He said that if I was not willing to part with my father's bundle, that he would marry me, but when I would not, then he said that I was a witch!'

" 'Where is the bundle now?' I asked her.

" 'I hid it near our winter camp before we came into the mountains. But there was sickness in the mountains and Waba-mooin said that it also was my fault. So they drove me out with sticks and stones. That is why they would not take me back.'

" 'Then,' I said, 'when Waba-mooin goes back to the winter camp, he will find the Medicine bundle.'

" 'He will never find it,' she said, 'but he will be the only Shaman in the village and will have all the gifts. But listen, M'toulin, by now the people are back in their winter home. It is more than two days from here. If you go without me, they will give you food and shelter, but with me you will have only hard words and stones. Therefore, I leave you, M'toulin.' She stood up, made a sign of farewell.

" 'You must show me the way to your village first,' I insisted.

"I saw that she meant what she said, and because I was too weak to run after her, I pretended. I thought that would hold her.

"We should have set out that moment, but a strange lightness came in my head. I do not know just what happened. I think the storm must have begun again early in the afternoon. There was a great roaring as of wind and the girl bending over me, wavering and growing thin like smoke. Twice I saw the great head of the moose thrust among the hemlock boughs, and heard Nukēwis urging and calling me. She lifted my hands and clasped them round the antlers of the moose; I could feel his warm breath. . . . He threw up his head, drawing me from my bed, wonderfully light upon my feet. We seemed to move through the storm. I could feel the hairy shoulder of the moose and across his antlers Nukēwis calling me. I felt myself carried along like a thin bubble of life in the storm that poured down from the Adirondack like Niagara. At last I slipped into darkness.

"I do not know how long this lasted, but presently I was aware of a light that began to grow and spread around me. It came from the face of the moose, and when I looked up out of my darkness it changed to the face of a great kind man. He had on the headdress of a chief priest, the tall headdress of eagle plumes and antlers. I had hold of one of them, and his arm was around and under me. But I knew very well who held me.

" 'You have appeared to me at last,' I said to him.

" 'I have appeared, my son.' His voice was kind as the sound of summer waters.

" 'I looked for you long, O Taryenya-wagon!'

" 'You looked for me among your little brothers of the wild,' he said, 'and for you the Vision was among men, my son.'

" 'How, among men?'

" 'What you did for that poor girl when you put your good thought between her and harm. That you must do for men.'

" 'I am to be a Shaman, then?' I thought of my father.

" 'According to a man's power,' said the Holder of the Heavens,—'as my power comes upon him . . .' "

The Onondaga puffed silently for a while on his pipe.

Dorcas Jane fidgeted. "But I don't understand," she said at last; "just what was it that happened?"

"It was my Mystery," said the Onondaga; "my Vision that came to me out of the fasting and the sacrifice. You see, there had been very little food since leaving Crooked Water, and Nukēwis—"

"You gave it all to her." Dorcas nodded. "But still I don't understand?"

"The moose had begun to travel down the mountain, and like a good brother he came back for me. Nukēwis lifted me up and bound me to his antlers, holding me from the other side, but I was too weak to notice.

"We must have traveled that way for hours through the storm until we reached the tall woods below the limit of the snow. When I came to myself, I was lying on a bed of fern in a bright morning and Nukēwis was cooking quail which she had snared with a slip noose made of her hair. I ate—I could eat now that I had had my Vision—and grew strong. All the upper mountain was white like a tent of deerskin, but where we were there was only thin ice on the edges of the streams.

"We stayed there for one moon. I wished to get my strength back, and besides, we wished to get married, Nukēwis and I."

"But how could you, without any party?" Dorcas wished to know. She had never seen anybody get married, but she knew it was always spoken of as a Wedding Party.

"We had the party four months later when we got back to my own village," explained the Onondaga. "For that time I built a hut, and when I had led her across the door, as our custom was, I scattered seeds upon her—seeds of the pine tree. Then we sat in our places on either side the fire, and she made me cake of acorn meal, and we made a vow as we ate it that we would love one another always.

"We were very happy. I hunted and fished, and the old moose fed in our meadow. Nukēwis used to gather armfuls of grass for him. When we went back to my wife's village he trotted along in the trail behind us like a dog. Nukēwis wished to go back after her father's Medicine bag, and being a woman she did not wish to go to my mother without her dower. There were many handsome skins and baskets in her father's hut which had been given to him when he was Medicine Man. She felt sure Waba-mooin would not have touched them. And as for me, I was young enough to want Waba-mooin to see that I was also a Shaman.

"We stole into Nukēwis's hut in the dark, and when it was morning a light snow was over the ground to cover our tracks, and there was our smoke going up and the great moose standing at our door chewing his cud and over the door the Medicine bag of Nukēwis's father. How the neighbors were astonished! They ran for Waba-mooin, and when I saw him coming in all his Shaman's finery, I put on the old Medicine Man's shirt and his pipe and went out to smoke with him as one Shaman with another."

The Onondaga laughed to himself, remembering. "It was funny to see him try to go through with it, but there was nothing else for him to do. I ought to have punished him a little for what he did to Nukēwis, but my heart was too full of happiness and my Mystery. And perhaps it was punishment enough to have me staying there in the village with all the folk bringing me presents and neglecting Waba-mooin. I think he was glad when we set out for my own village in the Moon of the Sap Running.

"I knew my mother would be waiting for me, and besides, I wished my son to be born an Onondaga."

"And what became of the old moose?"

"Somewhere on the trail home we lost him. Perhaps he heard his own tribe calling . . . and perhaps . . . He was the Holder of the Heavens to me, and from that time neither I nor my wife ate any moose meat. That is how it is when the Holder of the Heavens shows Himself to his children. But when I came by the tree where I had cut the first score of my search for Him, I cut a picture of the great moose, with my wife and I on either side of him."

The Onondaga pointed with his feathered pipe to a wide-boled chestnut a rod or two down the slope. "It was that I was looking for to-day," he said. "If you look you will find it."

And continuing to point with the long feathered stem of his pipe, the children rose quietly hand in hand and went to look.

XI
THE PEARLS OF COFACHIQUE: HOW LUCAS DE AYLLON CAME TO LOOK FOR THEM AND WHAT THE CACICA FAR-LOOKING DID TO HIM; TOLD BY THE PELICAN

One morning toward the end of February the children were sitting on the last bench at the far end of the Bird Gallery, which is the nicest sort of place to sit on a raw, slushy day. You can look out from it on one side over the flamingo colony of the Bahamas, and on the other straight into the heart of the Cuthbert Rookery in Florida. Just opposite is the green and silver coral islet of Cay Verde, with the Man-of-War Birds nesting among the flat leaves of the sea-grape.

If you sit there long enough and nobody comes by to interrupt, you can taste the salt of the spindrift over the banks of Cay Verde, and watch the palmetto leaves begin to wave like swords in the sea wind. That is what happened to Oliver and Dorcas Jane. The water stirred and shimmered and the long flock of flamingoes settled down, each to its own mud hummock on the crowded summer beaches. All at once Oliver thought of something.

"I wonder," he said, "if there are trails on the water and through the air?"

"Why, of course," said the Man-of-War Bird; "how else would we find our islet among so many? North along the banks till we sight the heads of Nassau, then east of Stirrup Cay, keeping the scent of the land flowers to windward, to the Great Bahama, and west by north to where blue water runs between the Biscayne Keys to the mouth of the Miami. That is how we reach the mainland in season, and back again to Cay Verde."

"It sounds like a long way," said Oliver.

"That's nothing," said the tallest Flamingo. "We go often as far east as the Windward Islands, and west to the Isthmus. But the ships go farther. We have never been to the place where the ships come from."

It was plain that the Flamingo was thinking of a ship as another and more mysterious bird. The Man-of-War Bird seemed to know better. The children could see, when he stretched out his seven-foot spread of wing, that he was a great traveler.

"What *I* should like to know," he said, "is how the ships find their way. With us we simply rise higher and higher, above the fogs, until we see the islands scattered like green nests and the banks and shoals which from that height make always the same pattern in the water, brown streaks of weed, gray shallows, and deep water blue. But the ships, though they never seem to leave the surface of the water, can make a shorter course than we in any kind of weather."

Oliver was considering how he could explain a ship's compass to the birds, but only the tail end of his thinking slipped out. "They call some of them men-of-war, too," he chuckled.

"You must have thought it funny the first time you saw one," said Dorcas Jane.

"Not me, but my ancestors," said the Man-of-War Bird; "*they* saw the Great Admiral when he first sailed in these waters. They saw the three tall galleons looming out of a purple mist on the eve of discovery, their topsails rosy with the sunset fire. The Admiral kept pacing, pacing; watching, on the one hand, lest his men surprise him with a mutiny, and on the other, glancing overside for a green bough or a floating log, anything that would be a sign of land. We saw him come in pride and wonder, and we saw him go in chains."

Like all the Museum people, the Man-of-War Bird said "we" when he spoke of his ancestors.

"There were others," said the Flamingo. "I remember an old man looking for a fountain."

"Ponce de Leon," supplied Dorcas Jane, proud that she could pronounce it.

"There is no harm in a fountain," said a Brown Pelican that had come sailing into Cuthbert Rookery with her wings sloped downward like a parachute. "It was the gold-seekers who filled the islands with the thunder of their guns and the smoke of burning huts."

The children turned toward the Pelican among the mangrove trees, crowded with nests of egret and heron and rosy hornbill.

The shallow water of the lagoon ran into gold-tipped ripples. In every one the low sun laid a tiny flake of azure. Over the far shore there was a continual flick and flash of wings, like a whirlwind playing with a heap of waste paper. Crooked flights of flamingoes made a moving reflection on the water like a scarlet snake, but among the queer mangrove stems, that did not seem to know whether they were roots or branches, there was a lovely morning stillness. It was just the place and hour for a story, and while the Brown Pelican opened her well-filled maw to her two hungry nestlings, the Snowy Egret went on with the subject.

"They were a gallant and cruel and heroic and stupid lot, the Spanish gold-seekers," she said. "They thought nothing of danger and hunger, but they could not find their way without a guide any further than their eyes could see, and they behaved very badly toward the poor Indians."

"We saw them all," said the Flamingo,—"Cortez and Balboa and Pizarro. We saw Panfilo Narvaez put in at Tampa Bay, full of zeal and gold hunger, and a year later we saw him at Appalache, beating his stirrup irons into nails to make boats to carry him back to Havana. We alone know why he never reached there."

The Pelican by this time had got rid of her load of fish and settled herself for conversation. "Whatever happened to them," she said, "they came back,—Spanish, Portuguese, and English,— back they came. I remember how Lucas de Ayllon came to look for the pearls of Cofachique—"

"Pearls!" said the children both at once.

"Very good ones," said the Pelican, nodding her pouched beak; "as large as hazel nuts and with a luster like a wet beach at evening. The best were along the Savannah River where some of my people had had a rookery since any of them could remember. Ayllon discovered the pearls when he came up from Hispaniola looking for slaves, but it was an evil day for him when he came again to fill his pockets with them, for by that time the lady of Cofachique was looking for Ayllon."

"For Soto, you mean," said the Snowy Egret,—"Hernando de Soto, the Adelantado of Florida, and that is *my* story."

"It is all one story," insisted the Pelican. "Ayllon began it. His ship put in at the Savannah at the time of the pearling, when the best of our young men were there, and among them Young Pine, son of Far-Looking, the Chief Woman.

"The Indians had heard of ships by this time, but they still believed the Spaniards were Children of the Sun, and trusted them. They had not yet learned what a Spaniard will do for gold. They did not even know what gold was, for there was none of it at Cofachique. The Cacique came down to the sea to greet the ships, with fifty of his best fighting men behind him, and when the Spaniard invited them aboard for a feast, he let Young Pine go with them. He was as straight as a pine, the young Cacique, keen and strong-breasted, and about his neck he wore a twist of pearls of three strands, white as sea foam. Ayllon's eyes glistened as he looked at them, and he gave word that the boy was not to be mishandled. For as soon as he had made the visiting Indians drunk with wine, which they had never tasted before and drank only for politeness, the Spaniard hoisted sail for Hispaniola.

"Young Pine stood on the deck and heard his father calling to him from the shore, and saw his friends shot as they jumped overboard, or were dragged below in chains, and did not know what to do at such treachery. The wine foamed in his head and he hung sick against the rail until Ayllon came sidling and fidgeting to find out where the pearls came from. He fingered the strand on Young Pine's neck, making signs of friendship.

"The ship was making way fast, and the shore of Cofachique was dark against the sun. Ayllon had sent his men to the other side of the ship while he talked with Young Pine, for he did not care to have them learn about the pearls.

"Young Pine lifted the strand from his neck, for by Ayllon's orders he was not yet in chains. While the Spaniard looked it over greedily, the boy saw his opportunity. He gave a shout to the sea-birds that wheeled and darted about the galleon, the shout the fishers give when they throw offal to the gulls, and as the wings gathered and thickened to hide him from the guns, he dived straight away over the ship's side into the darkling water.

"All night he swam, steering by the death-fires which the pearlers had built along the beaches, and just as the dawn came up behind him to turn the white-topped breakers into green fire, the land swell caught him. Four days later a search party looking for those who had jumped overboard, found his body tumbled among the weeds along the outer shoals and carried it to his mother, the Cacica, at Talimeco.

"She was a wonderful woman, the Chief Woman of Cofachique, and terrible," said the Pelican. "It was not for nothing she was called Far-Looking. She could see the thoughts of a man while they were still in his heart, and the doings of men who were far distant. When she wished to know what nobody could tell her, she would go into the Silence; she would sit as still as a brooding pelican; her limbs would stiffen and her eyes would stare—

"That is what she did the moment she saw that the twist of

"She could see the thoughts of a man while they were still in his heart."

pearls was gone from her son's neck. She went silent with her hand on his dead breast and looked across the seas into the cruel heart of the Spaniard and saw what would happen. 'He will come back,' she said; 'he will come back to get what I shall give him for *this.*'

"She meant the body of Young Pine, who was her only son," said the Pelican, tucking her own gawky young under her breast, "and that is something a mother never forgets. She spent the rest of her time planning what she would do to Lucas de Ayllon when he came back.

"There was a lookout built in the palmetto scrub below the pearling place, and every day canoes scouted far to seaward, with runners ready in case ships were sighted. Talimeco was inland about a hundred miles up the river and the Cacica herself seldom left it.

"And after four or five years Ayllon, with the three-plied rope of pearls under his doublet, came back.

"The Cacica was ready for him. She was really the Chief Woman of Cofachique,—the Cacique was only her husband,—and she was obeyed as no ordinary woman," said the Brown Pelican.

"She was not an ordinary woman," said the Snowy Egret, fluffing her white spray of plumes. "If she so much as looked at you and her glance caught your eye, then you had to do what she said, whether you liked it or not. But most of her people liked obeying her, for she was as wise as she was terrible. That was why she did not kill Lucas de Ayllon at the pearling place as the Cacique wished her to do. 'If we kill him,' said the Chief Woman, 'others will come to avenge him. We must send him home with such a report that no others of his kind will visit this coast again.' She had everything arranged for that."

The Egret settled to her nest again and the Pelican went on with the story.

"In the spring of the year Ayllon came loafing up the Florida coast with two brigantines and a crew of rascally adventurers, looking for slaves and gold. At least Ayllon said he was looking for slaves, though most of those he had carried away the first time had either jumped overboard or refused their food and died. But he had not been willing to tell anybody about the pearls, and he had to have some sort of excuse for returning to a place where he could n't be expected to be welcomed.

"And that was the first surprise he had when he put to shore on the bluff where the city of Savannah now stands, with four small boats, every man armed with a gun or a crossbow.

"The Indians, who were fishing between the shoals, received the Spaniards kindly; sold them fish and fresh fruit for glass beads, and showed themselves quite willing to guide them in their search for slaves and gold. Only there was no gold: nothing but a little copper and stinging swarms of flies, gray clouds of midges and black ooze that sucked the Spaniards to their thighs, and the clatter of scrub palmetto leaves on their iron shirts like the sound of wooden swords, as the Indians wound them in and out of trails that began in swamps and arrived nowhere. Never once did they come any nearer to the towns than a few poor fisher huts, and never a pearl showed in any Indian's necklace or earring. The Chief Woman had arranged for that!

"All this time she sat at Talimeco, in her house on the temple mound—"

"Mounds!" interrupted the children both at once. "Were they Mound-Builders?"

"They built mounds," said the Pelican, "for the Cacique's house and the God-House, and for burial, with graded ways and embankments. The one at Talimeco was as tall as three men on horseback, as the Spaniards discovered later—Soto's men, not Ayllon's. *They* never came within sound of the towns nor in sight of the league-long fields of corn nor the groves of mulberry trees. They lay with their goods spread out along the beach without any particular order and without any fear of the few poor Indians they saw.

"That was the way the Chief Woman had arranged it. All the men who came down to the ships were poorly dressed and the women wrinkled, though she was the richest Cacica in the country, and had four bearers with feather fans to accompany her. All

this time she sat in the Silences and sent her thoughts among the
Spaniards so that they bickered among themselves, for they were
so greedy for gold that no half-dozen of them would trust another
half-dozen out of their sight. They would lie loafing about the
beaches and all of a sudden anger would run among them like thin
fire in the savannahs, which runs up the sap wood of the pines,
winding, and taking flight from the top like a bird. Then they
would stab one another in their rages, or roast an Indian because
he would not tell them where gold was. For they could not get it
out of their heads that there was gold. They were looking for
another Peru.

"Toward the last, Ayllon had to sleep in his ship at night so
jealous his captains were of him. He had a touch of the swamp
fever which takes the heart out of a man, and finally he was obliged
to show them the three-plied rope of pearls to hold them. To just a
few of his captains he showed it, but the Indian boy he had taken
to be his servant saw them fingering it in the ship's cabin and sent
word to the Chief Woman."

The sun rose high on the lagoon as the Pelican paused in her
story, and beyond the rookery the children could see blue water
and a line of surf, with the high-pooped Spanish ships rising and
falling. Beyond that were the low shore and the dark wood of
pines and the shining leaves of the palmettoes like a lake spattered
with the light—split by their needle points. They could see the
dark bodies of the Indian runners working their way through it to
Talimeco. The Pelican went on with the story.

" 'Now it is time,' said the Cacica, and the Cacique's Own—that
was a band of picked fighting men—took down their great shields
of woven cane from the god-house and left Talimeco by night.
And from every seacoast town of Cofachique went bowmen and
spearsmen. They would be sitting by their hearth-fires at evening,
and in the morning they would be gone. At the same time there
went a delegation from Talimeco to Lucas de Ayllon to say that the
time of one of the Indian feasts was near, and to invite him and his
men to take part in it. The Spaniards were delighted, for now they

thought they should see some women, and maybe learn about gold. But though scores of Indians went down, with venison and maize cakes in baskets, no women went at all, and if the Spaniards had not been three fourths drunk, that would have warned them.

"When Indians mean fighting they leave the women behind," explained the Pelican, and the children nodded.

"The Spaniards sat about the fires where the venison was roasting, and talked openly of pearls. They had a cask of wine out from the ship, and some of their men made great laughter trying to dance with the young men of Cofachique. But one of the tame Indians that Ayllon had brought from Hispaniola with him, went privately to his master. 'I know this dance,' he said; 'it is a dance of death.' But Ayllon dared do nothing except have a small cannon on the ship shot off, as he said, for the celebration, but really to scare the Indians."

"And they were scared?"

"When they have danced the dance of death and vengeance there is nothing can scare Indians," said the Brown Pelican, and the whole rookery agreed with her.

"At a signal," she went on, "when the Spaniards were lolling after dinner with their iron shirts half off, and the guns stacked on the sand, the Indians fell upon them with terrible slaughter. Ayllon got away to his ships with a few of his men, but there were not boats enough for all of them, and they could not swim in their armor. Some of them tried it, but the Indians swam after them, stabbing and pulling them under. That night Ayllon saw from his ships the great fires the Indians made to celebrate their victory, and the moment the day popped suddenly out of the sea, as it does at that latitude, he set sail and put the ships about for Hispaniola, without stopping to look for survivors.

"But even there, I think, the Cacica's thought followed him. A storm came up out of the Gulf, black with thunder and flashing green fire. The ships were undermanned, for the sailors, too, had been ashore feasting. One of the brigantines—but not the one which carried Ayllon—staggered awhile in the huge seas and went under."

"And the pearls, the young chief's necklace, what became of that?" asked Dorcas.

"It went back to Talimeco with the old chief's body and was buried with him. You see, that had been the signal. Ayllon had the necklace with him in the slack of his doublet. He thought it would be a good time after the feast to show it to the Cacique and inquire where pearls could be found. He had no idea that it had belonged to the Cacique's son; all Indians looked very much alike to him. But when the Cacique saw Young Pine's necklace in the Spaniard's hand, he raised the enemy shout that was the signal for his men, who lay in the scrub, to begin the battle. Ayllon struck down the Cacique with his own sword as the nearest at hand. But the Cacique had the pearls, and after the fighting began there was no time for the Spaniard to think of getting them back again. So the pearls went back to Talimeco, with axes and Spanish arms, to be laid up in the god-house for a trophy. It was there, ten years later, that Hernando de Soto found them. As for Ayllon, his pride and his heart were broken. He died of that and the fever he had brought back from Cofachique, but you may be sure he never told exactly what happened to him on that unlucky voyage. Nobody had any ear in those days for voyages that failed; they were all for gold and the high adventure."

"What I want to know," said Dorcas, "is what became of the Cacica, and whether she saw Mr. de Soto coming and why, if she could look people in the eye and make them do what she wanted, she did n't just see Mr. de Ayllon herself and tell him to go home again."

"It was only to her own people she could do that," said the Pelican. "She could send her dream to them too, if it pleased her, but she never dared to put her powers to the test with the strangers. If she had tried and failed, then the Indians would have been certain of the one thing they were never quite sure of, that the Spaniards were the Children of the Sun. As for the horses, they never did get it out of their minds that they might be eaten by them. I think the Cacica felt in her heart that the strangers were only men, but it was too important to her to be feared by her own people to take any chances of showing herself afraid of the Spaniards. That was why she never saw Ayllon, and when it was at last necessary that Soto should be met, she left that part of the business to the young Princess."

"That," said the Snowy Egret, "should be my story! The egrets were sacred at Cofachique," she explained to the children; "only the chief family wore our plumes. Our rookery was in the middle swamp a day inland from Talimeco, safe and secret. But we used to go past the town every day fishing in the river. That is how we knew the whole story of what happened there and at Tuscaloosa."

Dorcas remembered her geography. "Tuscaloosa is in Alabama," she said; "that's a long way from Savannah."

"Not too long for the Far-Looking. She and the Black Warrior—that's what Tuscaloosa means—were of one spirit. In the ten or twelve years after the Cacique, her husband, was killed, she put the fear of Cofachique on all the surrounding tribes, as far as Tuscaloosa River.

"There was an open trail between the two chief cities of Cofachique and Mobila, which was called the Tribute Road because of the tribes that traveled it, bringing tribute to one or another of the two Great Ones. But not any more after the Princess who was called the Pearl of Cofachique walked in it."

"Oh, Princesses!" sighed Dorcas Jane, "if we could just see one!"

The Snowy Egret considered. "If the Pelicans would dance for you—"

"Have the Pelicans a *dance*?"

"Of all the dances that the Indians have," said the Egret, "the first and the best they learned from the Wing People. Some they learned from the Cranes by the water-courses, and some from the bucks prancing before the does on the high ridges; old, old dances of the great elk and the wapiti. In the new of the year everything dances in some fashion, and by dancing everything is made one, sky and sea, and bird and dancing leaf. Old time is present, and all old feelings are as the times and feelings that will be. These are the things men learned in the days of the Unforgotten, dancing to make the world work well together by times and seasons. But the Pelicans can always dance a little; anywhere in their rookeries you might see them bowing and balancing. Watch, now, in the clear foreshore."

True enough, on the bare, ripple-packed sand that glimmered like the inside of a shell, several of the great birds were making absurd dips and courtesies toward one another; they spread their wings like flowing draperies and began to sway with movements of strange dignity. The high sun filmed with silver fog, and along the heated air there crept an eerie feel of noon.

"When half a dozen of them begin to circle together," said the Snowy Egret, "turn round and look toward the wood."

At the right moment the children turned, and between the gray and somber shadows of the cypress they saw her come. All in white she was—white cloth of the middle bark of mulberries, soft as linen, with a cloak of oriole feathers black and yellow, edged with sables. On her head was the royal circlet of egret plumes nodding above the yellow circlet of the Sun. When she walked, it made them think of the young wind stirring in the corn. Around her neck she wore, in the fashion of Cofachique, three strands of pearls reaching to the waist, in which she rested her left arm.

"That was how the Spaniards saw her for the first time, and found her so lovely that they forgot to ask her name; they called her 'The Lady of Cofachique,' and swore there was not a lovelier lady in Europe nor one more a princess.

"Which might easily be true," said the Egret, "for she was brought up to be Cacica in Far-Looking's place, after the death of her son Young Pine."

The Princess smiled on the children as she came down the cypress trail. One of her women, who moved unobtrusively beside her, arranged cushions of woven cane, and another held a fan of

painted skin and feather work between her and the sun. A tame
egret ruffled her white plumes at the Princess's shoulder.

"I was telling them about the pearls of Cofachique," said the
Egret who had first spoken to the children, "and of how Hernando
de Soto came to look for them."

"Came and looked," said the Princess. One of her women
brought a casket carved from a solid lump of cypress, on her knee.
Around the sides of the casket and on the two ends ran a decora-
tion of woodpeckers' heads and the mingled sign of the sun and
the four quarters which the Corn Woman had drawn for Dorcas
on the dust of the dancing-floor.

The Princess lifted the lid and ran her fine dark fingers through
a heap of gleaming pearls. "There were many mule loads such as
these in the god-house at Talimeco," she said; "we filled the caskets
of our dead Caciques with them. What is gold that he should have
left all these for the mere rumor of it?"

She was sad for a moment and then stern. "Nevertheless, I think
my aunt, the Cacica, should have met him. She would have seen
that he was a man and would have used men's reasons with him.
She made Medicine against him as though he were a god, and in
the end his medicine was stronger than ours."

"If you could tell us about it—" invited Dorcas Jane.

XII
HOW THE IRON SHIRTS CAME TO
TUSCALOOSA: A TELLING OF THE TRIBUTE
ROAD BY THE LADY OF COFACHIQUE

"There was a bloom on the sea like the bloom on a wild grape when the Adelantado left his winter quarters at Anaica Apalache," said the Princess. "He sent Maldonado, his captain, to cruise along the Gulf coast with the ships, and struck north toward Cofachique. That was in March, 1540, and already his men and horses were fewer because of sickness and skirmishes with the Indians. They had for guide Juan Ortiz, one of Narvaez's men who had been held captive by the Indians these eight years, and a lad Perico who remembered a trading trip to Cofachique. And what he could not remember he invented. He made Soto believe there was gold there. Perhaps he was thinking of copper, and perhaps, since the Spaniards had made him their servant, he found it pleasanter to be in an important position.

"They set out by the old sea trail toward Altapaha, when the buds at the ends of the magnolia boughs were turning creamy, and the sandhill crane could be heard whooping from the lagoons miles inland. First went the captains with the Indian guides in chains, for they had a way of disappearing in the scrub if not watched carefully, and then the foot soldiers, each with his sixty days' ration on his back. Last of all came a great drove of pigs and dogs of Spain, fierce mastiffs who made nothing of tearing an Indian in pieces, and had to be kept in leash by Pedro Moron, who was as keen as a dog himself. He could smell Indians in hiding and wood smoke three leagues away. Many a time when the expedition was all but lost, he would smell his way to a village.

"They went north by east looking for gold, and equal to any adventure. At Achese the Indians, who had never heard of white men, were so frightened that they ran away into the woods and would not come out again. Think what it meant to them to see strange bearded men, clad in iron shirts, astride of fierce, unknown animals,—for the Indians could not help but think that the horses would eat them. They had never heard of iron either. Nevertheless, the Spaniards got some corn there, from the high cribs of cane set up on platforms beside the huts.

"Everywhere Soto told the Caciques that he and his men were the Children of the Sun, seeking the highest chief and the richest province, and asked for guides and carriers, which usually he got. You may be sure the Indians were glad to be rid of them so cheaply.

"The expedition moved toward Ocute, with the bloom of the wild vines perfuming all the air, and clouds of white butterflies beginning to twinkle in the savannahs."

"But," said Dorcas, who had listened very attentively, "I thought Savannah was a place."

"Ever so many places," said the Princess; "flat miles on miles of slim pines melting into grayness, sunlight sifting through their plumy tops, with gray birds wheeling in flocks, or troops of red-headed woodpeckers, and underfoot nothing but needles and gray sand. Far ahead on every side the pines draw together, but where one walks they are wide apart, so that one seems always about to approach a forest and never finds it. These are the savannahs.

"Between them along the water-courses are swamps; slow, black water and wide-rooted, gull-gray cypress, flat-topped and all adrip with moss. And everywhere a feeling of snakes—wicked water-snakes with yellow rims around their eyes.

"They crossed great rivers, Ockmulgee, Oconee, Ogechee, making a bridge of men and paddling their way across with the help of saddle cruppers and horses' tails. If the waters were too deep for that, they made piraguas—dug-out canoes, you know—and rafts of cane. By the time they had reached Ocute the Span-iards were so hungry they were glad to eat dogs which the Indians gave them, for there was such a scarcity of meat on all that journey that the sick men would sometimes say, 'If only I had a piece of meat I think I would not die!'"

"But where was all the game?" Oliver insisted on knowing.

"Six hundred men with three hundred horses and a lot of Indian carriers, coming through the woods, make a great deal of noise," said the Princess. "The Spaniards never dared to hunt far from the trail for fear of getting lost. There were always lurking Indians ready to drive an arrow through a piece of Milan armor as if it were pasteboard, and into the body of a horse over the feather of the shaft, so that the Spaniards wondered, seeing the little hole it made, how the horse had died.

"Day after day the expedition would wind in and out of the trail, bunching up like quail in the open places, and dropping back in single file in the canebrake, with the tail of the company so far from the head that when there was a skirmish with the Indians at either end, it would often be over before the other end could catch up. In this fashion they came to Cofaque, which is the last prov-ince before Cofachique."

"Oh," said Dorcas, "and did the Chief Woman see them com-ing? The one who was Far-Looking!"

"She saw too much," said the Egret, tucking her eggs more warmly under her breast. "She saw other comings and all the evil that the White Men would bring and do."

"Whatever she saw she did her best to prevent," said the Prin-cess. "Three things she tried. Two of them failed. There are two trails into the heart of Cofachique, one from the west from Tuscaloosa, and the other from Cofaque, a very secret trail through swamp and palmetto scrub, full of false clues and blind leads.

"Far-Looking sat in the god-house at Talimeco, and sent her thought along the trail to turn the strangers back; but what is the thought of one woman against six hundred men! It reached nobody but the lad Perico, and shook him with a midnight terror, so that he screamed and threw himself about. The Spaniards came running with book and bell, for the priest thought the boy was plagued by a devil. But the soldiers thought it was all a pretense to save himself from being punished for not knowing the trail to Cofachique.

"Nobody really knew it, because the Cofachiquans, who were at war with Cofaque, had hidden it as a fox covers the trail to her lair. But after beating about among the sloughs and swamps like a rabbit in a net, and being reduced to a ration of eighteen grains of corn, the Spaniards came to the river about a day's journey above the place where Lucas de Ayllon's men had died. They caught a few stray Indians, who allowed themselves to be burnt rather than show the way to their towns,—for so the Cacica had ordered them,—and at last the expedition came to a village where there was corn.

"But I should n't think the Indians would give it to them," said Dorcas.

"Indians never refuse food, if they have it, even to their enemies," said the Princess.

The children could see that this part of the story was not pleasant remembering for the Lady of Cofachique. She pushed the pearls away as though they wearied her, and her women came crowding at her shoulder with soft, commiserating noises like doves. They were beautiful and young like her, and wore the white dress of Cofachique, a skirt of mulberry fiber and an upper garment that went over the left shoulder and left the right arm bare except for the looped bracelets of shell and pearl. Their long hair lay sleek across their bosoms and, to show that they were privileged to wait upon the Chief Woman, they had each a single egret's plume in the painted bandeau about her forehead.

"Far-Looking was both aunt and chief to me," said the Princess; "it was not for me to question what she did. Our country had been long at war with Cofaque, at cost of men and corn. And Soto, as he came through that country, picked up their War Leader Patofa, and the best of their fighting men, for they had persuaded him that only by force would he get anything from the Cacica of Cofachique. The truth was that it was only by trusting to the magic of the white men that Patofa could get to us. The Adelantado allowed him to pillage such towns as they found before he thought better of it and sent Patofa and his men back to Cofaque, but by that time the thing had happened which made the Cacica's second plan impossible. Our fighting men had seen what the Spaniards could do, and I had seen what they could be."

Proudly as she said it, the children could see, by the way the Princess frowned to herself and drummed with her fingers on the cypress wood, that the old puzzle of the strangers who were neither gods nor men worked still in her mind.

"The Cacica's first plan," she went on, "which had been to lose them in the swamps and savannahs, had failed. Her second was to receive them kindly and then serve them as she had served Ayllon.

"They made their camp at last across the river from Talimeco, and I with my women went out to meet them as a great Cacique should be met, in a canoe with an awning, with fan-bearers and flutes and drums. I saw that I pleased him," said the Princess. "I gave him the pearls from my neck, and had from him a ring from his finger set with a red stone. He was a handsome and a gallant gentleman, knowing what was proper toward Princesses."

"And all this time you were planning to kill him?" said Dorcas, shocked.

The Princess shook her head.

"Not I, but the Cacica. She told me nothing. Talimeco was a White Town; how should I know that she planned killing in it. She sat in the Place of the Silences working her mischief and trusted me to keep the Spaniards charmed and unsuspicious. How should I know what she meant? I am chief woman of Cofachique, but I am not far-looking.

"I showed the Adelantado the god-house with its dead Caciques all stuffed with pearls, and the warrior-house where the arms of Ayllon were laid up for a trophy. It would have been well for him to be contented with these things. I have heard him say they would have been a fortune in his own country, but he was bitten with the love of gold and mad with it as if a water moccasin had set its fangs in him. I had no gold, and I could not help him to get Far-Looking into his power.

"That was his plan always, to make the chief person of every city his hostage for the safety of his men. I would have helped him if I could," the Princess admitted, "for I thought him glorious, but the truth was, I did not know.

"There was a lad, Islay, brought up with me in the house of my aunt, the Cacica, who went back and forth to her with messages to the Place of the Silences, and him I drove by my anger to lead the Spaniards that way. But as he went he feared her anger coming to meet him more than he feared mine that waited him at home. One day while the Spanish soldiers who were with him admired the arrows which he showed them in his quiver, so beautifully made, he plunged the sharpest of them into his throat. He was a poor thing," said the Princess proudly, "since he loved neither me nor my aunt enough to serve one of us against the other. We succeeded only in serving Soto, for now there was no one to carry word for the Cacica to the men who were to fall upon the Spaniards and destroy them as they had destroyed Ayllon.

"Perhaps," said the Princess, "if she had told me her plan and her reason for it, things would have turned out differently. At any rate, she need not have become, as she did finally, my worst enemy, and died fighting me. At that time she was as mother and chief to me, and I could never have wished her so much bitterness as she must have felt sitting unvisited in the Place of the Silences, while I took

the Adelantado pearling, and the fighting men, who should have
fallen upon him at her word, danced for his entertainment.

"She had to come out at last to find what had happened to Islay,
for whose death she blamed me, and back she went without a word
to me, like a hot spider to spin a stronger web. This time she
appealed to Tuscaloosa. They were of one mind in many things,
and between them they kept all the small tribes in tribute.

"It was about the time of the year when they should be coming
with it along the Tribute Road, and the Cacica sent them word
that if they could make the Spaniards believe that there was gold
in their hills, she would remit the tribute for one year. There was
not much for them to do, for there were hatchets and knives in the
tribute, made of copper, in which Soto thought he discovered
gold. It may be so: once he had suspected it, I could not keep him
any longer at Talimeco. The day that he set out there went another
expedition secretly from the Cacica to Tuscaloosa. 'These men,'
said the message, 'must be fought by men.' And Tuscaloosa smiled
as he heard it, for it was the first time that the Cacica had admitted there was anything that could not be done by a woman. But
at that she had done her cleverest thing, because, though they
were friends, the Black Warrior wanted nothing so much as an
opportunity to prove that he was the better warrior.

"It was lovely summer weather," said the Princess, "as the Spaniards passed through the length of Cofachique; the mulberry trees
were dripping with ripe fruit, the young corn was growing tall, and
the Indians were friendly. They passed over the Blue Ridge where
it breaks south into woody hills. Glossy leaves of the live-oak
made the forest spaces vague with shadows; bright birds like flame
hopped in and out and hid in the hanging moss, whistling clearly;
groves of pecans and walnuts along the river hung ropy with long
streamers of the purple muscadines.

"You have heard," said the Lady of Cofachique, hesitating for
the first time in her story, and yet looking so much the Princess
that the children would never have dared think anything displeasing to her, "that I went a part of the way with the Adelantado on

the Tribute Road?" Her lovely face cleared a little as they shook their heads.

"It is not true," she said, "that I went for any reason but my own wish to learn as much as possible of the wisdom of the white men and to keep my own people safe in the towns they passed through. I had my own women about me, and my own warriors ran in the woods on either side, and showed themselves to me in the places where the expedition halted, unsuspected by Soto. It was as much as any Spaniard could do to tell one half-naked Indian from another.

"The pearls, too,"—she touched the casket with her foot,—"the finest that Soto had selected from the god-house, I kept by me. I never meant to let them go, though there were some of them I gave to a soldier . . . there were slaves, too, of Soto's who found the free life of Cofachique more to their liking than the fruitless search for gold. . . ."

"She means," said the Snowy Egret, seeing that the Princess did not intend to say any more on that point, "that she gave them for bribes to one of Soto's men, a great bag full, though there came a day when he needed the bag more than the pearls and he left them scattered on the floor of the forest. It was about the slaves who went with her when she gave Soto the slip in the deep woods, that she quarreled afterward with the old Cacica."

"At the western border of Cofachique, which is the beginning of Tuscaloosa's land," went on the Princess, "I came away with my women and my pearls; we walked in the thick woods and we were gone. Where can a white man look that an Indian cannot hide from him? It is true that I knew by this time that the Cacica had sent to Tuscaloosa, but what was that to me? The Adelantado had left of his own free will, and I was not then Chief Woman of Cofachique. At the first of the Tuscaloosa towns the Black Warrior awaited them. He sat on the piazza of his house on the principal mound. He sat as still as the Cacica in the Place of Silences, a great turban stiff with pearls upon his head, and over him the standard of Tuscaloosa like a great round fan on a slender stem, of fine featherwork laid on deerskin. While the Spaniards wheeled and raced their horses in front of him, trying to make an impression, Soto could not get so much as the flick of an eyelash out of the Black Warrior. Gentleman of Spain as he was and the King's own representative, he had to dismount at last and conduct himself humbly.

"The Adelantado asked for obedience to his King, which Tuscaloosa said he was more used to getting than giving. When Soto wished for food and carriers, Tuscaloosa gave him part, and, dissembling, said the rest were at his capital of Mobila. Against the advice of his men Soto consented to go there with him.

"It was a strong city set with a stockade of tree-trunks driven into the ground, where they rooted and sent up great trees in which wild pigeons roosted. It was they that had seen the runners of Cofachique come in with the message from Far-Looking. All the wood knew, and the Indians knew, but not the Spaniards. Some of them suspected. They saw that the brush had been cut from the ground outside the stockade, as if for battle.

"One of them took a turn through the town and met not an old man nor any children. There were dancing women, but no others. This is the custom of the Indians when they are about to fight,— they hide their families.

"Soto was weary of the ground," said the Princess. "This we were told by the carriers who escaped and came back to Cofachique. He wished to sit on a cushion and sleep in a bed again. He came riding into the town with the Cacique on a horse as a token of honor, though Tuscaloosa was so tall that they had trouble finding a horse that could keep his feet from the ground, and it must have been as pleasant for him as riding a lion or a tiger. But he was a great chief, and if the Spaniards were not afraid to ride neither would he seem to be. So they came to the principal house, which was on a mound. All the houses were of two stories, of which the upper was open on the sides, and used for sleeping. Soto sat with Tuscaloosa in the piazza and feasted; dancing girls came out in the town square with flute-players, and danced for the guard.

"But one of Soto's men, more wary than the rest, walked about, and saw that the towers of the wall were full of fighting men. He saw Indians hiding arrows behind palm branches.

"Back he went to the house where Soto was, to warn him, but already the trouble had begun. Tuscaloosa, making an excuse, had withdrawn into the house, and when Soto wished to speak to him sent back a haughty answer. Soto would have soothed him, but one of Soto's men, made angry with the insolence of the Indian who had brought the Cacique's answer, seized the man by his cloak, and when the Indian stepped quickly out of it, answered as quickly with his sword. Suddenly, out of the dark houses, came a shower of arrows."

"It was the plan of the Cacica of Cofachique," explained the Egret. "The men of Mobila had meant to fall on the Spaniards while they were eating, but because of the Spanish gentleman's bad temper, the battle began too soon."

"It was the only plan of hers that did not utterly fail," said the Princess, "for with all her far-looking she could not see into the Adelantado's heart. Soto and his guard ran out of the town, every one with an arrow sticking in him, to join themselves to the rest of the expedition which had just come up. Like wasps out of a nest the Indians poured after them. They caught the Indian carriers, who were just easing their loads under the walls. With every pack and basket that the Spaniards had, they carried them back into the town, and the gates of the stockade were swung to after them."

"All night," said the Egret, "the birds were scared from their roost by the noise of the battle. Several of the horses were caught inside the stockade; these the Indians killed quickly. The sound of their dying neighs was heard at all the rookeries along the river."

"The wild tribes heard of it, and brought us word," said the Princess. "Soto attacked and pretended to withdraw. Out came the Indians after him. The Spaniards wheeled again and did terrible slaughter. They came at the stockade with axes; they fired the towers. The houses were all of dry cane and fine mats of cane for walls; they flashed up in smoke and flame. Many of the Indians threw themselves into the flames rather than be taken. At the last there were left three men and the dancing women. The women came into the open by the light of the burning town, with their hands crossed before them. They stood close and hid the men with their skirts, until the Spaniards came up, and then parted. So the last men of Mobila took their last shots and died fighting."

"Is that the end?" said Oliver, seeing the Princess gather up her pearls and the Egret preparing to tuck her bill under her wing. He did not feel very cheerful over it.

"It was the end of Mobila and the true end of the expedition," said the Princess. Rising she beckoned to her women. She had lost all interest in a story which had no more to do with Cofachique.

"Both sides lost," said the Egret, "and that was the sad part of it. All the Indians were killed; even the young son of Tuscaloosa was found with a spear sticking in him. Of the Spaniards but eighteen died, though few escaped unwounded. But they lost everything they had, food, medicines, tools, everything but the sword in hand and the clothes they stood in. And while they lay on the bare ground recovering from their wounds came Juan Ortiz, who had been sent seaward for that purpose, with word that Maldonado lay with the ships off the bay of Mobila,—that's Mobile, you know,—not six days distant, to carry them back to Havana.

"And how could Soto go back defeated? No gold, no pearls, no conquests, not so much as a map, even,—only rags and wounds and a sore heart. In spite of everything he was both brave and gallant, and he knew his duty to the King of Spain. He could not go back with so poor a report of the country to which he had been sent to establish the fame and might of His Majesty. Forbidding Juan Ortiz to tell the men about the ships, with only two days' food and no baggage, he turned away from the coast, from his home and his wife and safe living, toward the Mississippi. He had no hope in his heart, I think, but plenty of courage. And if you like," said the Egret, "another day we will tell you how he died there."

"Oh, no, please," said Dorcas, "it is so very sad; and, besides," she added, remembering the picture of Soto's body being lowered at night into the dark water, "it is in the School History."

"In any case," said the Egret, "he was a brave and gallant gentleman, kind to his men and no more cruel to the Indians than they were to one another. There was only one of the gentlemen of Spain who never had *any* unkindness to his discredit. That was Cabeza de Vaca; he was one of Narvaez's men, and the one from whom Soto first heard of Florida,—but that is also a sad story."

Neither of the children said anything. The Princess and her women lost themselves in the shadowy wood. The gleam here and there of their white dresses was like the wing of tall white birds. The sun sailing toward noon had burnt the color out of the sky into the deep water which could be seen cradling fresh and blue beyond the islets. One by one the pelicans swung seaward, beating their broad wings all in time like the stroke of rowers, going to fish in the clean tides outside of the lagoons.

The nests of the flamingoes lay open to the sun except where here and there dozed a brooding mother.

"Don't you know any not-sad stories?" asked Dorcas, as the Egret showed signs again of tucking her head under her wing.

"Not about the Iron Shirts," said the Egret. "Spanish or Portuguese or English; it was always an unhappy ending for the Indians."

"Oh," said Dorcas, disappointed; and then she reflected, "If they had n't come, though, I don't suppose we would be here either."

"I'll tell you," said the Man-of-War Bird, who was a great traveler, "they did n't all land on this coast. Some of them landed in Mexico and marched north into your country. I've heard things from gulls at Panuco. You don't know what the land birds might be able to tell you."

XIII
HOW THE IRON SHIRTS CAME LOOKING FOR THE SEVEN CITIES OF CIBOLA; TOLD BY THE ROAD-RUNNER

From Cay Verde in the Bahamas to the desert of New Mexico, by the Museum trail, is around a corner and past two windows that look out upon the west. As the children stood waiting for the Road-Runner to notice them, they found the view not very different from the one they had just left. Unending, level sands ran into waves, and strange shapes of rocks loomed through the desert blueness like steep-shored islands. It was vast and terrifying like the sea, and yet a very pleasant furred and feathered life appeared to be going on there between the round-headed cactus, with its cruel fishhook thorns, and the warning, blood-red blossoms that dripped from the ocatilla. Little frisk-tailed things ran up and down the spiney shrubs, and a woodpecker, who had made his nest in its pithy stalk, peered at them from a tall *sahuaro*.

The Road-Runner tilted his long rudder-like tail, flattened his crested head until it reminded them of a wicked snake, and suddenly made up his mind to be friendly.

"Come inside and get your head in the shade," he invited. "There's no harm in the desert sun so long as you keep something between it and your head. I've known Indians to get along for days with only the shade of their arrows."

The children snuggled under the feathery shadow of the mesquite beside him.

"We're looking for the trail of the Iron Shirts," said Oliver. "Alvar Nuñez Cabeza de Vaca," added Dorcas Jane, who always remembered names. The Road-Runner ducked once or twice by way of refreshing his memory.

"There was a black man with him, and they went about as Medicine Men to the Indians who believed in them, and at the same time treated them very badly. But that was nearly four hundred years ago, and they never came into this part of the country, only into Texas. And they had n't any iron shirts either, scarcely anything to put either on their backs or into their stomachs."

"Nevertheless," quavered a voice almost under Oliver's elbow, "they brought the iron shirts, and the long-tailed elk whose hooves are always stumbling among our burrows."

The children had to look close to make out the speckled fluff of feathers hunched at the door of its *hogan*.

"Meet my friend Thla-po-po-ke-a," said the Road-Runner, who had picked up his manners from miners and cowboys as well as from Spanish explorers.

The Burrowing Owl bobbed in her own hurried fashion. "Often and often," she insisted with a whispering *whoo-oo* running through all the sentences, "I've heard the soldiers say that it was Cabeza de Vaca put it into the head of the King of Spain to send Francisco Coronado to look for the Seven Cities. In my position one hears the best of everything," went on Po-po-ke-a. "That is because all the important things happen next to the ground. Men are born and die on the ground, they spread their maps, they dream dreams."

The children could see how this would be in a country where there was never a house or a tree and scarcely anything that grew more than knee-high to a man. The long sand-swells, and the shimmer of heat-waves in the air looked even more like the sea now that they were level with it. Off to the right what seemed a vast sheet of water spread out like quicksilver on the plain; it moved with a crawling motion, and a coyote that trotted across their line of vision seemed to swim in it, his head just showing above the slight billows.

"It's only mirage," said the Road-Runner; "even Indians are fooled by it if they are strange to the country. But it is quite true about the ground being the place to hear things. All day the Iron Shirts would ride in a kind of doze of sun and weariness. But when they sat at meals, loosening their armor buckles, then there would be news. We used to run with it from one camp to another—I can run faster than a horse can walk—until the whole mesa would hear of it."

"But the night is the time for true talking," insisted Po-po-ke-a. "It was then we heard that when Cabeza de Vaca returned to Spain he made one report of his wanderings to the public, and a secret report to the King. Also that the Captain-General asked to be sent on that expedition because he had married a young wife who needed much gold."

"At that time we had not heard of gold," said the Road-Runner; "the Spaniards talked so much of it we thought it must be something good to eat, but it turned out to be only yellow stones. But it was not all Cabeza de Vaca's doing. There was another story by an Indian, Tejo, who told the Governor of Mexico that he remembered going with his father to trade in the Seven Cities, which were as large as the City of Mexico, with whole streets of silver workers, and blue turquoises over the doors."

"If there is a story about it—" began Oliver, looking from one to the other invitingly, and catching them looking at each other in the same fashion.

"Brother, there is a tail to you," said the Burrowing Owl quickly, which seemed to the children an unnecessary remark, since the Road-Runner's long, trim tail was the most conspicuous thing about him. It tipped and tilted and waggled almost like a dog's, and answered every purpose of conversation.

Now he ducked forward on both legs in an absurd way he had. "To you, my sister—" which is the polite method of story asking in that part of the country.

"My word bag is as empty as my stomach," said Po-po-ke-a, who had eaten nothing since the night before and would not eat until night again. "*Sons eso*—to your story."

"*Sons eso, tse-n?,*" said the Road-Runner, and began.

"First," he said, "to Hawikuh, a city of the Zuñis, came Estevan, the black man who had been with Cabeza de Vaca, with a rattle in his hand and very black behavior. Him the Indians killed, and the priest who was with him they frightened away. Then came Coronado, with an army from Mexico, riding up the west coast and turning east from the River of the Brand, the one that is now called Colorado, which is no name at all, for all the rivers hereabout run red after rain. They were a good company of men and captains, and many of those long-tailed elk,—which are called horses, sister," said the Road-Runner aside to Po-po-ke-a,—"and the Indians were not pleased to see them."

"That was because there had been a long-tailed star seen over To-ya-lanne, the sacred mountain, some years before, one of the kind that is called Trouble-Bringer. They thought of it when they looked at the long tails of the new-fashioned elk," said Po-po-ke-a, who had not liked being set right about the horses.

"In any case," went on the Road-Runner, "there was trouble. Hawikuh was one of these little crowded pueblos, looking as if it had been crumpled together and thrown away, and though there were turquoises over the doors, they were poor ones, and there was no gold. And as Hawikuh, so they found all the cities of Cibola, and the cities of the Queres, east to the River of White Rocks."

Dorcas Jane nudged Oliver to remind him of the Corn Woman and Tse-tse-yote. All the stories of that country, like the trails, seemed to run into one another.

"Terrible things happened around Tiguex and at Cicuye, which is now Pecos," said the Road-Runner, "for the Spaniards were furious at finding no gold, and the poor Indians could never make up their minds whether these were gods to be worshiped, or a strange people coming to conquer them, who must be fought. They were not sure whether the iron shirts were to be dreaded as magic, or coveted as something they could use themselves. As for the horses, they both feared and hated them. But there was one man who made up his mind very quickly.

"He was neither Queres nor Zuñi, but a plainsman, a captive of their wars. He was taller than our men, leaner and sharp-looking. His god was the Morning Star. He made sacrifices to it. The Spaniards called him the Turk, saying he looked like one. We did not know what that meant, for we had only heard of turkeys which the Queres raised for their feathers, and he was not in the least like one of these. But he knew that the Spaniards were men, and was almost a match for them. He had the Inknowing Thought."

The Road-Runner cocked his head on one side and observed the children, to see if they knew what this meant.

"Is it anything like far-looking?" asked Dorcas.

"It is something none of my people ever had," said the Road-Runner. "The Indian who was called the Turk could look in a bowl of water in the sun, or in the water of the Stone Pond, and he could see things that happened at a distance, or in times past. He proved to the Spaniards that he could do this, but their priests said it was the Devil and would have nothing to do with it, which was a great pity. He could have saved them a great deal."

"Hoo, hoo!" said the Burrowing Owl; "he could not even save himself; and none of the things he told to the Spaniards were true."

"He was not thinking for himself," said the Road-Runner, "but for his people. The longer he was away from them the more he thought, and his thoughts were good, even though he did not tell the truth to the Iron Shirts. They, at least, did not deserve it. For when the people of Zuñi and Cicuye and Tiguex would not tell them where the sacred gold was hid, there were terrible things done. That winter when the days were cold, the food was low and the soldiers fretful. Many an Indian kept the secret with his life."

"Did the Indians really know where the gold was?" The children knew that, according to the geographies, there are both gold and silver in New Mexico.

"Some of them did, but gold was sacred to them. They called it the stone of the Sun, which they worshiped, and the places where it was found were holy and secret. They let themselves be burned rather than tell. Besides, they thought that if the Spaniards were convinced there was no gold, they would go away the sooner. One thing they were sure of: gods or men, it would be better for the people of the pueblos if they went away. Day and night the *tombes* would be sounding in the kivas, and prayer plumes planted in all the sacred places. Then it was that the Turk went to the Caciques sitting in council.

" 'If the strangers should hear that there is gold in my country, there is nothing would keep them from going there.'

" 'That is so,' said the Caciques.

" 'And if they went to my country,' said the Turk, 'who but I could guide them?'

" 'And how long,' said the Caciques, 'do you think a guide would live after they discovered that he had lied?' For they knew very well there was no gold in the Turk's country.

" 'I should at least have seen my own land,' said the Turk, 'and here I am a slave to you.'

"The Caciques considered. Said they, 'It is nothing to us where and how you die.'

"So the Turk caused himself to be taken prisoner by the Spaniards, and talked among them, until it was finally brought to the Captain-General's ears that in the Turk's country of Quivira, the people ate off plates of gold, and the Chief of that country took his afternoon nap under a tree hung with golden bells that rung him to sleep. Also that there was a river there, two leagues wide, and that the boats carried twenty rowers to a side with the Chief under the awning."

"That at least was true," said the Burrowing Owl; "there were towns on the Missi-sippu where the Chiefs sat in balconies on high mounds and the women fanned them with great fans."

"Not in Quivira, which the Turk claimed for his own country. But it all worked together, for when the Spaniards learned that the one thing was true, they were the more ready to believe the other. It was always easy to get them to believe any tale which had gold in it. They were so eager to set out for Quivira that they could scarcely be persuaded to take food enough, saying they would have all the more room on their horses for the gold.

"They forded the Rio Grande near Tiguex, traveled east to Cicuye on the Pecos River, and turned south looking for the Turk's country, which is not in that direction."

"But why—" began Oliver.

"Look!" said the Road-Runner.

The children saw the plains of Texas stretching under the heat haze, stark sand in wind-blown dunes, tall stakes of *sahuaro* marching wide apart, hot, trackless sand in which a horse's foot sinks to the fetlock, and here and there raw gashes in the earth for rivers that did not run, except now and then in fierce and ungovernable floods. Northward the plains passed out of sight in trackless, grass-covered prairies, day's journey upon day's journey.

"It was the Caciques' idea that the Turk was to lose the strangers there, or to weaken them beyond resistance by thirst and hunger and hostile tribes. But the buffalo had come south that winter for the early grass. They were so thick they looked like trees walking, to the Spaniards as they lay on the ground and saw the sky between their huge bodies and the flat plain. And the wandering bands of Querechos that the Expedition met proved friendly. They were the same who had known Cabeza de Vaca, and they had a high opinion of white men. They gave the Spaniards food and proved to them that it was much farther to the cities of the Missi-sippu than the Turk had said.

"By that time Coronado had himself begun to suspect that he should never find the golden bells of Quivira, but with the King and Doña Beatris behind him, there was nothing for him to do but go forward. He sent the army back to Tiguex, and, with thirty men and all the best horses, turned north in as straight a track as the land permitted, to the Turk's country. And all that journey he kept the Turk in chains.

"Even though he had not succeeded in getting rid of the Iron Shirts, the Turk was not so disappointed as he might have been. The Caciques did not know it, but killing the strangers or losing them had been only a part of his plan.

"All that winter at Tiguex the Turk had seen the horses die, or grow sick and well again; some of them had had colts, and he had come to the conclusion that they were simply animals like elk or deer, only more useful.

"The Turk was a Pawnee, one of those roving bands that build grass houses and follow the buffalo for food. They ran the herds into a *piskune* below a bluff, over which they rushed and were killed. Sometimes the hunters themselves were caught in the rush and trampled. It came into the Turk's mind, as he watched the Spaniards going to hunt on horseback, that the Morning Star, to whom he made sacrifices for his return from captivity, had sent him into Zuñi to learn about horses, and take them back to his people. Whatever happened to the Iron Shirts on that journey, he had not meant to lose the horses. Even though suspected and in chains he might still do a great service to his people.

"When the Querechos were driving buffalo, some of the horses were caught up in the 'surround,' carried away with the rush of the stampeding herd, and never recovered. Others that broke away in a terrible hailstorm succeeded in getting out of the ravine where the army had taken shelter, and no one noticed that it was always at the point where the Turk was helping to herd them, that the horses escaped. Even after he was put in chains and kept under the General's eye on the way to Quivira, now and then there would be a horse, usually a mare with a colt, who slipped her stake-rope. Little gray coyotes came in the night and gnawed them. But coyotes will not gnaw a rope unless it has been well rubbed with buffalo fat," said the Road-Runner.

"I should have thought the Spaniards would have caught him at it," said Oliver.

"White men, when they are thinking of gold," said the Road-Runner, "are particularly stupid about other things. There was a man of the Wichitas, a painted Indian called Ysopete, who told them from the beginning that the Turk lied about the gold. But the Spaniards preferred to believe that the Indians were trying to keep the gold for themselves. They did not see that the Turk was losing their horses one by one; no more did they see, as they neared Quivira, that every day he called his people.

"There are many things an Indian can do and a white man not catch him at it. The Turk would sit and feed the fire at evening, now a bundle of dry brush and then a handful of wet grass, smoke and smudge, such as hunters use to signal the movements of the quarry. He would stand listening to the captains scold him, and push small stones together with his foot for a sign. He could slip in the trail and break twigs so that Pawnees could read. When strange Indians were brought into camp, though he could only speak to them in the language of signs, he asked for a Pawnee called Running Elk, who had been his friend before he was carried captive into Zuñi Land. They had mingled their blood after the custom of friendship and were more than brothers to one another. And though the Iron Shirts looked at him with more suspicion every day, he was almost happy. He smelled sweet-grass and the dust of his own country, and spoke face to face with the Morning Star.

"I do not understand about stars," said the Road-Runner. "It seems that some of them travel about and do not look the same from different places. In Zuñi Land where there are mountains, the Turk was not always sure of his god, but in the Pawnee country it is easily seen that he is the Captain of the Sky. You can lie on the ground there and lose sight of the earth altogether. Mornings the

Turk would look up from his chains to see his Star, white against the rosy stain, and was comforted. It was the Star, I suppose, that brought him his friend.

"For four or five days after Running Elk discovered that the Turk was captive to the Iron Shirts, he would lurk in the tall grass and the river growth, making smoke signals. Like a coyote he would call at night, and though the Turk heard him, he dared not answer. Finally he hit upon the idea of making songs. He would sing and nobody could understand him but Running Elk, who lay in the grass, and finally had courage to come into the camp in broad day, selling buffalo meat and wild plums.

"There was a bay mare with twin colts that the Turk wished him to loose from her rope and drive away, but Running Elk was afraid. Cold mornings the Indian could see the smoke of the horses' nostrils and thought that they breathed fire. But the Turk made his friend believe at last that the horse is a great gift to man, by the same means that he had made the Spaniards think him evil, by the Inknowing Thought.

"'It is as true,' said the Turk, 'that the horse is only another sort of elk, as that my wife is married again and my son died fighting the Ho-he.' All of which was exactly as it had happened, for his wife had never expected that he would come back from captivity. 'It is also true,' the Turk told him, 'that very soon I shall join my son.'

"For he was sure by this time that when the Spaniards had to give up the hope of gold, they would kill him. He told Running Elk all the care of horses as he had learned it, and where he thought those that had been lost from Coronado's band might be found. Of the Iron Shirts, he said that they were great Medicine, and the Pawnees were by all means to get one or two of them.

"By this time the Expedition had reached the country of the Wichitas, which is Quivira, and there was no gold, no metal of any sort but a copper gorget around the Chief's neck, and a few armbands. The night that Coronado bought the Chief's gorget to send to his king, as proof that he had found no gold, Running Elk heard the Turk singing. It was no song of secret meaning; it was his own song, such as a man makes to sing when he sees his death facing him.

"All that night the Turk waited in his chains for the rising of his Star. There was something about which he must talk to it. He had made a gift of the horse to his people, but there was no sacrifice to wash away all that was evil in the giving and make it wholly blessed. All night the creatures of the earth heard the Turk whisper at his praying, asking for a sacrifice.

"And when the Star flared white before the morning, a voice was in the air saying that he himself was to be the sacrifice. It was the voice of the Morning Star walking between the hills, and the Turk was happy. The doves by the water-courses heard him with the first flush of the dawn waking the Expedition with his death song. Loudly the Spaniards swore at him, but he sang on steadily till they came to take him before the General, whose custom it was to settle all complaints the first thing in the morning. The soldiers thought that since it was evident the Turk had purposely misled them about the gold and other things, he ought to die for it. The General was in a bad humor. One of his best mares with her colts had frayed her stake-rope on a stone that night and escaped. Nevertheless, being a just man, he asked the Turk if he had anything to say. Upon which the Turk told them all that the Caciques had said, and what he himself had done, all except about the horses, and especially about the bay mare and Running Elk. About that he was silent. He kept his eyes upon the Star, where it burned white on the horizon. It was at its last wink, paling before the sun, when they killed him."

The children drew a long breath that could hardly be distinguished from the soft whispering *whoo-hoo* of the Burrowing Owl.

"So in spite of his in-knowing he could not save himself," Dorcas Jane insisted, "and his Star could not save him. If he had looked in the earth instead of the heavens he would have found gold and the Spaniards would have given him all the horses he wanted."

"You forget," said the Road-Runner, "that he knew no more than the Iron-Shirts did, where the gold was to be found. There were not more than two or three in any one of the Seven Cities that ever knew. Ho-tai of Matsaki was the last of those, and his own wife let him be killed rather than betray the secret of the Holy Places."

"Oh, if you please—" began the children.

"It is a town story," said the Road-Runner, "but the Condor that has his nest on El Morro, he might tell you. He was captive once in a cage at Zuñi." The Road-Runner balanced on his slender legs and cocked his head trailwise. Any kind of inactivity bored him dreadfully. The burrowing owls were all out at the doors of their *hogans*, their heads turning with lightning swiftness from side to side; the shadows were long in the low sun. "It is directly in the trail from the Rio Grande to Acoma, the old trail to Zuñi," said the Road-Runner, and without waiting to see whether or not the children followed him, he set off.

XIV
HOW THE MAN OF TWO HEARTS KEPT
THE SECRET OF THE HOLY PLACES;
TOLD BY THE CONDOR

"In the days of our Ancients," said the Road-Runner between short
skimming runs, "this was the only trail from the river to the Middle
Ant Hill of the World. The eastern end of it changed like the tip of
a wild gourd vine as the towns moved up and down the river or the
Queres crossed from Katzimo to the rock of Acoma; but always
Zuñi was the root, and the end of the first day's journey was the
Rock."

Each time he took his runs afresh, like a kicking stick in a race,
and waited for the children to catch up. The sands as they went
changed from gray to gleaming pearl; on either side great islands
of stone thinned and swelled like sails and took on rosy lights and
lilac shadows.

They crossed a high plateau with somber cones of extinct vol-
canoes, crowding between rivers of block rock along its rim.
Northward a wilderness of pines guarded the mesa; dark junipers,
each one with a secret look, browsed wide apart. They thickened
in the cañons from which arose the white bastions of the Rock.

Closer up, El Morro showed as the wedge-shaped end of a high mesa, soaring into cliffs and pinnacles, on the very tip of which they could just make out the hunched figure of the great Condor.

"El Morro, 'the Castle,' the Spaniards called it," said the Road-Runner, casting himself along the laps of the trail like a feathered dart. "But to our Ancients it was always 'The Rock.' On winter journeys they camped on the south side to get the sun, and in summers they took the shade on the north. They carved names and messages for those that were to come after, with flint knives, with swords and Spanish daggers. Men are all very much alike," said the Road-Runner.

On the smooth sandstone cliffs the children could make out strange, weathered picture-writings, and twisty inscriptions in much abbreviated Spanish which they could not read.

The white sand at the foot of the Rock was strewn with flakes of charcoal from the fires of ancient camps. A little to the south of the cliff, that towered two hundred feet and more above them, shallow footholds were cut into the sandstone.

"There were pueblos at the top in the old days," said the Road-Runner, "facing across a deep divide, but nobody goes there now except owls that have their nests in the ruins, and the last of the Condors, who since old time have made their home in the pinnacles of the Rock. He'll have seen us coming." The children looked up as a sailing shadow began to circle about them on the evening-colored sands. "You can see by the frayed edges of his wing feathers that he has a long time for remembering," said the Road-Runner.

The great bird came slowly to earth, close by the lone pine that tasseled out against the south side of El Morro and the Road-Runner ducked several times politely.

"My children, how is it with you these days?" asked the Condor with great dignity.

"Happy, happy, Grandfather. And you?"

The Condor assured them that he was very happy, and seeing that no one made any other remark, he added, after an interval, looking pointedly at the children, "It is not thinking of nothing that strangers come to the house of a stranger."

"True, Grandfather," said the Road-Runner; "we are thinking of the gold, the seed of the Sun, that the Spaniards did not find. Is there left to you any of the remembrance of these things?"

"*Hai, hai!*" The Condor stretched his broad wings and settled himself comfortably on a nubbin of sandstone. "Of which of these who passed will you hear?" He indicated the inscriptions on the rock, and then by way of explanation he said to the children, "I am town-hatched myself. Lads of Zuñi took my egg and hatched it under a turkey hen, at the Ant Hill. They kept my wings clipped, but once they forgot, so I came away to the ancient home of my people. But in the days of my captivity I learned many tales and the best manner of telling them. Also the Tellings of my own people who kept the Rock. They fit into one another like the arrow point to the shaft. Look!"—he pointed to an inscription protected by a little brow of sandstone, near the lone pine. "Juan de Oñate did that when he passed to the discovery of the Sea of the South. He it was who built the towns, even the chief town of Santa Fé.

"There signed with his sword, Vargas, who reconquered the pueblos after the rebellion—yes, they rebelled again and again. On the other side of the Rock you can read how Governor Nieto carried the faith to them. They came and went, the Iron Shirts, through two hundred years. You can see the marks of their iron hats on some of the rafters of Zuñi town to this day, but small was the mark they left on the hearts of the Zuñi."

"Is that so!" said the Road-Runner, which is a polite way of saying that you think the story worth going on with; and then cocking his eye at the inscription, he hinted, "I have heard that the Long Gowns, the Padres who came with them, were master-workers in hearts."

"It is so," said the Condor. "I remember the first of them who managed to build a church here, Padre Francisco Letrado. Here!"

He drew their attention to an inscription almost weathered away, and looking more like the native picture-writings than the signature of a Spanish gentleman. He read:—

"They passed on the 23d of March of 1832 years to the avenging of the death of Father Letrado." It was signed simply "Lujan."

"There is a Telling of that passing and of that soldier which has to do with the gold that was never found."

"*Sons eso*," said the Road-Runner, and they settled themselves to listen.

"About the third of a man's life would have passed between the time when Oñate came to the founding of Santa Fé, and the building of the first church by Father Letrado. There were Padres before that, and many baptizings. The Zuñis were always glad to learn new ways of persuading the gods to be on their side, and they thought the prayers and ceremonies of the Padres very good Medicine indeed. They thought the Iron Shirts were gods themselves, and when they came received them with sprinklings of sacred meal. But it was not until Father Letrado's time that it began to be understood that the new religion was to take the place of their own, for to the Indians there is but one spirit in things, as there is one life in man. They thought their own prayers as good as any that were taught them.

"But Father Letrado was zealous and he was old. He made a rule that all should come to the service of his church and that they should obey him and reverence him when they met, with bowings and kissings of his robe. It is not easy to teach reverence to a free people, and the men of the Ant Hill had been always free. But the worst of Father Letrado's rulings was that there were to be no more prayers in the kivas, no dancings to the gods nor scatterings of sacred pollen and planting of plumes. Also—this is not known, I think—that the sacred places where the Sun had planted the seed of itself should be told to the Padres."

"He means the places where the gold is found mixed with the earth and the sand," explained the Road-Runner to Dorcas Jane and Oliver.

"In the days of the Ancients," said the Condor, "when such a place was found, it was told to the Priests of the Bow, and kept in reverence by the whole people. But since the Zuñis had discovered what things white men will do for gold, there had been fewer and fewer who held the secret. The Spaniards had burnt too many of those who were suspected of knowing, for one thing, and they had a drink which, when they gave to the Indians, let the truth out of their mouths as it would not have gone when they were sober.

"At the time Father Letrado built his first chapel there was but one man in Hawikuh who knew.

"He was a man of two natures. His mother had been a woman of the Matsaki, and his father one of the Oñate's men, so that he was half of the Sun and half of the Moon, as we say,—for the Zuñis called the first half-white children, Moon-children,—and his heart was pulled two ways, as I have heard the World Encompassing Water is pulled two ways by the Sun and the Moon. Therefore, he was called Ho-tai the Two-Hearted.

"What finally pulled his heart out of his bosom was the love he had for his wife. Flower-of-the-Maguey, she was called, and she was beautiful beyond all naming. She was daughter to the Chief Priest of the Bow, and young men from all the seven towns courted her. But though she was lovely and quiet she was not as she seemed to be. She was a Passing Being." The Condor thoughtfully stretched his wings as he considered how to explain this to the children.

"Such there are," he said. "They are shaped from within outward by their own wills. They have the power to take the human form and leave it. But it was not until she had been with her mother to To-yalanne, the sacred Thunder Mountain, as is the custom when maidens reach the marriageable age, that her power came to her. She was weary with gathering the sacred flower pollen; she lay under a maguey in the warm sun and felt the light airs play over her. Her breath came evenly and the wind lifted her long hair as it lay along her sides.

"Strangely she felt the pull of the wind on her hair, all along her body. She looked and saw it turn short and tawny in the sun, and

the shape of her limbs fitted to the sandy hollows. Thus she understood that she was become another being, Moke-iche, the puma.
She bounded about in the sun and chased the blue and yellow
butterflies. After a time she heard the voice of her mother calling,
and it pulled at her heart. She let her heart have way and became a
maid again. But often she would steal out after that, when the wind
brought her the smell of the maguey, or at night when the moon
walked low over To-yalanne, and play as puma. Her parents saw
that she had power more than is common to maidens, but she was
wise and modest, and they loved her and said nothing.

"'Let her have a husband and children,' they said, 'and her
strangeness will pass.' But they were very much disappointed at
what happened to all the young men who came a-courting.

"This is the fashion of a Zuñi courting: The young man says to
his Old Ones, 'I have seen the daughter of the Priest of the Bow at
the Middle Ant Hill, what think ye?' And if they said, 'Be it well!'
he gathered his presents into a bundle and went to knock at the
sky-hole of her father's house.

"'She!' he said, and 'Hai!' they answered from within. 'Help me
down,' he would say, which was to tell them that he had a bundle
with him and it was a large one. Then the mother of the girl would
know what was afoot. She would rise and pull the bundle down
through the sky-hole—all pueblo houses are entered from the top,
did you not know?" asked the Condor.

The children nodded, not to interrupt; they had seen as they
came along the trail the high terraced houses with the ladders
sticking out of the door-holes.

"Then there was much politeness on both sides, politeness of
food offered and eaten and questions asked, until the girl's parents
were satisfied that the match would be a good one. Finally, the Old
Ones would stretch themselves out in their corners and begin to
scrape their nostrils with their breath—thus," said the Condor,
making a gentle sound of snoring; "for it was thought proper for
the young people to have a word or two together. The girl would

set the young man a task, so as not to seem too easily won, and to prove if he were the sort of man she wished for a husband.

" 'Only possibly you love me,' said the daughter of the Chief Priest of the Bow. 'Go out with the light to-morrow to hunt and return with it, bringing your kill, that I may see how much you can do for my sake.'

"But long before light the girl would go out herself as a puma and scare the game away. Thus it happened every time that the young man would return at evening empty-handed, or he would be so mortified that he did not return at all, and the girl's parents would send the bundle back to him. The Chief Priest and his wife began to be uneasy lest their daughter should never marry at all.

"Finally Ho-tai of the pueblo of Matsaki heard of her, and said to his mother, 'That is the wife for me.'

" '*Shoom!*' said his mother; 'what have you to offer her?' for they were very poor.

" '*Shoom* yourself!' said Ho-tai. 'He that is poor in spirit as well as in appearance, is poor indeed. It is plain she is not looking for a bundle, but for a man.' So he took what presents he had to the house of the Chief Priest of the Bow, and everything went as usual; except that when Ho-tai asked them to help him in, the Chief Priest said, 'Be yourself within,' for he was growing tired of court- ings that came to nothing. But when Ho-tai came cheerfully down the ladder with his gift, the girl's heart was touched, for he was a fine gold color like a full moon, and his high heart gave him a proud way of walking. So when she had said, 'Only possibly you love me, but that I may know what manner of husband I am getting, I pray you hunt for me one day,' and when they had bidden each other 'wait happily until the morning,' she went out as a puma and searched the hills for game that she might drive to- ward the young man, instead of away from him. But because she could not take her eyes off of him, she was not so careful as she should be not to let him see her. Then she went home and put on all her best clothes, the white buckskins, the turquoises and silver bracelets, and waited. At evening, Ho-tai, the Two-Hearted, came with a fine buck on his shoulders, and a stiff face. Without a word he gave the buck to the Priest's wife and turned away. 'Hai,' said the mother, 'when a young man wins a girl he is permitted to say a few words to her!'—for she was pleased to think that her daughter had got a husband at last.

"'I did not kill the buck by myself,' said Ho-tai; and he went off to find the Chief Priest and tell him that he could not marry his daughter. Flower-of-the-Maguey, who was in her room all this time peeking through the curtain, took a water jar and went down to the spring where Ho-tai could not help but pass her on his way back to his own village.

"'I did not bring back your bundle,' she said when she saw him; 'what is a bundle to a woman when she has found a man?'

"Then his two hearts were sore in him, for she was lovely past all naming. 'I do not take what I cannot win by my own labor,' said he; 'there was a puma drove up the game for me.'

"'Who knows,' said she, 'but Those Above sent it to try if you were honest or a braggart?' After which he began to feel differently. And in due course they were married, and Ho-tai came to live in the house of the Chief Priest at Hawikuh, for her parents could not think of parting with her.

"They were very happy," said the Condor, "for she was wisely slow as well as beautiful, and she eased him of the struggle of his two hearts, one against the other, and rested in her life as a woman."

"Does that mean she was n't a puma any more?" asked Dorcas Jane.

The Condor nodded, turning over the Zuñi words in his mind for just the right phrase. "Understanding of all her former states came to her with the years. There was nothing she dreaded so much as being forced out of this life into the dust and whirl of Becoming. That is one reason why she feared and distrusted the Spanish missionaries when they came, as they did about that time.

"One of her husband's two hearts pulled very strongly toward the religion of the Spanish Padres. He was of the first that were baptized by Father Letrado, and served the altar. He was also the first of those upon whose mind the Padre began to work to persuade him that in taking the new religion he must wholly give up the old.

"At the end of that trail, a day's journey," said the Condor, indicating the narrow foot-tread in the sand, which showed from tree to tree of the dark junipers, and seemed to turn and disappear at every one, "lies the valley of Shiwina, which is Zuñi.

"It is a narrow valley, watered by a muddy river. Red walls of mesas shut it in above the dark wood. To the north lies Thunder Mountain, wall-sided and menacing. Dust devils rise up from the plains and veil the crags. In the winter there are snows. In the summer great clouds gather over Shiwina and grow dark with rain. White corn tassels are waving, blue butterfly maidens flit among the blossoming beans.

"Day and night at midsummer, hardly the priests have their rattles out of their hands. You hear them calling from the house-tops, and the beat of bare feet on the dancing places. But the summer after Father Letrado built his chapel of the Immaculate Virgin at Halona and the chapel and parish house of the Immaculate Conception at Hawikuh, he set his face against the Rain Dance, and especially against the Priests of the Rain. Witchcraft and sorcery he called it, and in Zuñi to be accused of witchcraft is death.

"The people did not know what to do. They prayed secretly where they could. The Priests of the Rain went on with their preparations, and the soldiers of Father Letrado—for he had a small detachment with him—broke up the dance and profaned the sacred places. Those were hard days for Ho-tai the Two-Hearted. The gods of the strangers were strong gods, he said, let the people wait and see what they could do. The white men had strong Medicine in their guns and their iron shirts and their long-tailed, smoke-breathing beasts. They did not work as other gods. Even if there was no rain, the white gods might have another way to save the people.

"These were the things Father Letrado taught him to say, and the daughter of the Chief Priest of the Bow feared that his heart would be quite pulled away from the people of Zuñi. Then she went to her father the Chief Priest, who was also the keeper of the secret of the Holy Places of the Sun, and neared the dividing of the ways of life.

"'Let Ho-tai be chosen Keeper in your place,' she said, 'so all shall be bound together, the Medicine of the white man and the brown.'

"'Be it well,' said the Priest of the Bow, for he was old, and had respect for his daughter's wisdom. Feeling his feet go from him toward the Spirit Road, he called together the Priests of the Bow, and announced to them that Ho-tai would be Keeper in his stead.

"Though Two-Hearted was young for the honor, they did not question it, for, like his wife, they were jealous of the part of him that was white—which, for her, there was no becoming—and they thought of this as a binding together. They were not altogether sure yet that the Spaniards were not gods, or at the least Surpassing Beings.

"But as the rain did not come and the winter set in cold with a shortage of corn, more and more they neglected the bowings and the reverences and the service of the mass. Nights Father Letrado would hear the muffled beat of the drums in the kivas where the old religion was being observed, and because it was the only heart open to him, he twisted the heart of Ho-tai to see if there was not some secret evil, some seed of witchcraft at the bottom of it which he could pluck out."

"That was great foolishness," said the Road-Runner; "no white man yet ever got to the bottom of the heart of an Indian."

"True," said the Condor, "but Ho-tai was half white, and the white part of him answered to the Padre's hand. He was very miserable, and in fact, nobody was very happy in those days in

Hawikuh. Father Martin who passed there in the moon of the Sun Returning, on his way to establish a mission among the People of the Coarse Hanging Hair, reported to his superior that Father Letrado was ripe for martyrdom.

"It came the following Sunday, when only Ho-tai and a few old women came to mass. Sick at the sound of his own voice echoing in the empty chapel, the Padre went out to the plaza of the town to scold the people into services. He was met by the Priests of the Rain with their bows. Being neither a coward nor a fool, he saw what was before him. Kneeling, he clasped his arms, still holding the crucifix across his bosom, and they transfixed him with their arrows.

"They went into the church after that and broke up the altar, and burned the chapel. A party of bowmen followed the trail of Father Martin, coming up with him after five days. That night with the help of some of his own converts, they fell upon and killed him. There was a half-breed among them, both whose hearts were black. He cut off the good Padre's hand and scalped him."

"Oh," said Oliver, "I think he ought not to have done that!"

The Condor was thoughtful.

"The hand, no. It had been stretched forth only in kindness. But I think white men do not understand about scalping. I have heard them talk sometimes, and I know they do not understand. The scalp was taken in order that they might have the scalp dance. The dance is to pacify the spirit of the slain. It adopts and initiates him into the tribe of the dead, and makes him one with them, so that he will not return as a spirit and work harm on his slayers. Also it is a notice to the gods of the enemy that theirs is the stronger god, and to beware. The scalp dance is a protection to the tribe of the slayer; to omit one of its observances is to put the tribe in peril of the dead. Thus I have heard; thus the Old Ones have said. Even Two-Hearted, though he was sad for the killing, danced for the scalp of Father Martin.

"Immediately it was all over, the Hawikuhkwe began to be afraid. They gathered up their goods and fled to K'iakime, the

Place of the Eagles, on Thunder Mountain, where they had a stronghold. There were Iron Shirts at Santa Fé and whole cities of them in the direction of the Salt Containing Waters. Who knew what vengeance they might take for the killing of the Padres? The Hawikuhkwe intrenched themselves, and for nearly two years they waited and practiced their own religion in their own way.

"Only two of them were unhappy. These were Ho-tai of the two hearts, and his wife, who had been called Flower-of-the-Maguey. But her unhappiness was not because the Padres had been killed. She had had her hand in that business, though only among the women, dropping a word here and there quietly, as one drops a stone into a deep well. She was unhappy because she saw that the dead hand of Father Letrado was still heavy on her husband's heart.

"Not that Ho-tai feared what the soldiers from Santa Fé might do to the slayer, but what the god of the Padre might do to the whole people. For Padre Letrado had taught him to read in the Sacred Books, and he knew that whole cities were burned with fire for their sins. He saw doom hanging over K'iakime, and his wife could not comfort him. After awhile it came into his mind that it was his own sin for which the people would be punished, for the one thing he had kept from the Padre was the secret of the gold.

"It is true," said the Condor, "that after the Indians had forgotten them, white men rediscovered many of their sacred places, and many others that were not known even to the Zuñis. But there is one place on Thunder Mountain still where gold lies in the ground in lumps like pine nuts. If Father Letrado could have found it, he would have hammered it into cups for his altar, and immediately the land would have been overrun with the Spaniards. And the more Ho-tai thought of it, the more convinced he was that he should have told him.

"Toward the end of two years when it began to be rumored that soldiers and new Padres were coming to K'iakime to deal with the killing of Father Letrado, Ho-tai began to sleep more quietly at night. Then his wife knew that he had made up his mind to tell, if it seemed necessary to reconcile the Spaniards to his people, and it was a knife in her heart.

"It was her husband's honor, and the honor of her father, Chief Priest of the Bow; and besides, she knew very well that if Ho-tai told, the Priests of the Bow would kill him. She said to herself that her husband was sick with the enchantments of the Padres, and she must do what she could for him. She gave him seeds of forgetfulness."

"Was that a secret too?" asked Dorcas, for the Condor seemed not to remember that the children were new to that country.

"It was *peyote*. Many know of it now, but in the days of Our Ancients it was known only to a few Medicine men and women. It is a seed that when eaten wipes out the past from a man's mind and gives him visions. In time its influence will wear away, and it must be eaten anew, but if eaten too often it steals a man's courage and his strength as well as his memory.

"When she had given her husband a little in his food, Flower-of-the-Maguey found that he was like a child in her hands.

" 'Sleep,' she would say, 'and dream thus, and so,' and that is the way it would be with him. She wished him to forget both the secret of the gold in the ground and the fear of the Padres.

"From the time that she heard that the Spaniards were on their way to K'iakime, she fed him a little *peyote* every day. To the others it seemed that his mind walked with Those Above, and they were respectful of him. That is how Zuñis think of any kind of madness. They were not sure that the madness had not been sent for just this occasion when they had need of the gods, and so, as it seemed to them, it proved.

"The Spaniards asked for parley, and the Caciques permitted the Padres to come up into the council chambers, for they knew that the long gowns covered no weapons. The Spaniards had learned wisdom, perhaps, and perhaps they thought Father Letrado somewhat to blame. They asked nothing but permission to reëstablish their missions, and to have the man who had scalped Father Martin handed over to them for Spanish justice.

"They sat around the wall of the kiva, with Ho-tai in his place, hearing and seeing very little. But the parley was long, and, little by little, the vision of his own gods which the *peyote* had given him began to wear away. One of the Padres rose in his place and began a long speech about the sin of killing, and especially of killing priests. He quoted his Sacred Books and talked of the sin in their hearts, and, little by little, the talk laid hold on the wandering mind of Ho-tai. 'Thus, in this killing, has the secret evil of your hearts come forth,' said the Padre, and 'True, He speaks true,' said Ho-tai, upon which the Priests of the Hawikuhkwe were astonished. They thought their gods spoke through his madness.

"Then the Padre began to exhort them to give up this evil man in their midst and rid themselves of the consequences of sin, which he assured them were most certain and as terrible as they were sure. Then the white heart of Ho-tai remembered his own anguish, and spoke thickly, as a man drunk with *peyote* speaks.

"'He must be given up,' he said. It seemed to them that his voice came from the under world.

"But there was a great difficulty. The half-breed who had done the scalping had, at the first rumor of the soldiers coming, taken himself away. If the Hawikuhkwe said this to the Spaniards, they knew very well they would not be believed. But the mind of Ho-tai had begun to come back to him, feebly as from a far journey.

"He remembered that he had done something displeasing to the Padre, though he did not remember what, and on account of it there was doom over the valley of the Shiwina. He rose staggering in his place.

"'Evil has been done, and the evil man must be cast out,' he said, and for the first time the Padres noticed that he was half white. Not one of them had ever seen the man who scalped Father Letrado, but it was known that his father had been a soldier. This man was altogether such a one as they expected. His cheeks were drawn, his hair hung matted over his reddened eyes, as a man's might, tormented of the spirit. 'I am that man,' said Ho-tai of the Two Hearts, and the Caciques put their hands over their mouths with astonishment."

"But they never," cried Oliver,—"they never let him be taken?"

"A life for a life," said the Condor, "that is the law. It was necessary that the Spaniards be pacified, and the slayer could not be found. Besides, the people of Hawikuh thought Ho-tai's offer to go in his place was from the gods. It agrees with all religions that a man may lay down his life for his people."

"Could n't his wife do anything?"

"What could she? He went of his own will and by consent of the Caciques. But she tried what she could. She could give him *peyote* enough so that he should remember nothing and feel nothing of what the Spaniards should do to him. But to do that she had to make friends with one of the soldiers. She chose one Lujan, who had written his name on the Rock on the way to K'iakime. By him she sent a cake to Ho-tai, and promised to meet Lujan when she could slip away from the village unnoticed.

"Between here and Acoma," said the Condor, "is a short cut which may be traveled on foot, but not on horseback. Returning with Ho-tai, manacled and fast between two soldiers, the Spaniards meant to take that trail, and it was there the wife of Ho-tai promised to meet Lujan at the end of the second day's travel.

"She came in the twilight, hurrying as a puma, for her woman's heart was too sore to endure her woman's body. Lujan had walked apart from the camp to wait for her; smiling, he waited. She was still very beautiful, and he thought she was in love with him. Therefore, when he saw the long, hurrying stride of a puma in the trail, he thought it a pity so beautiful a woman should be frightened. The arrow that he sped from his cross-bow struck in the yellow flanks. 'Well shot,' said Lujan cheerfully, but his voice was drowned by a scream that was strangely like a woman's. He remembered it afterward in telling of the extraordinary thing that had happened to him, for when he went to look, where the great beast had leaped in air and fallen, there was nothing to be found there. Nothing.

"If she had been in her form as a woman when he shot her," said the Condor, "that is what he would have found. But she was a Passing Being, not taking form from without as we do, of the outward touchings of things, and her shape of a puma was as mist which vanishes in death as mist does in the sun. Thus shortens my story."

"Come," said the Road-Runner, understanding that there would be no more to the Telling. "The Seven Persons are out, and the trail is darkling."

The children looked up and saw the constellation which they knew as the Dipper, shining in a deep blue heaven. The glow was gone from the high cliffs of El Morro, and the junipers seemed to draw secretly together. Without a word they took hands and began to run along the trail after the Road-Runner.

XV
HOW THE MEDICINE OF THE ARROWS WAS BROKEN AT REPUBLICAN RIVER; TOLD BY THE CHIEF OFFICER OF THE DOG SOLDIERS

This is the story the Dog Soldier told Oliver one evening in April, just after school let out, while the sun was still warm and bright on the young grass, and yet one somehow did not care about playing. Oliver had slipped into the Indian room by the west entrance to look at the Dog Dancers, for the teacher had just told them that our country was to join the big war which had been going on so long on the other side of the Atlantic, and the boy was feeling rather excited about it, and yet solemn.

The teacher had told them about the brave Frenchmen who had stood up in the way of the enemy saying, "They shall not pass," and they had n't. It made Oliver think of what he had read on the Dog Dancer's card—how in a desperate fight the officer would stick an arrow or a lance through his long scarf, where it trailed upon the ground, pinning himself to the earth until he was dead or his side had won the victory.

Oliver thought that that was exactly the sort of thing that he would do himself if he were a soldier, and when he read the card over again, he sat on a bench with his back to the light looking at the Dog Dancers, and feeling very friendly toward them. It had just occurred to him that they, too, were Americans, and he liked to think of them as brave and first-class fighters.

From where he sat he could see quite to the end of the east corridor which was all of a quarter of a mile away. Nobody moved in it but a solitary guard, looking small and flat like a toy man at that distance, and the low sun made black and yellow bars across the floor. In a moment more, while Oliver was wondering where that woodsy, smoky smell came from, they were all around him, all the Dog Warriors, of the four degrees, with their skin-covered lances curved like the beak of the Thunder Bird, and the rattles of dew-claws that clashed pleasantly together. Some of them were painted red all over, and some wore tall headdresses of eagle feathers, and every officer had his trailing scarf of buckskin worked in patterns of the Sacred Four. Around every neck was the whistle made of the wing-bone of a turkey, and every man's forehead glistened with the sweat of his dancing. The smell that Oliver had noticed was the smoke of their fire and the spring scent of the young sage. It grew knee-high, pale green along the level tops, stretching away west to the Backbone-of-the-World, whose snowy tops seemed to float upon the evening air. Off to the right there was a river dark with cottonwoods and willows.

"But where are we?" Oliver wished to know, seeing them all pause in their dancing to notice him in a friendly fashion.

"Cheyenne Country," said one of the oldest Indians. "Over there"—he pointed to a white thread that dipped and sidled along the easy roll of the hills—"is the Taos Trail. It joins the Santa Fé at the Rio Grande and goes north to the Big Muddy. It crosses all the east-flowing rivers near their source and skirts the Pawnee Country."

"And who are you—Cheyennes or Arapahoes?" Oliver could not be sure, though their faces and their costumes were familiar.

"Cheyennes *and* Arapahoes," said the oldest Dog Dancer, easing himself down to the buffalo robe which one of the rank and file of the warriors had spread for him. "Camp-mates and allies, though we do not call ourselves Cheyennes, you know. That is a Sioux name for us,—Red Words, it means;—what you call foreign-speaking, for the Sioux cannot speak any language but their own. We call ourselves Tsis-tsis-tas, Our Folk." He reached back for his pipe which a young man brought him and loosened his tobacco pouch from his belt, smiling across at Oliver, "Have you earned your smoke, my son?"

"I'm not allowed," said Oliver, eyeing the great pipe which he was certain he had seen a few moments before in the Museum case.

"Good, good," said the old Cheyenne; "a youth should not smoke until he has gathered the bark of the oak."

Oliver looked puzzled and the Dog Warrior smiled broadly, for gathering oak bark is a poetic Indian way of speaking of a young warrior's first scalping.

"He means you must not smoke until you have done something to prove you are a man," explained one of the Arapahoes, who was painted bright red all over and wore a fringe of scalps under his ceremonial belt. Pipes came out all around the circle and some one threw a handful of sweet-grass on the fire.

"What I should like to know," said Oliver, "is why you are called Dog Dancer?"

The painted man shook his head.

"All I know is that we are picked men, ripe with battles, and the Dog is our totem. So it has been since the Fathers' Fathers." He blew two puffs from his pipe straight up, murmuring, "O God, remember us on earth," after the fashion of ceremonial smoking.

"God and us," said the Cheyenne, pointing up with his pipe-stem; and then to Oliver, "The Tsis-tsis-tas were saved by a dog once in the country of the Ho-Hé. That is Assiniboine," he explained, following it with a strong grunt of disgust which ran all around the circle as the Dog Chief struck out with his foot and started a little spurt of dust with his toe, throwing dirt on the name of his enemy. "They are called Assiniboine, stone cookers, because they cook in holes in the ground with hot stones, but to us they were the Ho-Hé. The first time we met we fought them. That was in the old time, before we had guns or bows either, but clubs and pointed sticks. That was by the Lake of the Woods where we first met them."

"Lake of the Woods," said Oliver, "that's farther north than the headwater of the Mississippi."

"We came from farther and from older time," said the Dog Soldier. "We thought the guns were magic at first and fell upon our faces. Nevertheless, we fought the Ho-Hé and took their guns away from them."

"So," said the officer of the Yellow Rope, as the long buckskin badge of rank was called. "We fought with Blackfoot and Sioux. We fought with Comanches and Crows, and expelled them from the Land. With Kiowas we fought; we crossed the Big Muddy and long and bitter wars we had with Shoshones and Pawnees. Later we fought the Utes. We are the Fighting Cheyennes.

"That is how it is when a peaceful people are turned fighters. For we are peaceful. We came from the East, for one of our wise men had foretold that one day we should meet White Men and be conquered by them. Therefore, we came away, seeking peace, and we did not know what to do when the Ho-Hé fell upon us. At last we said, 'Evidently it is the fashion of this country to fight. Now, let us fight everybody we meet, so we shall become great.' That is what has happened. Is it not so?"

"It is so!" said the Dog Dancers. "Hi-hi-yi," breaking out all at once in the long-drawn wolf howl which is the war-cry of the Cheyennes. Oliver would have been frightened by it, but quite as suddenly they returned to their pipes, and he saw the old Dog Chief looking at him with a kindly twinkle.

"You were going to tell me why you are called Dog Soldiers," Oliver reminded him.

"Dog is a good name among us," said the old Cheyenne, "but it is forbidden to speak of the Mysteries. Perhaps when you have been admitted to the Kit Foxes and have seen fighting—"

"We've got a war of our own, now," said Oliver hopefully.

The Indians were all greatly interested. The painted Arapahoe blew him a puff from his pipe. Send you good enemies," he said, trailing the smoke about in whatever direction enemies might come from. "And a good fight!" said the Yellow Rope Officer; "for men grow soft where there is no fighting."

"And in all cases," said the Dog Chief, "respect the Mysteries. Otherwise, though you come safely through yourself, you may bring evil on the Tribe. . . . I remember a Telling . . . No," he said, following the little pause that always precedes a story; "since you are truly at war I will tell a true tale. A tale of my own youth and the failure that came on Our Folks because certain of our young men forgot that they were fighting for the Tribe and thought only of themselves and their own glory."

He stuffed his pipe again with fine tobacco and bark of red willow and began.

"Of one mystery of the Cheyennes every man may speak a little—of the Mystery of the Sacred Medicine Arrows. Four arrows there are with stone heads painted in the four colors, four feathered with eagle plumes. They give power to men and victory in battle. It is a man mystery; no woman may so much as look at it. When we go out as a Tribe to war, the Arrows go with us tied to the lance of the Arrow-Keeper.

"The Medicine of the Arrows depended on the Mysteries which are made in the camp before the Arrows go out. But if any one goes out from the camp toward the enemy before the Mysteries are completed, the protection of the Arrows is destroyed. Thus it happened when the Potawatami helped the Kitkahhahki, and the Cheyennes were defeated. This was my doing, mine and Red Morning and a boy of the Suh-tai who had nobody belonging to him.

"We three were like brothers, but I was the elder and leader. I waited on War Bonnet when he went to the hunt, and learned warcraft from him. That was how it was with us as we grew up,—we

attached ourselves to some warrior we admired; we brought back
his arrows and rounded up his ponies for him, or washed off the
Medicine paint after battle, or carried his pipe.

"War Bonnet I loved for the risks he would take. Red Morning
followed Mad Wolf, who was the best of the scouts; and where we
two went the Suh-tai was not missing. This was long after we had
learned all the tricks of the Ho-Hé by fighting them, after the Iron
Shirts brought the horse to us, and we had crossed the Big Muddy
into this country.

"We were at war with the Pawnees that year. Not," said the Dog
Chief with a grin, "that we were ever at peace with them, but the
year before they had killed our man Alights-on-the-Cloud and
taken our iron shirt."

"Had the Cheyennes iron shirts?" Oliver was astonished.

"Alights-on-the-Cloud had one. When he rode up and down in
front of the enemy with it under his blanket, they thought it great
Medicine. There were others I have heard of; they came into the
country with the men who had the first horses, but this was ours. It
was all fine rings of iron that came down to the knees and covered
the arms and the head so that his long hair was inside.

"It was the summer before we broke the Medicine of the Arrows
that the Tsis-tsis-tas had gone out against the Pawnees. Arapahoes,
Sioux, Kiowas, and Apaches, they went out with us.

"Twice in the year the Pawnees hunted the buffaloes, once in
the winter when the robes were good and the buffaloes fat, and
once in the summer for food. All the day before we had seen a
great dust rising and all night the ground shook with the buffaloes
running. There was a mist on the prairie, and when it rose our
scouts found themselves almost in the midst of the Pawnees who
were riding about killing buffaloes.

"It was a running fight; from noon till level sun they fought, and
in the middle of it, Alights-on the Cloud came riding on a roan
horse along the enemy line, flashing a saber. As he rode the Pawnees gave back, for the iron shirt came up over his head and their
arrows did him no harm. So he rode down our own line, and

returning charged the Pawnees, but this time there was one man who did not give back. Carrying-the-Shield-in-Front said to those around him: 'Let him come on, and do you move away from me so he can come close. If he possesses great Medicine, I shall not be able to kill him; but if he does not possess it, perhaps I shall kill him.'

"So the others fell back, and when Alights-on-the-Cloud rode near enough so that Carrying-the-Shield-in-Front could hear the clinking of the iron rings, he loosed his arrow and struck Alights-on-the-Cloud in the eye.

"Our men charged the Pawnees, trying to get the body back, but in the end they succeeded in cutting the iron shirt into little pieces, and carrying it away. This was a shame to us, for Alights-on-the-Cloud was well liked, and for a year there was very little talked of but how he might be avenged.

"Early the next spring a pipe was carried. Little Robe carried it along the Old North Trail to Crows and the Burnt Thigh Sioux and the Northern Cheyennes. South also it went to Apaches and Arapahoes. And when the grape was in leaf we came together at Republican River and swore that we would drive out the Pawnees.

"As it turned out both Mad Wolf and War Bonnet were among the first scouts chosen to go and locate the enemy, and though we had no business there, we three, and two other young men of the Kiowas, slipped out of the camp and followed. They should have turned us back as soon as we were discovered, but Mad Wolf was good-natured, and they were pleased to see us so keen for war.

"There was a young moon, and the buffalo bulls were running and fighting in the brush. I remember one old bull with long streamers of grapevines dragging from his horns who charged and scattered us. We killed a young cow for meat, and along the next morning we saw wolves running away from a freshly killed carcass. So we knew the Pawnees were out.

"Yellow Bear, an Arapahoe Dog Soldier, who was one of the scouts, began to ride about in circles and sing his war-song, saying that we ought not to go back without taking some scalps, or counting coup, and we youngsters agreed with him. We were disappointed when the others decided to go back at once and report. I remember how Mad Wolf, who was the scout leader, sent the others all in to notify the camp, and how, as they rode, from time to time they howled like wolves, then stopped and turned their heads from side to side.

"There was a great ceremonial march when we came in, the Dog Soldiers, the Crooked Lances, the Fox Soldiers, and all the societies. First there were two men—the most brave in the society—leading, and then all the others in single file and two to close. The women, too—all the bright blankets and the tall war bonnets—the war-cries and the songs and the drums going like a man's heart in battle.

"Three days," said the Dog Chief, "the preparation lasted. Wolf Face and Tall Bull were sent off to keep in touch with the enemy, and the women and children dropped behind while the men unwrapped their Medicine bundles and began the Mysteries of the *Issiwun*, the Buffalo Hat, and *Mahuts*, the Arrows. It was a long ceremony, and we three, Red Morning, the Suh-tai boy, and I, were on fire with the love of fighting. You may believe that we made the other boys treat us handsomely because we had been with the scouts, but after a while even that grew tame and we wandered off toward the river. Who cared what three half-grown boys did, while the elders were busy with their Mysteries.

"By and by, though we knew very well that no one should move toward the enemy while the Arrows were uncovered, it came into our heads what a fine thing it would be if we could go out after Wolf Face and Tall Bull, and perhaps count coup on the Pawnees before our men came up with them. I do not think we thought of any harm, and perhaps we thought the Medicine of the Arrows was only for the members of the societies. But we saw afterward that it was for the Tribe, and for our wrong the Tribe suffered.

"For a while we followed the trail of Tall Bull, toward the camp of Pawnees. But we took to playing that the buffaloes were Pawnees and wore out our horses charging them. Then we lost the trail, and when at last we found a village the enemy had moved on following the hunt, leaving only bones and ashes. I do not know what we should have done," said the Dog Chief, "if we had come up with them: three boys armed with hunting-knives and bows, and a lance which War Bonnet had thrown away because it was too light for him. Red Morning had a club he had made, with a flint set into the side. He kept throwing it up and catching it as he rode, making a song about it.

"After leaving the deserted camp of the Pawnees, we rode about looking for a trail, thinking we might come upon some small party. We had left our own camp before finding out what Wolf Face and Tall Bull had come back to tell them, that the enemy, instead of being the whole Nation of Pawnees as we supposed, was really only the tribe of the Kitkahhahki, helped out by a band of the Potawatami. The day before our men attacked the Kitkahhahki, the Potawatami had separated from them and started up one of the creeks, while the Pawnees kept on up the river. We boys stumbled on the trail of the Potawatami and followed it.

"Now these Potawatami," said the Dog Chief, "had had guns a long time, and better guns than ours. But being boys we did not know enough to turn back. About midday we came to level country around the headwaters of the creek, and there were four Potawatami skinning buffaloes. They had bunched up their horses and tied them to a tree while they cut up the kill. Red Morning said for us to run off the horses, and that would be almost as good as a scalp-taking. We left our ponies in the ravine and wriggled through the long grass. We had cut the horses loose and were running them, before the Potawatami discovered it. One of them called his own horse and it broke out of the bunch and ran toward him. In a moment he was on his back, so we three each jumped on a horse and began to whip them to a gallop. The Potawatami made for the Suh-tai, and rode even with him. I think he saw it was only a boy, and neither of them had a gun. But suddenly as their horses came neck and neck Suh-tai gave a leap and landed on the Pota-watami's horse behind the rider. It was a trick of his with which he used to scare us. He would leap on and off before you had time to think. As he clapped his legs to the horse's back he stuck his knife into the Potawatami. The man threw up his arms and Suh-tai tumbled him off the horse in an instant.

"This I saw because Red Morning's horse had been shot under him, and I had stopped to take him up. By this time another man had caught a horse and I had got my lance again which I had left leaning against a tree. I faced him with it as he came on at a dead run, and for a moment I thought it had gone clean through him, but really it had passed between his arm and his body and he had twisted it out of my hand.

"Our horses were going too fast to stop, but Red Morning, from behind me, struck at the head of the man's horse as it passed with his knife-edged club, and we heard the man shout as he went down. I managed to get my horse about in time to see Suh-tai, who had caught up with us, trying to snatch the Potawatami's scalp, but his knife turned on one of the silver plates through which his scalp-lock was pulled, and all the Suh-tai got was a lock of the hair. In his excitement he thought it was the scalp and went shaking it and shouting like a wild man.

"The Potawatami pulled himself free of his fallen horse as I came up, and it did me good to see the blood flowing from under his arm where my lance had scraped him. I rode straight at him, meaning to ride him down, but the horse swerved a little and got a long wiping stroke from the Potawatami's knife, from which, in a minute more, he began to stagger. By this time the other men had got their guns and begun shooting. Suh-tai's bow had been shot in two, and Red Morning had a graze that laid his cheek open. So we got on our own ponies and rode away.

"We saw other men riding into the open, but they had all been chasing buffaloes, and our ponies were fresh. It was not long before we left the shooting behind. Once we thought we heard it break out again in a different direction, but we were full of our own affairs, and anxious to get back to the camp and brag about them.

As we crossed the creek Suh-tai made a line and said the words that made it Medicine. We felt perfectly safe.

"It was our first fight, and each of us had counted coup. Suh-tai was not sure but he had killed his man. Not for worlds would he have wiped the blood from his knife until he had shown it to the camp. Two of us had wounds, for my man had struck at me as he passed, though I had been too excited to notice it at the time . . . 'Eyah!' said the Dog Chief,—'a man's first scar . . . !' We were very happy, and Red Morning taught us his song as we rode home beside the Republican River.

"As we neared our own camp we were checked in our rejoicing; we heard the wails of the women, and then we saw the warriors sitting around with their heads in their blankets—as many as were left of them. My father was gone, he was one of the first who was killed by the Potawatami."

The Dog Chief was silent a long time, puffing gently on his pipe, and the Officer of the Yellow Rope began to sing to himself a strange, stirring song.

Looking at him attentively Oliver saw an old faint scar running across his face from nose to ear.

"Is your name Red Morning?" Oliver wished to know.

The man nodded, but he did not smile; they were all of them smoking silently with their eyes upon the ground. Oliver understood that there was more and turned back to the Dog Chief.

"Were n't they pleased with what you had done?" he asked.

"They were pleased when they had time to notice us," he said, "but they did n't know—they did n't know that we had broken the Medicine of the Arrows. It did n't occur to us to say anything about the time we had left the camp, and nobody asked us. A young warrior, Big Head he was called, had also gone out toward the enemy before the Mystery was over. They laid it all to him.

"And at that time we did n't know ourselves, not till long afterward. You see, we thought we had got away from the Potawatami because our ponies were fresh and theirs had been running buffaloes. But the truth was they had followed us until they heard the noise of the shooting where Our Folks attacked the Kitkahhahki. It was the first they knew of the attack and they went to the help of their friends.

"Until they came Our Folks had all the advantage. But the Potawatami shoot to kill. They carry sticks on which to rest the guns, and their horses are trained to stand still. Our men charged them as they came, but the Potawatami came forward by tens to shoot, and loaded while other tens took their places . . . and the Medicine of the Arrows had been broken. The men of the Pota-watami took the hearts of our slain to make strong Medicine for their bullets and when the Cheyennes saw what they were doing they ran away.

"But if we three had not broken the Medicine, the Potawatami would never have been in that battle.

"Thus it is," said the Dog Soldier, putting his pipe in his belt and gathering his robes about him, "that wars are lost and won, not only in battle, but in the minds and the hearts of the people, and by the keeping of those things that are sacred to the people, rather than by seeking those things that are pleasing to one's self. Do you understand this, my son?"

"I think so," said Oliver, remembering what he had heard at school. He felt the hand of the Dog Chief on his shoulder, but when he looked up it was only the Museum attendant come to tell him it was closing time.

THE END

APPENDIX

THE BEGINNING OF THE TRAIL

The appendix is that part of a book in which you find the really important things, put there to keep them from interfering with the story. Without an appendix you might not discover that all of the important things in this book really *are* true.

All the main traveled roads in the United States began as animal or Indian trails. There is no map that shows these roads as they originally were, but the changes are not so many as you might think. Railways have tunneled under passes where the buffalo went over, hills have been cut away and swamps filled in, but the general direction and in many places the actual grades covered by the great continental highways remain the same.

THE BUFFALO COUNTRY

Licks are places where deer and buffaloes went to lick the salt they needed out of the ground. They were once salt springs or lakes long dried up.

Wallows were mudholes where the buffaloes covered themselves with mud as a protection from mosquitoes and flies. They would lie down and work themselves into the muddy water up to their eyes. Crossing the Great Plains, you can still see round green places that were wallows in the days of the buffalo.

The Pawnees are a roving tribe, in the region of the Platte and Kansas Rivers. If they were just setting out on their journey when the children heard them they would sing:—

> "Dark against the sky, yonder distant line
> Runs before us.
> Trees we see, long the line of trees
> Bending, swaying in the wind.

> "Bright with flashing light, yonder distant line
> Runs before us.
> Swiftly runs, swift the river runs,
> Winding, flowing through the land."

But if they happened to be crossing the river at the time they would be singing to *Kawas*, their eagle god, to help them. They had a song for coming up on the other side, and one for the mesas, with long, flat-sounding lines, and a climbing song for the mountains.

You will find all these songs and some others in a book by Miss Fletcher in the public library.

TRAIL TALK

You will find the story of the Coyote and the Burning Mountain in my book *The Basket Woman*.

The Tenasas were the Tennessee Mountains. Little River is on the map.

Flint Ridge is a great outcrop of flint stone in Ohio, near the town of Zanesville. Sky-Blue-Water is Lake Superior.

Cahokia is the great mound near St. Louis, on the Illinois side of the river.

When the Lenni-Lenape speaks of a Telling of his Fathers about the mastodon or the mammoth, he was probably thinking of the story that is pictured on the Lenape stone, which seems to me to be the one told by Arrumpa. Several Indian tribes had stories of a large extinct animal which they called the Big Moose, or the Big Elk, because moose and elk were the largest animals they knew.

ARRUMPA'S STORY

I am not quite certain of the places mentioned in this story, because the country has so greatly changed, but it must have been in Florida or Georgia, probably about where the Savannah River is now. It is in that part of the country we have the proof that man was here in America at the same time as the mammoth.

Shell mounds occur all along the coast. No doubt the first permanent trails led to them from the hunting-grounds. Every year the tribe went down to gather sea-food, and left great piles of shells many feet deep, sometimes covering several acres. It is from these mounds that we discover the most that we know about early man in the United States.

There are three different opinions as to where the first men in America came from. First, that they came from some place in the North that is now covered with Arctic ice; second, that they came from Europe and Africa by way of some islands that are now sunk beneath the Atlantic Ocean; third, that they came from Asia across Behring Strait and the Aleutian Islands.

The third theory seems the most reasonable. But also it is very likely that some people did come from the lost islands in the Atlantic, and left traces in South America and the West Indies. It may be that Dorcas Jane and Oliver will yet meet somebody in the Museum country who can tell them about it.

The Great Cold that Arrumpa speaks about must have been the Ice Age, that geologists tell us once covered the continent of North America, almost down to the Ohio River. It came and went slowly, and probably so changed the climate that the elephants, tigers, camels, and other animals that used to be found in the United States could no longer live in it.

THE COYOTE'S STORY

Tamal-Pyweack—Wall-of-Shining-Rocks—is an Indian name for the Rocky Mountains. *Backbone-of-the-World* is another.

The Country of the Dry Washes is between the Rockies and the Sierra Nevadas, toward the south. A dry wash is the bed of a river that runs only in the rainy season. As such rivers usually run very swiftly, they make great ragged gashes across a country.

There are several places in the Rockies called *Wind Trap*. The Crooked Horn might have been Pike's Peak, as you can see by the pictures. The white men had to rediscover this trail for themselves, for the Indians seemed to have forgotten it, but the railroad that passes through the Rockies, near Pike's Peak, follows the old trail of the Bighorn.

It is very likely that the Indian in America had the dog for his friend as soon as he had fire, if not before it. Most of the Indian stories of the origin of fire make the coyote the first discoverer and bringer of fire to man. The words that Howkawanda said before he killed the Bighorn were probably the same that every Indian hunter uses when he goes hunting big game: "O brother, we are about to kill you, we hope that you will understand and forgive us." Unless they say something like that the spirit of the animal killed might do them some mischief.

THE CORN WOMAN'S STORY

Indian corn, *mabiz*, or maize, is supposed to have come originally from Central America. But the strange thing about it is that no specimen of the wild plant from which it might have developed has ever been found. This would indicate that the development must have taken place a very long time ago, and the parent corn may have belonged to the age of the mastodon and other extinct creatures.

Different tribes probably brought it into the United States at different times. Some of it came up the Atlantic Coast, across the West Indies. The fragments of legend from which I made the story of the Corn Woman were found among the Indians that were living in Virginia, Kentucky, and Tennessee at the time the white men came.

Chihuahua is a province and city in Old Mexico, the trail that leads to it one of the oldest lines of tribal migration on the continent.

To be given to the Sun meant to have your heart cut out on a sacrificial stone, usually on the top of a hill, or other high place. The Aztecs were an ancient Mexican people who practiced this kind of sacrifice as a part of their religion. If it was from them the Corn Woman obtained the seed, it must have been before they moved south to Mexico City, where the Spaniards found them in the sixteenth century.

A *teocali* was an Aztec temple.

MOKE-ICHA'S STORY

A *tipi* is the sort of tent used by the Plains Indians, made of tanned skins. It is sometimes called a *lodge*, and the poles on which the skins are hung are usually cut from the tree which for this reason is called the lodge-pole pine. It is important to remember things like this. By knowing the type of house used, you can tell more about the kind of life lived by that tribe than by any other one thing. When the poles were banked up with earth the house was called an *earth lodge*. If thatched with brush and grass, a *wickiup*. In the eastern United States, where huts were covered with bark, they were generally called *wigwams*. In the desert, if the house was built of sticks and earth or brush, it was called a *hogan*, and if of earth made into rude bricks, a *pueblo*.

The Queres Indians live all along the Rio Grande in pueblos, since there is no need of their living now in the cliffs. You can read about them at Ty-uonyi in "The Delight-Makers."

A *kiva* is the underground chamber of the house, or if not underground, at least without doors, entered from the top by means of a ladder.

Shipapu, the place from which the Queres and other pueblo Indians came, means, in the Queres language, "Black Lake of Tears," and according to the Zuñi, "Place of Encompassing Mist," neither of which sounds like a pleasant place to live. Nevertheless, all the Queres expect to go there when they die. It is the Underworld from which the Twin Brothers led them when the mud of the earliest world was scarcely dried, and they seem to have gone wandering about until they found Ty-uonyi, where they settled.

The stone puma, which Moke-icha thought was carved in her honor, can still be seen on the mesa back from the river, south of Ty-uonyi. But the Navajo need not have made fun of the Cliff-Dwellers for praying to a puma, since the Navajos of to-day still say their prayers to the bear. The Navajos are a wandering tribe, and pretend to despise all people who live in fixed dwellings.

The "ghosts of prayer plumes," which Moke-icha saw in the sky, is the Milky Way. The Queres pray by the use of small feathered sticks planted in the ground or in crevices of the rocks in high and lonely places. As the best feathers for this purpose are white, and as everything is thought of by Indians as having a spirit, it was easy for them to think of that wonderful drift of stars across the sky as the spirits of prayers, traveling to Those Above. If ever you should think of making a prayer plume for yourself, do not on any account use the feathers of owl or crow, as these are black prayers and might get you accused of witchcraft.

The *Uakanyi*, to which Tse-tse wished to belong, were the Shamans of War; they had all the secrets of strategy and spells to protect a man from his enemies. There were also Shamans of hunting, of medicine and priestcraft.

It was while the Queres were on their way from Shipapu that the Delight-Makers were sent to keep the people cheerful. The white mud with which they daubed themselves is a symbol of light, and the corn leaves tied in their hair signify fruitfulness, for the corn needs cheering up also. There must be something in it, for you notice that clowns, whose business it is to make people laugh, always daub themselves with white.

THE MOUND-BUILDER'S STORY

The Mound-Builders lived in the Mississippi Valley about a thousand years ago. They built chiefly north of the Ohio River, until they were driven out by the Lenni-Lenape about five hundred years before the English and French began to settle that country. They went south and are probably the same people we know as Creeks and Cherokees.

Tallegewi is the only name for the Mound-Builders that has come down to us, though some people insist that it ought to be *Allegewi*, and the singular instead of being *Tallega* should be *Allega*.

The *Lenni-Lenape* are the tribes we know as Delawares. The name means "Real People."

The *Mingwe* or *Mingoes* are the tribes that the French called Iroquois, and the English, Five Nations. They called themselves

"People of the Long House." *Mingwe* was the name by which they were known to other tribes, and means "stealthy," "treacherous." All Indian tribes have several names.

The *Onondaga* were one of the five nations of the Iroquois. They lived in western New York.

Shinaki was somewhere in the great forest of Canada. *Namae-sippu* means "Fish River," and must have been that part of the St. Lawrence between Lakes Erie and Huron.

The *Peace Mark* was only one of the significant ways in which Indians painted their faces. The marks always meant as much to other Indians as the device on a knight's shield meant in the Middle Ages.

Scioto means "long legs," in reference to the river's many branches.

Wabashiki means "gleaming white," on account of the white limestone along its upper course.

Maumee and *Miami* are forms of the same word, the name of the tribe that once lived along those waters.

Kaskaskia is also the name of a tribe and means, "They scrape them off," or something of that kind, referring to the manner in which they get rid of their enemies, the Peorias.

The Indian word from which we take *Sandusky* means "cold springs," or "good water, here," or "water pools," according to the person who uses it.

You will find all these places on the map.

"*G'we!*" or "*Gowe!*" as it is sometimes written, was the war cry of the Lenape and the Mingwe on their joint wars. At least that was the way it sounded to the people who heard it. Along the eastern front of these nations it was softened to "*Zowie!*" and in that form you can hear the people of eastern New York and Vermont still using it as slang.

THE ONONDAGA'S STORY

The *Red Score* of the Lenni-Lenape was a picture writing made in red chalk on birch bark, telling how the tribe came down out of Shinaki and drove out the Tallegewi in a hundred years' war. Several imperfect copies of it are still in existence and one nearly perfect interpretation made for the English colonists. It was in the nature of short-hand memoranda of the most interesting items of their tribal history, but unless Oliver and Dorcas Jane meet somebody in the Museum country who knew the Tellings that went with the Red Score, it is unlikely we shall ever know just what did happen.

Any early map of the Ohio Valley, or any good automobile map of the country south and east of the Great Lakes, will give the *Muskingham-Mahoning Trail*, which was much used by the first white settlers in that country. The same is true of the old Iroquois Trade Trail, as it is still a well-traveled country road through the heart of New York State.

Muskingham means "Elk's Eye," and referred to the clear brown color of the water. *Mahoning* means "Salt Lick," or, more literally, "There a Lick."

Mohican-ittuck, the old name for the Hudson River, means the river of the Mohicans, whose hunting-grounds were along its upper reaches.

Niagara probably means something in connection with the river at that point, the narrows, or the neck. According to the old spelling it should have been pronounced Nee-ä-gär'-ä, but it is n't.

Adirondack means "Bark-Eaters," a local name for the tribe that once lived there and in seasons of scarcity ate the inner bark of the birch tree.

Algonquian is a name for one of the great tribal groups, several members of which occupied the New England country at the beginning of our history. The name probably means "Place of the

Fish-Spearing," in reference to the prow of the canoe, which was occupied by the man with the fish spear. The Eastern Algonquians were all canoers.

Wabaniki means "Eastlanders," people living toward the East.

The American Indians, like all other people in the world, believed in supernatural beings of many sorts, spirits of woods and rocks, Underwater People and an Underworld. They had stories of ghosts and flying heads and giants. Most of the tribes believed in animals that, when they were alone, laid off their animal skins and thought and behaved as men. Some of them thought of the moon and stars as other worlds like ours, inhabited by people like us who occasionally came to earth and took away with them mortals whom they loved. In the various tribal legends can be found the elements of almost every sort of European fairy tale.

Shaman is not an Indian word at all, but has been generally adopted as a term of respect to indicate men or women who became wise in the things of the spirit. Sometimes a knowledge of healing herbs was included in the Shaman's education, and often he gave advice on personal matters. But the chief business of the Shaman was to keep man reconciled with the spirit world, to persuade it to be on his side, or to prevent the spirits from doing him harm. A Shaman was not a priest, nor was he elected to office, and in some tribes he did not even go to war, but stayed at home to protect the women and children. Any one could be a Shaman who thought himself equal to it and could persuade people to believe in him.

Taryenya-wagon was the Great Spirit of the Five Nations, who was also called "Holder of the Heavens."

Indian children always belong to the mother's side of the house. The only way in which the Shaman's son could be born an Onondaga was for the mother to be adopted into the tribe before the son was born. Adoptions were very common, orphans, prisoners of war, and even white people being made members of the tribe in this way.

THE SNOWY EGRET'S STORY

The Great Admiral was, of course, Christopher Columbus. You will find all about him and the other Spanish gentlemen in the school history.

Something special deserves to be said about Panfilo de Narvaez, since it was he who set the Spanish exploration of the territory of the United States in motion. He landed on the west coast of Florida in 1548, and after penetrating only a little way into the interior was driven out by the Indians. But he left Juan Ortiz, one of his men, a prisoner among them, who was afterward discovered by Soto and became his interpreter and guide.

There is no good English equivalent for Soto's title of *Adelantado*. It means the officer in charge of a newly discovered country.

Cay is an old Spanish word for islet. "Key" is an English version of the same word. *Cay Verde* is "Green Islet."

The pearls of *Cofachique* were fresh-water pearls, very good ones, too, such as are still found in many American rivers and creeks.

The Indians that Soto found were very likely descended from the earlier Mound-Builders of the Ohio Valley. They showed a more advanced civilization, which was natural, since it was four or five hundred years after the Lenni-Lenape drove them south. Later they were called "Creeks" by the English, on account of the great number of streams in their country.

Cacique and *Cacica* were titles brought up by the Spaniards from Mexico and applied to any sort of tribal rulers. They are used in all the old manuscripts and have been adopted generally by modern writers, since no one knows just what were the native words.

The reason the Egret gives for the bird dances—that it makes the world work together better—she must have learned from an Indian, since there is always some such reason back of every primitive dance. It makes the corn grow or the rain fall or the heart of the enemy to weaken. The Cofachiquans were not the only people who learned their dances from the water birds, as the ancient Greeks had a very beautiful one which they took from the cranes and another from goats leaping on the hills.

THE PRINCESS'S STORY

Hernando de Soto landed first at Tampa Bay in Florida, and after a short excursion into the country, wintered at Anaica Apalache, an Indian town on Apalachee Bay, the same at which Panfilo de Narvaez had beaten his spurs into nails to make the boats in which he and most of his men perished. It was between Tampa and Anaica Apalache that Soto met and rescued Juan Ortiz, who had been all that time a prisoner and slave to the Indians.

When the Princess says that Talimeco was a White Town, she means that it was a Town of Refuge, a Peace Town, in which no killing could be done. Several Indian tribes had these sanctuaries.

In an account of Soto's expedition, which was written sometime afterward from the stories of survivors, it is said by one that the Princess went with him of her own accord, and by another that she was a prisoner. The truth probably is that if she had not gone willingly, she would have been compelled. There is also mention of the man to whom she gave the pearls for assisting at her escape, six pounds of them, as large as hazel nuts, though the man himself would never tell where he got them.

The story of Soto's death, together with many other interesting things, can be read in the translation of the original account made by Frederick Webb Hodge.

THE ROAD-RUNNER'S STORY

Cabeza de Vaca was one of Narvaez's men who was cast ashore in one of the two boats ever heard from, on the coast of Texas. He wandered for six years in that country before reaching the Spanish settlements in Old Mexico, and it was his account of what he saw there and in Florida that led to the later expeditions of both Soto and Coronado.

Francisco de Coronado brought his expedition up from Old Mexico in 1540, and reached Wichita in the summer of 1541. His party was the first to see and describe the buffalo. There is an account of the expedition written by Castenada, one of his men, translated by Frederick Webb Hodge, which is easy and interesting reading.

The Seven Cities were the pueblos of Old Zuñi, some of which are still inhabited. Ruins of the others may be seen in the Valley of Zuñi in New Mexico. The name is a Spanish corruption of *Ashiwi*, their own name for themselves. We do not know why the early explorers called the country "Cibola."

The Colorado River was first called *Rio del Tizon*, "River of the Brand," by the Spaniards, on account of the local custom of carrying fire in rolls of cedar bark. Coronado's men were the first to discover the Grand Cañon.

Pueblo, the Spanish word for "town," is applied to all Indians living in the terraced houses of the southwest. The Zuñis, Hopis, and Queres are the principal pueblo tribes.

You will find *Tiguex* on the map, somewhere between the Tyuonyi and the place where the Corn Woman crossed the Rio Grande. *Cicuye* is on the map as Pecos, in Texas.

The Pawnees at this time occupied the country around the Platte River. Their name is derived from a word meaning "horn," and refers to their method of dressing the scalp-lock with grease and paint so that it stood up stiffly, ready to the enemy's hand. Their name for themselves is Chahiksichihiks, "Men of men."

THE CONDOR'S STORY

The *Old Zuñi Trail* may still be followed from the Rio Grande to the Valley of Zuñi. *El Morro*, or "Inscription Rock," as it is called, is between Acoma and the city of Old Zuñi which still goes by the name of "Middle Ant Hill of the World."

In a book by Charles Lummis, entitled *Strange Corners of Our Country*, there is an excellent description of the Rock and copies of the most interesting inscriptions, with translations.

The Padres of Southwestern United States were Franciscan Friars who came as missionaries to the Indians. They were not all of them so unwise as Father Letrado.

Peyote, the dried fruit of a small cactus, the use of which was only known in the old days to a few of the Medicine Men. The effect was like that of opium, and gave the user visions.

THE DOG SOLDIER'S STORY

The Cheyenne Country, at the time of this story, was south of the Pawnees, along the Taos Trail. All Plains Indians move about a great deal, so that you will not always hear of them in the same neighborhood.

You can read how the Cheyennes were saved from the Ho-Hé by a dog, in a book by George Bird Grinnell, called the *Fighting Cheyennes*. There is also an account in that book of how their Medicine Bundle was taken from them by the Pawnees, and how, partly by force and partly by trickery, three of the arrows were recovered.

The Medicine Bundle of the tribe is as sacred to them as our flag is to us. It stands for something that cannot be expressed in any other way. They feel sure of victory when it goes out with them, and think that if anything is done by a member of the tribe that is contrary to the Medicine of the Tribe, the whole tribe will suffer for it. This very likely is the case with all national emblems; at any rate, it would probably be safer while our tribe is at war not to do anything contrary to what our flag stands for. All that is left of the Cheyenne Bundle is now with the remnant of the tribe in Oklahoma. The fourth arrow is still attached to the Morning Star Bundle of the Pawnees, where it may be seen each year in the spring when the Medicine of the Bundle is renewed.

This is the song the Suh-tai boy—the Suh-tai are a sub-tribe of the Cheyenne—made for his war club:—

> "Hickory bough that the wind makes strong,—
> I made it—
> Bones of the earth, the granite stone,—
> I made it—
> Hide of the bull to bind them both,—
> I made it—
> Death to the foe who destroys our land,—
> We make it!"

The line that the Suh-tai boy drew between himself and the pursuing Potawatomi was probably a line of sacred meal, or tobacco dust, drawn across the trail while saying, "Give me protection from my enemies; let none of them pass this line. Shield my heart from them. Let not my life be threatened." Unless the enemy possesses a stronger Medicine, this makes one safe.

GLOSSARY OF INDIAN AND SPANISH NAMES

ä sounds like "a" in *father*

ā sounds like "a" in *bay*

ă sounds like "a" in *fat*

à sounds like "a" in *sofa*

e sounds like "a" in *ace*

ĕ sounds like "e" in *met*

ē sounds like "e" in *me*

ẽ sounds like "e" in *her*

i sounds like "e" in *eve*

ĭ sounds like "i" in *pin*

ī sounds like "i" in *pine*

ō sounds like "o" in *note*

ŏ sounds like "o" in *not*

ū sounds like "oo" in *food*

ŭ sounds like "u" in *nut*

Ä′cō-mä

A-che′-se

À-de-län-tä′-dō

Äl-tä-pä′-hä

Äl′-vär Nuñez (noon′-yāth) Cä-be′-zä (thä) de Vä′-cä

Än-ä-i′-cä

Ä-păch′-ē

Ä-pä-lä′-che

Ä-pŭn-kē′-wĭs

Är-äp′-ä-hōes

Är-rūm′-pä

Bäl-bō′-ä

Bis-cāy′ne

Cabeza de Vaca (cä-be′-thä de Vä′-cä)

Cä-ci′-cä

Cä-ci que′

Cä-hō′-kĭ-à

Cāy Vẽrd′-e

Cen-te-ō′-tli

Chä-hĭk-si-chi′-hĭks

Cheyenne (shī-ĕn′)

Chi-ä′

Chihuahua (chi-wä'-wä)

Ci'-bō-lä

Ci'-cū-ye

Ci'-nō-äve

Cō-chi'-ti

Cō-fä-chi'-que

Cō-fäque'

Cō-măn'-che

Cōr-tez'

Di-ne'

El Mōr'-rō

Es'-te-vän

Frän-cis'-cō de Cō-rō-nä'-dō

Frän-ces'-cō Le-trä'-dō

Gä-hōn'-gä

Gän-dä'-yäh

Hä-lō'-nä

Hä'-wi-kūh

Hĕr-nän'-dō de Sō'-tō

His-pä-ni-ō'-lä

Hō'-gãn

Hō-he'

Hō-pi'

Hō-tai' (tī)

How-kä-wän'-dä

I'-rō-quois

Is'-läy

Is-si-wūn'

Juan de Oñate (hwän de ōn-yä'-te)

Juan Ortiz (hwän ōr'-tiz)

Kä-bey'-de

Kä-nä'-wáh

Kăs-kăs'-kĭ-ä

Kät'-zi-mō

K'ia-ki'-mä

Kī'-ō-wās

Kĭt-käh-häh'-ki

Ki'-vä

Kō-kō'-mō

Koos-koos'-kĭ

Kō-shä'-re

Lĕn'-ni-Lĕn-ăpe'

Lū'-cäs de Ayllon (īl'-yōn)

Lujan (lū-hän')

Mahiz (mä-iz')

Mä'-hūts

Mäl-dō-nä'-dō

Mät'-sä-ki

Mĕn'-gwē

Mesquite (mes-kēēt')

Mĭn'-gō

Mō-hi'-cän-ĭt'-tŭck

Mō-ke-ĭch'-ä

M'tōū'-lĭn

Mŭs-kĭng'-hăm

Nä-māe-sip'pū

Narvaez (när-vä'-eth)

Navajo (nä'-vä-hō)

Ni-e'-tō

Nō'-päl

Nū-kē'-wĭs

Occatilla (ōc-cä-til'-yä)

Ōck-mŭl'-gēē

Ō'-cō-nee

Ō-cŭt'-e

Ō-dōw'-ăs

Ō-ge'-chee

Olla (ōl'-yä)

Ōng-yä-tăs′-se

Ŏn-ŏn-dā′-gä

Ō-pä′-tä

Ō-wĕn-ūng′-ä

Pän-fi′-lō de När-vä′-ez (eth)

Pän-ū′-cō

Paw-nēē′

Pe′-cōs

Pe′-drō Mō′-rōn

Pe-ri′-cō

Pe-yō′-te

Pi-rä′-guäs

Pitahaya (pĭt-ä-hī′-ä)

Pi-zär′-rō

Ponce (pōn′-the) de Le-ōn′

Pŏt-ä-wät′-ä-mi

Pueblo (pwĕb′-lō)

Que-re′-chōs

Que′-res

Que-re-sän′

Qui-vi′-rä

Ri′-tō de lōs Frijoles (fri-hō′-les)

Sahuaro (sä-wä′-rō)

Scioto (sī-ō′-tō)

Shä′-man

Shi-năk′-i

Ship-ä-pū′

Shi-wi′-nä

Shō-shō′-nes

Shūng-ä-ke′-lä

Sōns e′-sō, tse′-nä

Sūh-tai′ (tī)

Tä′-kū-Wä′-kĭn

Täl-i-me′-cō

Täl-le′-gä

Täl-le-ge′-wi

Tä′-mäl-Pỹ-wē-ăck′

Tä′-ōs

Tär-yĕn-ya-wăg′-ōn

Tejo (tä′-hō)

Tĕn′-ä-säs

Te-ō-cäl′-es

Thlä-pō-pō-ke′-ä

Ti-ä′-kĕns

Tiguex (ti′-gash)

Ti′-pi

Tōm′-bes

Tō-yä-län′-ne

Tse-tse-yō′-te

Tsis-tsis′-täs

Tŭs-cä-lōōs′-ä

Tỹ-ū-ōn′-yi

Ū-ä-kän-yi′

Vär′-gäs

Wä-bä-mōō′-ĭn

Wä-bä-ni′-ki

Wä-bä-shi′-ki

Wăp′-ĭ-tĭ

Wich′-i-täs

Zuñi (zūn′-yee)

AFTERWORD
Melody Graulich

PLOTTING NORTH AMERICAN HISTORY
WITH A NEW COMPASS

In 1931 Mary Austin pointed out that "in the United States, the first-born literature of our native land, such as becomes among all other peoples a proud and universally accepted literary heritage," is disregarded, that most Americans "know more of Beowulf than of the Red Score of the Delaware, more of Homer than of the Creation Myth of the Zuni, more of Icelandic sagas than of the hero myths of the Iroquois and Navajo."[1] Throughout her long and prolific career, which included over 30 books and some 250 periodical publications, she attempted to address this ignorance in many genres—essays, poems, plays, stories—but nowhere so thoroughly as in *The Trail Book* (1918), her effort to expose children—and adults—to a multicultural history of North America, made up of "prehistoric trail stories, each one illustrating one of the pre-Columbian cultures" and their encounters with various emigrants to the continent.[2]

Having often suggested that America's school curriculum, much like its high culture, was dominated by the influence of Europe and New England, Austin approached the settlement of the continent from new directions, on trails originating in "prehistoric" times. From the North, "the Great Cold crept nearer" and "pressed the people west and south so that the tribes bore hard on one another."[3] Cultural exchanges took place "long before there were Pale Faces" on "trade trails and graded ways," which Mound-Builders used for trading purposes "as far south as Little River in the Tenasas Mountains, and north to the Sky-Blue Water"(*The Trail Book*, 12). Maps on skins preserved trails earlier discovered by such explorers as Howkawanda, apparently a Paiute from "The Country of the Dry Washes," who mapped a trail heading *east* over the mountains to the Buffalo Country. Cabeza de Vaca, castaway from the Panfilo de Narvaez expedition in 1548 and author of an account of his travels that has received much recent critical attention, wanders through several stories. The Spanish-named mesa El Morro, in what is now southern New Mexico, provides Austin with a written history of the movement of Spanish and Mexicans *north* long before "pioneers" crossing the plains from east to west carved their names on Independence Rock, but El Morro—already well inscribed by tribal peoples, who called it "The Rock"(244)—was no blank slate. Commerce had gone on between northerners and southerners long before the arrival of the Spanish in the "New World," as Austin points out in "Dorcas Jane Hears How the Corn Came to the Valley of the Missi-Sippu," a story about the northern migration of corn: "[T]he trail that leads to [Chihuahua is] one of the oldest lines of tribal migration on the continent" (290). As Austin's book title so well suggests, the inhabitants of North America have always been on the move.

In Austin's view, American history had been too firmly entrenched, temporally and spatially: Narrated in English, it began in 1607, with a brief preface in 1492, on the East Coast, the West becoming relevant only after it had been "purchased" in 1803 and "explored" soon thereafter. Long interested in oral storytelling, she recognized that stories, too, were always on the move, always changing—or should be—and she wanted to give American history a push in some new directions, into, for instance, the relatively pathless territory of environmental history. Her use of talking animals as narrators serves as a reminder that the history of the continent began before settlement by humans, and that animals and plants migrate and establish trails, a theme explored especially in "Dorcas Jane Hears How the Corn Came to the Valley of the Missi-Sippu." In her informational appendix to *The Trail Book*, she points out, "All the main traveled roads in the United States began as animal or Indian trails. . . . Railways have tunneled under passes where the buffalo went over, hills have been cut away and swamps filled in, but the general direction and in many places the actual grades covered by the great continental highways remain the same"(287). Set in a natural history museum, *The Trail Book* introduces readers to Austin's version of the "natural" history of a continent marked by movement, environmental change, *and* continuity.

Some of Austin's earliest writing was devoted to helping children learn the natural history and rhythms of the land on which they were growing up. Working as a traveling schoolteacher throughout southeastern California, she based her curriculum on "Western" materials, "going from coyotes to carrion crows and other features of the trail" (*The Trail Book*, 291). Feeling that children "were brought up [exclusively] . . . in the literature and lore of New England" (*Earth Horizon*, 97), their immediate experience rendered apparently irrelevant, she made up poems with them, which she soon published in children's magazines like *St. Nicholas* and eventually collected in *The Children Sing in the Far West* (1928). In her preface to that collection, she wrote that she wanted the "children [to] have [songs] for their own. Partly because I was teaching school and felt obliged to have something for my pupils about the land they lived in, and partly because I loved the land so much I couldn't bear not having grown up in it, I made most of the poems in this collection with the help of the children in my school." Children, she felt, had knowledge to share; they "let [her] into the secret of how the great Southwest feels to those who have never known any other country."[4] Because she found most children's books filled with "the same inchoate jumble of environmental elements," she revised familiar folk songs to respond to environmental particularities.[5] When one child wanted to know if a new threat to the California agricultural industry, the Australian ladybug, was "in any way related to the ladybug" of the familiar rhyme, Austin responded with

> The scale bug is down in the orchard alone,
> He is eating his way to the topmost limb,
> Ladybug, ladybug, go and eat him! (*Earth Horizon*, 214)

Because Austin saw landscape as a text that could be read only after long and patient observation, she argues that children's imaginative development should be grounded in their native language.

Austin also collected stories throughout her years in Southern California, and she put her thinking about children's educational needs into practice in her first children's book, *The Basket Woman* (1904), a collection of "western myths for school use" that she hoped would sustain the child's "intimacy with nature" and "happy sense of the community of life and interest in the Wild."[6] In *The Basket Woman*, she hoped to make myth "a part of the child's experience" by setting the stories in locales "common and accessible" to that experience, thus emphasizing a relationship with a particularized landscape—in this case, the Owens Valley on the eastern slope of the Sierra Nevada in Southern California (vii, ix). Yet Austin certainly did not intend her stories only for California schoolchildren. She believed that while children's responsiveness and curiosity evolved in relation to the natural world around them, they readily extended their interest to other fully realized landscapes. In a later essay, "Regionalism in American Fiction," she wrote that what children "like as background for a story is an explicit, well mapped strip of country, as intensively lived into as any healthy child lives into his own neighborhood"(102).

Indeed, Austin believed her children's books relied on the familiar—the child's relationship to place—to introduce the unfamiliar. In that same essay, she argued that "every American child" should be introduced to the "world of American Indian lore," and she extended her insistence upon the influence of region to native peoples, complaining that most "authors fail to know that everything an Indian does or thinks is patterned by the particular parcel of land which is his tribal home"("Regionalism," 103, 104). Though this passage demonstrates Austin's sometimes unfortunate tendency to generalize and essentialize in her nonfiction, the assertion is central to her children's books, in which she seldom makes the same mistake. In *The Basket Woman*, she does not tell generalized "Indian" tales but focuses on the historical and mythological stories of the Paiutes who lived on the slopes of the eastern Sierra, people with whom Austin spent considerable time between 1891 and 1899. She began to learn about the Paiutes, she said, by learning about "the land they lived in."[7] Writing her autobiography *Earth Horizon* forty years later, she still emphasized how much they had influenced her intellectual evolution. By spending time with them, she claimed, she learned "to interpret the significance of common things" (262), and by learning about their art, "she learned to write"(*Earth Horizon*, 289). One lesson particularly influenced what she wanted to convey to children: By participating in Paiute women's everyday activities, she "began to learn that to get at the meaning of work you must make all its motions, both of body and mind" (247). The Paiute women integrated experience and intellectual activity in their work, two elements which Austin would bring together in *The Basket Woman*, a work whose message urged that same integration in children's intellectual development.

Austin opens *The Basket Woman* with two stories told by the Basket Woman, a compassionate and insightful Paiute woman, to a young boy, Alan, who has recently moved to a Western ranch. Initially afraid of Indians because of what "he had heard" about them, Alan comes to know and love the Basket Woman through her stories that "enter his mind when he lay in his bed at night, and saw the stars in the windy sky shine through the cabin window," and they eventually become so much a part of his experience that he feels "part of the story himself" and even believes he dreams them (109–10). The Basket Woman becomes an important influence on Alan's consciousness, an inner voice that shapes his perceptions. She tells him—and the reader—tales of her people and personifies the natural world to emphasize that it is sentient, alive with spiritual meaning.

As the Basket Woman initiates Alan into a fuller appreciation of the interrelationship of all living things, the little boy becomes someone with whom Austin's young readers can identify. Although not all the stories are explicitly narrated by the Basket Woman, she is the implicit storyteller, and the stories are told within the framework of a developing human relationship. The collection's structure thus attempts to recreate the oral tradition Austin so valued and conveys the feeling that stories help create human bonds as well as an enduring connection to and respect for the natural world. In her preface, Austin encouraged parents and teachers to read her stories to children, and so, too, does the Basket Woman become a mother figure, nurturing especially Alan's imagination. In *The Trail Book*, Austin would once again create a dramatized audience—this time using two young children—and recount stories from oral traditions, but she would expand her cast of narrators to tell a more sweeping story.

Austin's interest in nurturing children's imaginations certainly originated in a childhood she felt was pinched and starved. Born in 1868 in Carlinville, Illinois, Austin at age ten lost her father, who had encouraged her interest in stories and read her books, along with her beloved sister, Jennie. Throughout her childhood she feuded with her strong-willed Methodist mother, who expressed a clear preference for her brother and whom Austin portrayed in her autobiography, *Earth Horizon* (1932), as repressive, rejecting, and dissatisfied. She emphasized particularly her mother's lack of physical affection, representing herself as starved for love and support, "in need of mothering." Describing herself as an isolated lonely child who turned to her imagination—to making believe—for solace, she recounts a scene where her mother sought to silence her creativity, telling the child that "storying was wicked" and "she'd have to punish you or you would grow up a story-teller" (42–43). In her adult life, Austin felt her mother was "not much interested" in her writing (316). Trying to get her mother's approval and affection yet always "falling short . . . as a young lady," Austin suffered throughout her adolescence for her assertiveness, her curiosity, and her supposed physical unattractiveness (169).

Austin responded to her feelings of being unacceptable and unwanted with a poignant act of self-naming, "Mary-by-herself." Yet instead of creating the characteristic imaginary friend, Austin discovered another self that would allow her to reshape the isolation of Mary-by-herself into independence, "I-Mary," who "suffered no need of being taken up and comforted; to be I-Mary was more solid and satisfying than to be Mary-by-herself" (47). Significantly "I-Mary was associated with the pages of books," appearing most often as the child was reading (46).

Given the role Austin believed books played in alleviating her loneliness and sense of inadequacy, she viewed them as powerful and transformational forces in children's personal lives. Yet though she associated books with liberation, in *Earth Horizon* she critiques traditional elementary school pedagogy, which she said was based on "incredible sessions of desk-sitting and the stultification of young intelligence by hours of mock business, occasionally punctuated by boring recitations," resulting in "seven hours of unanticipated dullness" (58, 59). Especially in her children's books, Austin created models of what she saw as experiential and collaborative learning. Her devotion to this ideal is metaphorically suggested by an anecdote in *Earth Horizon* whereby the seven- or eight-year-old child realizes she "wanted to write books that you could walk around in"(73). Rather than entrapping children in passive roles as consumers of information with little connection to their lived experiences, Austin's stories and books would provide them with "trails" to walk in self-exploration. And indeed, the Basket Woman does in fact tell Alan stories as they walk along trails and visit her nation.

Austin found her own new trails when she moved west with her family to homestead in 1888. Insecure but ambitious, unhappy and frustrated, she soon came to associate the West with feelings of personal and spiritual liberation. "Its treeless spaces," she wrote, "uncramp the soul."[8] With no books available that adequately addressed her experience, "spellbound" (*Earth Horizon*, 195) with "wanting to know" a "country [that] failed to explain itself" (194) but simultaneously revealed "the bare core of things" (*Land of Little Rain*, 8), she turned to the land itself as text she could both read and walk around in. Conventional thinking was inadequate in this country that gave her "the courage to sheer off what is not worth while," where she made the "revolutionary discovery" that there "was something you could do about unsatisfactory conditions besides being heroic or a martyr to them, something more satisfactory than enduring or complaining, and that was getting out to hunt for the remedy" (*Land of Little Rain*, 78; *Earth Horizon*, 195).

In numerous stories Austin shows women hunting for a way out of the corsets, literal and metaphorical, of Victorian "young ladihood." One of her most remarkable stories ("The Walking Woman") seems to plot the course to a more spacious life and subjectivity. The unnamed narrator, herself a seeker, meets the Walking Woman, a desert wanderer who had "begun by walking off an illness" and was "healed at last by the large soundness of nature."[9] Although her choices have sometimes led to heartbreak, she inspires the narrator: "She was the Walking Woman. That was it. She had walked off all sense of society-made values, and, knowing the best when the best came to her, was able to take it" (97). Rejecting socially constructed limitations but receptive to new possibilities, the Walking Woman embodies freedom of movement. The narrator comes to see her as a pathfinder: Recalling the rumors that the Walking Woman is "twisted," a metaphor for her deviance, the narrator looks at her footsteps and discovers that "the track of her two feet bore evenly and white" (98).

Like the Walking Woman, Austin found both joy and sorrow in the West. After embarking on a marriage that would prove to be unhappy, she gave birth to a daughter, Ruth, during a difficult childbirth in which the child was probably brain damaged. Austin was emotionally wrenched as she gradually realized her daughter could not develop speech or coordination. She received help from a Paiute neighbor, Seyavi, who would later serve as the model for the Basket Woman. Along with her own child, Seyavi nursed Ruth and later brought the silent child "meadowlarks' tongues, which make the speech nimble and quick" (*Earth Horizon*, 246). The meadowlark tongues could not help Ruth but Seyavi, herself a storyteller and an artist, led Austin to find her own language to describe the desert and its inhabitants and also to learn what would become one of the key themes in her work, which she articulated in the first story she wrote about Seyavi, "The Basket Maker": "To understand the fashion of any life, one must know the land it is lived in and the procession of the year."[10]

As Austin taught school and struggled to support herself and her daughter, writing at night the children's stories that would become *The Basket Woman*, she came to realize that she was bad for her child—too impatient, too nervous, her expectations too high. Eventually, with the support of a young woman doctor, Helen McKnight Doyle, who had moved to the region, she made the difficult decision to institutionalize Ruth in 1904, just as she published *The Basket Woman*. The ironies would not have escaped Austin. Perceiving herself as a "failure" as a mother, she was successful in telling stories for children not her own, and her increasing success as a writer helped pay for the care she could not provide her own daughter. Throughout her life she continued to yearn for a connection with children, dedicating *The Trail Book* to her niece, Mary, and writing at the end of her life, "Nobody had wanted children more than [she] did" (*Earth Horizon*, 274).

After finding a permanent home for Ruth and leaving her husband, Austin moved to artist colonies in Pasadena and Carmel, California, where she wrote several books. After an extended trip to Europe, she finally settled in New York to be close to her publishers and the political movements of her time. There she was active in the progressive and feminist movements, becoming friendly with numerous writers and intellectuals. She also wrote one of her most enduring books, the autobiographical novel *A Woman of Genius* (1912). In the opening sections of the novel devoted to her heroine's childhood, she once again attempted to understand "the processes at work behind the incidents of . . . growing up (31)," once again reiterating key themes of hers.[11] Austin's narrator, Olivia, ruminates on how her relationship with the natural world endures in her memory, shaping her sense of self: "[T]hough I cannot remember how my father looked nor who taught me long division, I recall perfectly how the reddening blackberry leaves lay under the hoar frost in Hadley's pasture, and the dew between the pale gold wires of the grass on summer mornings"(9). Yet none of her school reading addressed this fundamental relationship: "[M]ost of our reading . . . had no relativity to the process of life in Ohianna [the novel's fictional setting]; we had things as far removed from it as Dante and Euripides, things no nearer than *The Scarlet Letter* and *David Copperfield*" (43).

Perhaps Austin had it in mind to address these educational shortcomings when she wrote *The Trail Book* during her New York years. Whereas *The Basket Woman* is based almost entirely on Austin's personal experience with the Paiutes, *The Trail Book*, with its larger scope, grows out of her years of research on the history of numerous Indian nations, some of it done in New York. Although she complained while living in the city that she met no one there with whom she could "talk Indian," when she began writing *The Trail Book*, she "talked with the staff of the American Museum of Natural History. They let [her] go into the Museum at night and take things out of the cases, and wear them and be told things about them" (*Earth Horizon*, 331). This experience was the genesis for the organizing motif of the book.

Shortly after publishing *The Trail Book*, Austin began to spend part of the year in New Mexico, feeling what she called "the call of the West, which is never quite silenced in the soul of anyone who had heard it."[12] In 1925 she made a permanent move to Santa Fe. She continued to be a productive writer, but she also became involved in what one critic called "almost every enterprise which shows any tendency to enrich and deepen the life of the West."[13] She defended the water and land rights of Pueblo people and helped organize the Indian Arts Fund and the Spanish Colonial Arts Society, both organizations intended to help maintain cultural traditions. And she remained committed to the importance of cultural diversity in school curricula, supporting bilingual education for Hispanic and native children. When she died in 1934, she bequeathed her house and copyrights to the Indian Arts Fund.

Like Austin's other short story collections, *The Trail Book* is a unified work of interrelated stories. Oliver and Dorcas Jane, the children of the night engineer at a natural history museum, accompany him to the museum at night, which they recognize as "another world where almost anything might happen" (6). The stories evolve out of their curiosity and sense of adventure: Once Oliver spots the "Buffalo Trail," he insists upon seeing "where it begins and where it goes"(6). For the remainder of the book, the young brother and sister follow the "trails" of their guides, the American Indians and animals (often traditional storytellers like Coyote) who make up the exhibits and who magically come alive in response to the children's imaginative questions and desire to learn. The unifying trail metaphor teaches them the connections between landscape and human experience. They learn that "like the trails . . . every word is an expression of a need" (126) and that "there is a story about everything" (49). (Lines like these are remarkably similar to the work of contemporary Laguna writer Leslie Marmon Silko.)

Beginning with a story from the now-extinct Mastodon, the trails lead them through myths about friendships between humans and talking animals into more recent times, "to the place in the Story of the Trails, which is known in the schoolbooks as 'History'"(127). There they hear stories such as "How the Iron Shirts Came to Tuscaloosa," about a figure the children have heard about in school—Hernando de Soto—but told from an entirely new perspective by the Princess of Cofachique, who Austin identifies as an ancestor of the Creeks. The trails, ultimately a metaphor for stories, reveal to them the interrelationships between myth, history, nature, and human culture and identity when they discover that "all the stories of that country, like the trails, seemed to run into one another" (230).

Austin stresses the interrelationships among the stories in numerous ways. The trails run from one diorama scene to another—"Cay Verde in the Bahamas to the desert of New Mexico, by the Museum trail, is around a corner" (225)—and figures from different scenes and even time periods comment on each others' stories, interjecting different viewpoints, additional information, and querulous comments, arguing about whose story it is to tell. Oliver and Dorcas Jane begin to notice relationships among the stories. When in "The Seven Cities of Cibola," the Road-Runner mentions the cities of the Queres—under attack by the Spanish, who take rather than trade—"Dorcas Jane nudged Oliver to remind him of the Corn Woman" (230), whose story records a positive exchange between the peoples of Mexico and the nation of the Missi-Sippu. The two stories contrast Coronado's greedy quest, based on rumor, for something made valuable only by human desire (gold), with the Corn Woman's unselfish desire, based on wisdom, to introduce her adopted tribe to the knowledge of her birth tribe (how to cultivate corn), and her sacrifice to procure for them seed corn, symbolic of life, which they can then trade with other tribes.

When Oliver and Dorcas Jane ask the narrators how their stories relate to earlier stories, they learn lessons about historical change and cultural differences. For instance, when they ask the Onondaga if his story has anything to do with the Mound-Builder's story, he comments, "That was a hundred years before my time, and is a Telling of the Lenni-Lenape. In the Red Score it is written, the Red Score of the Lenni-Lenape" (167). Although Austin used the word "prehistoric" to describe her book, lines such as this one demonstrate that she was well aware that native peoples had historical records. The Tallega, or Mound-Builder, shows the children a birch-bark roll of picture writing, a message sent from the Mound-Builders to the Lenni-Lenape. Although Oliver and Dorcas Jane's teachers would probably not teach the Red Score or the picture writing as history, Austin's inclusion of these passages after the moment when the children have reached "the place in the Story of the Trails, which is known in the schoolbooks as 'History'"(127) emphasizes her belief that they are significant historical documents. Austin's frequent references to divergences in place-names also denote cultural differences: For instance, when the Mound-Builder refers to the "River of White-Flashing," an Iroquois explains to the children that "He means the Ohio"(125).

Although Austin does chronicle some warfare between native peoples, she focuses her stories on transactions between nations; indeed, trade is one of her most recurrent themes. Yet the interchanges are disrupted with the arrival of the Spanish, replaced by greed and trickery and by the efforts of the Spanish to control others through power and dominance. If throughout *The Trail Book* Austin's implicit goal is to promote cultural relativism, the Spanish, then, are the book's villains, most particularly the "zealous" Father Letrado, who forbids prayers in kivas, dancing, and other rituals, calling them "witchcraft and sorcery" (256). Inadvertently, the Spanish do manage to bring about some positive changes: The Spanish do not find the gold they're searching for in "The Seven Cities of Cibola," but a Pawnee man, the Turk, cleverly steals horses from the expedition to bring to his people, along with the knowledge to care for them. Yet Austin's summary judgment comes in "How the Iron Shirts Came" when Dorcas Jane asks the narrating Egret, "'Don't you know any not-sad stories?'" and he replies, "'Not about the Iron Shirts. . . . Spanish or Portuguese or English; it was always an unhappy ending for the Indians" (223).

Inevitably Austin leads us to the question of whether American history moves inexorably toward an unhappy ending for the various native peoples whose stories she recounts. Though the setting of the natural history museum provides a wonderful formal device for connecting the stories, symbolically it seems to position the Indians as historical rather than contemporary figures, leading readers to the conclusion that the Mound-Builders, for instance, are as extinct as the Mastodon. If Austin's trail metaphor, as I have argued, stresses motion and (inter)change, the dioramas seem to counter that theme, static scenes composed from dead "objects," creating only the illusion of life and its continuation, implicitly— at the very least—representing history as having progressed from primitivism to civilization.

Austin visited the American Museum of Natural History around 1912–1918, during the period Donna Haraway explores in a well-known essay called "Teddy Bear Patriarchy," in which she describes how the creation of the museum and its dioramas tells a story about "the power of commerce and knowledge" and about "the social construction of scientific knowledge."[14] Arguing that the museum was built, in part, to educate and socialize children, she quotes the museum president, H. K. Osborn, as saying that the exhibits in the museum "'all tend to demonstrate the slow upward ascent and struggle of man from the lower to the higher stages, physically, morally, intellectually, and spiritually. Reverently and carefully examined, they put man upwards towards a higher and better future and away from the purely animal stage of life'" (281). In Haraway's reading, the museum, filled with the "best" specimens obtainable, was a reaction against immigration and an instrument of social control, and it was no accident that the Second International Congress of Eugenics was held there in 1921.

Because Austin was a progressive, several of the stories in *The Trail Book* do chronicle what she viewed as crucial moments of cultural advancement—the domestication of animals, the change from a hunting to an agricultural society. But she did not use *primitive* in a pejorative way, certainly believed that native peoples possessed high levels of civilization, and would never have described aboriginal Americans as morally, intellectually, or spiritually inferior to whites. *The Trail Book* urges readers to acknowledge the fact that history and culture existed in North America *before* 1492 and to pass that history on to the next generation.

Austin has at times been criticized for assuming the right, as a white author, to tell "Indian" stories, and some might suggest that her implicit argument for the integration of aboriginal stories into the larger story of "America" is an appropriative act, enriching the experience of white children by allowing them to see American Indian history as part of their "heritage" while perhaps confirming their prejudice that Indian peoples were "vanishing." But Austin well knew that many native peoples kept their history alive through the oral tradition; she simply did what was within her power to introduce a white audience to American Indian history because she felt that the encounters between peoples on the North American continent were at the crux of its history.

Austin has also been taken to task for claiming too much knowledge about Indian peoples. She was not a trained ethnographer but, as her appendix shows, she read widely and had considerable personal experience with various native peoples. Like Haraway, Austin explores the way "knowledge" is constructed in the American Museum of Natural History. The figures in her recreated dioramas are not silent, vulnerable to interpretation: They speak out forcefully, tell their own stories, argue about meaning; they *move*. Through them, Austin provides new—and multiple—origin stories for the United States. She is self-conscious about how "knowledge" has been produced by institutions and authorities in positions of cultural power. In her work, knowledge is not a fixed goal, a place where you arrive and settle down to stay, but always "in process." Significantly, knowledge as well as goods moves along her trade trails, its usefulness contingent upon the setting. And Austin allows the reader to research her stories by providing an appendix where she lists her sources (almost all are American Indian and Spanish texts that have been translated); she also promotes a multilingual history by including a glossary of the many Indian and Spanish words used throughout *The Trail Book*. (In *Earth Horizon* Austin says she "completely and absolutely knew" as a child "that she wanted to write books 'with footnotes-and-appendix.'" These were the kind of books "you could walk around in" [73].) Austin's appendix is a trail leading to new sources of knowledge for her young readers.

Oliver and Dorcas Jane are undoubtedly socialized in the American Museum of Natural History, but not to a position of racial or cultural superiority. They consistently exhibit a respectful curiosity about "others" and remain open to having their assumptions challenged. During their nights spent in the museum, they learn lessons in cultural relativity, where meanings are not fixed but fluid and contextual. In Austin's museum, encounters and changes take place.

The Trail Book provides not only an alternative "national" history but also gestures toward an alternative *literary* history. In an influential essay (1995), Annette Kolodny argued for the redefinition of American literary history as characterized by moments when "distinct human cultures first encounter one another's 'otherness,'" a literary history "circumscribed by a particular physical terrain in the process of change *because* of the forms that contact takes, all of it inscribed by the collisions and interpenetrations of language."[15] In recent work, Kolodny has turned to oral history and to "prehistoric" sources to discover the origins of this process, one Austin began to map in 1918. Through apparently simple stories for children, Austin introduced complex topics—cultural relativity, the construction of nationhood—that resonate for twenty-first-century adults. Like Oliver and Dorcas Jane and the children for whom the book was intended, adult readers of *The Trail Book* will find themselves moving along unfamiliar trails that lead to changing views of North America and its inhabitants.

NOTES

1. Mary Austin, "Aboriginal American Literature" (Huntington Library Austin Collection, box 25, n.d.).

2. Mary Austin, *Earth Horizon* (1932; reprint, Albuquerque: University of New Mexico Press, 1991), 349. Page numbers follow subsequent quotations in text.

3. Mary Austin, *The Trail Book* (Boston: Houghton Mifflin, 1918), 27. Page numbers follow subsequent quotations in text.

4. Mary Austin, *The Children Sing in the Far West* (Boston: Houghton Mifflin, 1928), vii.

5. Mary Austin, "Regionalism in American Fiction," *English Journal* XXI (Feb. 1932): 97–107, 104. Page numbers follow subsequent quotations in text.

6. Mary Austin, *The Basket Woman: A Book of Indian Tales* (1904; reprinted for classroom use with a new expanded preface by Mary Austin, Boston: Houghton Mifflin, 1910 [ii, x]; reprint, Reno: University of Nevada Press, 1999). Page numbers follow subsequent quotations in text.

7. Mary Austin, *The American Rhythm: Studies and Reexpressions of Amerindian Songs* (1923; reprint, Boston: Houghton Mifflin, 1930), 38. The full quotation reads, "Better than I knew any Indian, I knew the land they lived in."

8. Mary Austin, *The Land of Little Rain* (1903; reprint, Albuquerque: University of New Mexico Press, 1974), 91. Page numbers follow subsequent quotations in text.

9. Mary Austin, "The Walking Woman," in *Western Trails: A Collection of Stories by Mary Austin*, ed. Melody Graulich (Reno: University of Nevada Press, 1987), 91–98, 93. Page numbers follow subsequent quotations in text.

10. Mary Austin, "The Basket Maker," in *Western Trails*, 31–38.

11. Mary Austin, *A Woman of Genius* (1912; reprint, Old Westbury, N.Y.: Feminist Press, 1985), 31. Page numbers follow subsequent quotations in text.

12. Mary Austin, "Willa Sibert Cather," *El Palacio* (March/April 1909): 90.

13. Henry Smith, "The Feel of the Purposeful Earth: Mary Austin's Prophesy," *New Mexico Quarterly* 1 (Feb. 1931): 33.

14. Donna Haraway, "Teddy Bear Patriarchy: Taxidermy in the Garden of Eden, New York City, 1908–1936," in *Cultures of United States Imperialism*, ed. Amy Kaplan and Donald E. Pease (Durham, N.C.: Duke University Press, 1993): 237–91, 238, 277. Page numbers follow subsequent quotations in text.

15. Annette Kolodny, "Letting Go Our Grand Obsessions: Notes Toward a New Literary History of the American Frontiers," in *Subjects and Citizens*, ed. Michael Moon and Cathy Davidson (Durham, N.C.: Duke University Press, 1995), 9–26, 17, 11.